Dangerous Thirst 3

The Final Drink

By
Ja'Lisa Marie

Published in the United States by Ja'Lisa Marie

Copyright © 2022 by Ja'Lisa Marie.

ISBN: 979-8-9861560-2-6

First printing edition 2022.

Library of Congress Control Number:

Dangerous Thirst 3, The Final Drink is a work of fiction. It is not meant to depict, portray, or represent any particular real persons. All the characters, incidents, and dialogues are a product of the author's imagination and are not to be construed as real. Any references or similarities to actual or historical events, entities, real people, living or dead, or real locales are used fictitiously and are intended to give the novel a sense of reality. Any similarity in other names, characters, entities, places, and incidents is entirely coincidental.

Cover Layout & Design: Jay Covers

Printed in the United States of America

Email: jalisamarie.ink@gmail.com
FB: www.facebook.com/authorjalisa.marie.3
IG: www.instagram.com/authoressjalisa

Dedication

Last but absolutely NEVER least! I dedicate this entire series to my little family TK, Taquiece, Monae, Kyessah, and Ja'siah! Everything I do in life, I do for the love and security of my family. You all have been beyond patient, loving, and understanding during this journey. I thank y'all for not giving up on me during these times that I hide in my office for hours on in, skip family functions, and go into beast mode. Y'all make this journey that much more important and engaging to go through. From the bottom of my heart, THANK YOU! I Love Y'all something fierce!

Table of Contents

INTRODUCTION

Dear Brain Diary,

You know, we all start to die the day we are born. That scares me. And yet, here I am, a person who has never once thought about killing herself or doing drugs, yet I've wanted to do both. I look in my drawer from time to time, unwrap the red scarf and stare in disbelief that I, me, Royelle Amoire Kingsley, would have the audacity to reach out for drugs or fathom the idea that death by my own hands was the best way to go. And the crazy part is, I still have these syringes full of heroin in them, just in case I find the urge to do something stupid. Help me, Lord!!!

Here I am today though, excited that I beat the odds… sort of! If any of my family ever found out about this, they would probably disown me. And my poor mother, I'm sure she's turning in her grave right now saying, 'was machen sie?' That means 'what are you doing' in German. But what would you have done if you were in my shoes? Would you want your life anymore? What would you do to rid yourself of all the pain you were facing?

This is why I'm glad im in counseling because I should've been dead the moment I thought about death. But between therapy and journaling, I guess I'm doing ok. This morning, when I looked in the mirror, I didn't see a broke me. At least not today. Today, I could see a new me growing. I hate that I've had to

1

go through some much to get here, but I'm going to be all right. I don't have a choice. Adala didn't raise me to feel sorry for myself, and I've overcome plenty of obstacles before. None as big as this one, but I've done it, and I'm going to do it again.

But if I could talk to my teenage self, I would tell her to choose wisely. I would tell her that having standards is a must, not an option. She would know that everything that glitters isn't gold and that it's ok to compromise in some situations, but it's never ok to settle in order to please other people. I would tell her to always follow her first mind, keep God first, pray for everything without ceasing, ask for constant guidance, and know that the closest thing next to God is your mother. Her words will always be gold and nothing less, even in her death. Today as an adult, that same teenage girl has learned that nothing is promised, men ain't shit, death is inevitable, and kills the soul of those left behind.

This last year has been so challenging. I can honestly say that regaining my memory has tormented me in ways I could've never imagined. Not to mention, being in therapy with my Neuropsychologist Dr. Angeli has been anything but relaxing. She has pushed me to limits I didn't know a person could be pushed to. It's scary how she's managed to help me unlock pieces of my life that I had somehow internally suppressed for so long.

With every session, I'm learning that the doors of memories either serve as pleasure or pain, there is no in-between, and that's what scares me the most. While therapy helps me unravel many of my twisted memories and slowly heals some of my deepest wounds, it's still draining and uncomfortable at times.

The more we unlock, the deeper my regrets become. So much about myself that I didn't even know existed has been unleashed, and that's frightening too. But now, I've accepted it as an expectation. Without Dr. Angeli, after all that I've learned, I don't think I would've made it this far in my mental state.

Because of her and the hypnosis, I have finally returned to work, and my memory surrounding Trevion is coming back. Not everything. But plenty. I still haven't reached the place where the hate I have for him broods through my pores, and I'm afraid of what that might look when it does. I'm praying Dr. Angeli has a way to help me through that part because I'm sure it's coming. And to be honest, I don't want to hate him or anyone else for that matter. I don't want that burden on my back. But how does one not hate another person after everything that person has put them through?

Why hate him, one might ask. Well, ask yourself why you would hate someone who has ruined your life, lied to you about everything, put you in positions you would've never been in if it hadn't been for them. And they are also the reason you feel like you're going half insane. Not to mention, you still don't know why that person was so gun-ho on ruining you. What was it about you that they wanted so bad? Why you and not someone else? I mean, the list of questions goes on and on. I need answers and closure, but I'll never get it because the dead can't talk.

Xandra seems to think she can get me those answers, and I believe she may have tried, but it's been so long now since everything happened it feels like the hatch was buried along with him. It truly feels like he was a chosen demon. Here for a short while to create havoc and leave. I don't know. I just know I was his target, and honestly, he damn near had me. Had he not been murdered already, I might have killed him myself for all he put me through and lied to me about.

I often look at his picture and think, how could I have fallen for someone like him? So vicious, cruel, dishonest, and conniving? Dr. Angeli says it's because I saw in him what he wanted me to see, not who he really was. So, I continuously ask, who is Trevion? Was anything about who I spent the last five years of my life with real? Was any of what he ever said to me true? Why me? Why Royelle Amoire Blevins? He could've chosen anyone else in the world, but yet, he chose me to be the one thing I said I would never be for no man; blind. Silly of me to have not seen it.

During therapy, I constantly see that stupid yellow sticky note that I found on the bedroom floor. You know, the one written by someone other than me. Sometimes I want it to be water under the bridge; other times, I still want to perform a writing analysis on everybody connected to him. Impossible. I know. But it bothers me to think that it might be someone we both know.

I know I repeat myself often brain diary, and I've written this stuff

3

repeatedly. But just know, I do so for no other reason than to keep my mind from going back to that place it was in when I woke up from the coma. I want to keep it from going idle so that I don't get mad to the point that I do what I initially set out to do with those needles. I write often so that I am reminded and refreshed of his atrocities every day. Writing this is my way of remembering that what was good for the goose was never good for the gander.

All that said, I'm doing ok today. You know better than anybody else, that some days I wake up ready to fight the world, but today, I woke up in great spirits despite having to see and deal with Rayford in some capacity. Since this whole coma situation, he has been a royal pain in my ass. I don't know why he thinks I can't handle what I've always been managing since before the accident.

He's even crazier than I thought if he thinks I'm going to let this go without a fight. If I can help it, he will not be handling anything of momma's, regardless of my condition, which has improved immensely. But he would never know that because he's too busy fighting me about everything and asking about me nothing.

Why him, though, Lord? Why did momma fall for him? There wasn't anybody else in the Navy to choose from? It just had to be him, huh? I know we can't choose our family, but sometimes I wish he was someone else's father because this father here is broken. He turned out to be anything but a good man. Maybe that's why it was so easy for Trevion to manipulate his way into my life. Rayford never showed me how to protect myself against assholes that act just like him.

He's been anything but a father, more like an uncured migraine if you ask me. And now today, I must deal with him AGAIN! I just want this to be over. Be with me today, Lord, because that man is going to make me strangle him. Lord, I just ask that you please be with me today. Let my thoughts be your thoughts, and my words, be your words. Because if I use my own, things are not going to go as planned.

~ Royelle

CHAPTER 1

"*A*lexa, play the Travis Greene station," Royelle said.

As soon as she put the pen and journal down on the nightstand, Tasha Cobb's song, "*You know my name,*" came on. When the beat dropped, she closed her eyes and lowered her head. As the lyrics blared through her speakers, she slowly rocked side to side, allowing the words to penetrate her soul. When the break hit, she started to clap and cry, praising God as if it would be the last time. She was so loud she was sure her neighbors could hear her.

She jumped to her feet and started shouting, thanking God for saving her, protecting her, and helping her through the pain that she knew no one else could do but him. Even with therapy, she knew only God could save her. She was so full of rage and hate towards her father, Trevion, the police, and at times, she even wanted to hate God, but she knew he would see her through this trial as he had done with all the other ones before.

When the song finished, she dropped to her knees and began praying while Mary Mary's "*I Worship You*" played in the background. The sounds of her prayers were more of a wailing. It was a pain-releasing lament where the hurt could be seen, but the words were inaudible. She screamed, cried, and gave God all the pain she was experiencing at that moment. And the more she prayed and wept, the more she could feel the weight of her agony lift from around her.

As the song came to a close, she slowly stood to her feet and began walking towards the shower, thanking God and asking him to be the strength she needed to deal with Rayford. She turned the water on as hot as she could stand it and let the gospel music continue to play as a way to help her clear her mind. Once the long hot shower served its purpose, she got out and quickly changed the music.

The Alina Baraz radio was the one station that gave her a different variety of R & B music, with very little ratchetedness. And when she wanted tunes by violin only, she blasted the Damien Escobar station. Royelle was eclectic when it came to her music choices and, depending on how she woke up, determined the music choice for the day. It was never the same mix.

She stood in front of the mirror for several minutes, staring at herself. She recognized all of her beauty but questioned her mind. She hated that she had to be the one to regain all of what she lost. And even though her memory had gradually improved, she still had a ways to go. Every day brought on a new challenge for Royelle, but she was still pushing through.

Being in therapy and tapping into the world of the trauma surrounding her father had more of an effect on her adult life than she thought. All the things she had buried away concerning him were coming back to the surface, and if that wasn't enough, everything he had done while she was in the coma made it that much easier for her to hate him all the more. And although she never wanted to be on the opposing side of her father, someone had to be the responsible party, and she was always fit for the bill.

An hour after she left the house, she walked into the Downtown probate courtroom, and Rayford was there, on time, dressed to the nines, hoping and praying the judge would take a look at his appearance and side with him on the case. Royelle took one glance at him, walked past him without saying a mumbling word, and sat a few rows in front of him. When Rayford noticed her, he wanted to put her in her place for not speaking but refrained himself, knowing it wasn't the time or place. She couldn't speak for how he might've felt having a daughter who was more like a stranger, but she was sure it couldn't be a good feeling every time she challenged him in court.

"All Rise!" The court officer yelled out. "The honorable Judge Kim Scott presiding."

"You may all be seated." The judge said after she took her seat.

Even though Royelle's mind functioned well these days, she was still afraid she would fumble her words and ruin her chances of getting back the authority she once had over Adala. She quickly looked over her shoulder to see if her support team was there, but it was just her. As the judge read out and presided over other cases, Royelle checked her phone for voicemails and texts from her team, but her phone was dry. She started to grow concerned that maybe they had forgotten about the hearing. In believing so, she began to send out a group text but decided against it and put her phone back in her purse.

'You got this.' She thought to herself. She was tired of being dependent on others. It had been a year since all the drama with Trevion and eight months since she had been in therapy, channeling through her anger and working on coping mechanisms. By now, she felt like she could handle most things independently.

As the judge called out and ruled over other cases, Royelle sat patiently, trying to think of ways not to hate Rayford as much as she did. But childhood trauma could quickly turn into adult hate and dysfunction if not treated effectively. Thankfully, she had her mother, who taught her about sustainability, and Dr. Angeli, who helped her go through the proper steps to resolve her uncanny emotions.

"Docket #051217OC21. The Kingsley vs. Blevins case." The court clerk blurted out.

Royelle stood up and followed the directions of the court officer to her side of the podium, and Rayford did the same.

"Good Morning to you both." The judge said.

"Good Morning." They responded in unison.

The judge softly sighed as she opened their file to review the case notes. Again, everything appeared to be the same, except for the new notes and recommendations from Dr. Angeli.

"Mr. Blevins, we'll start with you." The judge said. " As stated before in our previous hearing regarding this same matter, I understand your reasoning for taking over the Power of Attorney during Royelle's initial ordeal, so how are you feeling since the last hearing? Do you think she is now capable of resuming the responsibility?"

Rayford hated the way the judge sounded and posed the question. It made him feel like the judge had already made up her mind about turning the rights back over to Royelle. With that in mind, he took a deep breath and quickly thought about what to say before speaking.

"Your honor." He started. "As you know, my daughter has been through a lot."

'Hmph. He would know, wouldn't he?' Royelle thought.

"I know she continues to go to therapy, and that's great. But after all she's been through, I don't think she's 100% ready to take on such a responsibility."

The more Rayford talked, the more bullshit he fed the judge. Royelle couldn't believe he was trying to convince the judge of some type of inabilities she might have after everything she had gone through and came out of. As far as Royelle was concerned, there was no stronger person fit for the job. Listening to him speak teed her off. She was mad at herself for not telling the judge the truth about Rayford when they stood before her the first time. Not doing so gave Rayford too much credit, and it showed. Had she spoken up sooner about everything he did to their mother while at Angel Zone, they wouldn't be standing before the judge now listening to Rayford's falsehoods.

But instead of getting mad, Royelle continued to stand straight in all her splendor and poise, not once taking her eyes off the judge. She remained calm but wanted to do two things: punch Rayford in the face for undermining her strengths and laugh hysterically at him for trying to convince the whole courtroom that he was a caring father and husband when in her eyes, he was anything but.

"Royelle." The judge called out to her. "I'd like to hear from you now."

Royelle was ecstatic! It was finally her turn to speak.

"Your honor, I didn't really get to say much the last time we were here, but the truth be told, my father and I have not seen eye to eye since before my mother's passing. There has always been tension between us surrounding her care. Unfortunately, because of all of his aspersions during her time at Angel Zone, I had to come here to gain Power of Attorney in the first place.

Now I understand why he was granted Power of Attorney during my time in the coma, but it wasn't without problems." Royelle continued.

"Problems?" What kind of problems?" The judge asked.

She intently listened as Royelle gave an account of all that had transpired before and after Adala passed away. Rayford cut sharp eyes towards Royelle as she used the big words he didn't understand, speaking about how no one could get ahold of him that fateful day because he was sleeping his drunkenness away. *"What the fuck do you know,"* is what he wanted to yell out had it not been for bad timing.

She continued with how he acted towards Xandra, and judging from the smile that curved the corners of his mouth, one could tell he enjoyed doing what he did to her. Not that it mattered to the judge, but Royelle needed to paint a clear picture of how evil he was. And when Royelle mentioned the inquiries about the life insurance policies, the look of concern replaced his sly grin.

"Do you have proof of the policy change request?" The judge questioned.

"Would screenshots of the letters be sufficed?"

"Pass them forward, please." The judge looked over at the court clerk to get the phone.

Royelle dug into her purse, grabbed her phone, opened up Raymelle's text containing all the open mail from the insurance company, and passed it to the court officer.

"Can you explain what it is I'm looking at?" The judge asked.

"Your honor, what you see are letters from the insurance company asking my mother to come in with her identification so that they may validate it is her requesting the increases to the policy. The problem is that the dates on those letters are dates that I was in a coma and my mother was at Angel Zone. Therefore, it would have been virtually impossible for either of us to make such a request."

The judge scrolled to look at the rest of the pictures, and all the letters were worded the same. The only difference between them was the correspondence dates, signifying that the request was made multiple times on different dates. Aside from that, the letters proved to the judge that the insurance company sensed some sort of fraud and flagged it immediately.

"Mr. Blevins. Do you know anything about these?" The judge gave him a straight, don't bullshit me, kind of look.

"No." Rayford quickly responded.

"Mrs. Kingsley, do you have anything else for me to see,"

"No, ma'am, that is all. But if I may, your honor."

"You may." The judge granted.

"I have never had any issues caring for my mother and her estates. Even after I woke up, I could still remember everything regarding her. I never made a late payment to Angel Zone or on her policies, for that matter. All her bank accounts are balanced and have been because I am the only one with access. Also, I have proof of where her funds were dispersed to. I've always been the responsible one in our family. To leave my father in charge of anything monetary-wise would be disastrous."

Rayford looked over at Royelle with a snoot look. If all it took were a stare to kill, Royelle would've been good as dead. To undermine him in the way she had was the same as emasculating him as far as he was concerned. He looked back over at the judge, waiting to hear what was coming next, but he felt the bullshit coming on.

"Mr. Blevins, do you have anything you'd like to add before I make my final ruling?"

"Yes. Your honor." He cleared his throat.

"As Royelle said, we do not see eye to eye because she always wants to be in charge. However, I can handle all my wife's affairs regardless of her opinion. Your honor, I did what I had to do while Royelle was in the hospital."

He stopped talking and waited for the judge to respond. As she continued reading the therapist's reports, everyone in the courtroom remained quiet, shocked at the battle between father and daughter. It was like watching an episode from reality TV for the onlookers, and they were all rooting for Royelle. Then, while they waited for the judge's decision, the courtroom doors flew open and in came a beautiful court clerk with an envelope in her hand. She signaled the court officer over and handed it to him.

"Please get this to the judge. It involves this particular case." She whispered.

The court officer walked the envelope over to the judge, and when she saw it was addressed by Marcos & Sweeney Esquire, it immediately heightened her curiosity. When the judge removed the documents, she carefully read and reviewed them. The room was pin-drop quiet. Everybody's focus shifted from the conflict between Royelle and Rayford to the judge and the documents in her hands. As she read them bit by bit, the picture became very clear to the judge about Adala's wishes regarding her assets. When the judge was fully satisfied with what she had read, she was ready to be done with the case.

"I have thoroughly reviewed all the documents before me, including those that just came in. What I have in front of me are signed, and notarized documents from the decedent sent over by the Law Offices of Marcos & Sweeney. These documents iron out in full detail her wishes."

Both Royelle and Rayford's eye's widened. Neither of them was expecting that surprise. It felt like a DejaVu moment for Rayford. It brought him right back to the time he was at the funeral home and learned about all of the things Adala had done behind his back, and this was just an added piece to that. He was sick!

" Now, the case concerning Adala's assets and the likes cannot be ruled here, as we are only discussing Power of Attorney matters. However, I've been asked to read this portion of the letter written and signed by Mrs. Blevins and notarized by this attorney's office. Mr. Blevins, would you like to read this privately, or would you like me to read it?"

"It's fine, your honor. Go ahead and read it. I have nothing to hide."

Rayford smiled, knowing that the letter would be in his favor, and he was eager to rub it in Royelle's face.

"Dear Ray, I always loved you. I lived my life to make you and our children happy. I remained loyal, humble, caring, and never changed a single day of my life or who I was, even when I knew you were lying, cheating, and doing unspeakable things, that I pray God forgives you for. I do not hate you. I forgive you for all that you have done. Because I have been prosperous here on earth and did what was expected of me as a mother

and a wife, I knew God would come for me first.

My work here on earth is done. I've raised three exceptional children, taught them morals, the importance of character, and the goodness of Jesus, and I prepared them on how to live without me. I'm grateful that God allowed me the opportunity to watch our kids grow so beautifully. They are each successful in their own right, and I can't thank you enough for your absence in their lives. It taught them some valuable lessons that I hope they take with them moving forward.

Rayford Blevins the III, you were everything I wanted in life, and because of my love for God, I stayed with you, even when you didn't want or deserve me and left us empty. So now I offer you what I always have; A life of love, prosperity, and excellent health. May it come to you quickly, and may God give it to you gracefully.

As for control over my estate, that has always been given to Royelle and will remain. Even if she didn't realize it or know why I gave her charge, she has always been the most responsible, and I know when the time comes, she will do exactly what I'm expecting her to do. Everything that I have left behind and saved is for MY CHILDREN! Rayford, I pray you find ways to live this life without any of my expected supplements. I wish you peace, amazing grace, and happiness. I Will Love You Always... Adala."

The judge looked up just in time to catch all the expressions of those sitting in the courtroom. Everyone was just as shocked as Royelle and Rayford to hear those words. Rayford was floored! Here he thought he was about to gain access to everything Adala owned, and it backfired. He was ashamed and embarrassed. Had he known that the letter contained that type of rejection and dismissal, he would've told the judge to keep it. Stunned by it all, Royelle stood quiet in tears. She knew her mother was always several steps ahead of Rayford, and this was just more proof of that.

Hearing those words flow as eloquently as they did, reaffirmed to Royelle that her mother was every ounce of the woman she had always known her to be. And had Rayford been paying more attention to his wife, he would've known it too. But he was being such an asshole most times that he didn't even realize he would soon need a life jacket to help him stay afloat from the same ship he left Adala drowning in.

"Your honor. May I speak?" Rayford asked.

"You may."

"How do you know Adala wrote that and not someone else? That doesn't sound like something my wife would say or write."

"I don't know what your wife would or wouldn't say or what she would or wouldn't write. What I know is legal documents when I see them. And this, sir, is a legally binding document."

"This is crazy," Rayford mumbled.

"It's not as crazy as you think." The judge shot back, surprising Rayford. "And I normally wouldn't do this, but I will do you one better."

Knowing the type of man Rayford had presented himself to be, the judge was not about to go back and forth with him or have him challenge her in her own courtroom. Instead, she passed the letter with the attorney's office phone number to the court clerk and asked her to dial it and place the call on speaker.

"Good Morning. Marcos here. How can I help you?" Attorney Marcos answered after the second ring.

"Good Morning Attorney Marcos, Judge Scott of the probate court here."

"Oh! Hello, Judge. How can I help you?" He eagerly asked.

"Yes. Thank you. I am calling with questions regarding letters that I received concerning…"

"Royelle Kingsley, I presume." Marcos interrupted.

"That is correct. Can you provide the court with more insight on what I have before me, please?"

Attorney Marcos explained the papers' purpose and the date they were brought in, signed, and notarized. He informed that he nor his partner were present today because they were not aware of the hearing due to it being a Power of Attorney hearing, not a contestant of the will. He went on to tell the court that they received a call from Raymelle informing them of what Royelle was up against, which is what prompted them to send a courier over with a copy of the letter. When Attorney Marcos was done, Judge Scott thanked him for his time, disconnected the call, and looked over at Rayford.

"Mr. Blevins, does this satisfy your question?" She asked.

Rayford slightly nodded his head in defeat.

"Well, if there is nothing else, after reviewing all that I have, I am awarding Royelle Kingsley as Power of Attorney over all of Adala Blevins' assets, which include but are not limited to financial responsibilities, medical, and properties. For the reading of the will, call the Attorney's office, and they will set a date and time."

"Your honor?!" Rayford blurted out.

"Sir?" She responded.

"I don't understand any of this. How do you know Royelle didn't write it and that she didn't pay the attorneys to be on her side? I don't know those attorneys, never heard of or met them a day in my life." Rayford spoke loudly.

"That's just it, sir. Your late wife meant for you not to know. And unless you can show me just cause as to why I should challenge this certified information from the attorney, or make me believe that your daughter would pay the attorneys to forge your late wife's demands for her children, then this court is adjourned, and I have nothing further."

"Your Honor!" He hollered.

The judge hit the gavel, and that was that, at least for the judge. For Rayford, daughter or no daughter, it was on. He was determined to get all of what he thought he was entitled to and stormed out of the courtroom with useless plots running through his mind. When Royelle finally gathered her things and stepped outside the courtroom, the team she thought had abandoned her was all standing outside the double doors waiting on her.

"Ahhh bitchhhh! Look at that smile! What you thought we were just gonna leave you stuck out like that?" Xandra laughed.

"Well, what was I supposed to think?" Royelle smiled big.

"You ain't supposed to think we ain't got you, that's for damn sure," Raymelle responded.

"How long have you all been here? Did he see y'all?" Royelle curiously asked.

"We saw you come in." Raymelle smiled. We knew you could do this shit, and you did!" He shoved her right shoulder. "But Nah. He didn't see us; we saw him. He'll be a'ight."

"In a minute, you won't even need us." Charlyn smiled. "Congrats on the win love."

"Thank you." Royelle smiled back.

Royelle was beyond ecstatic to see her three siblings and Charlyn. It gave her a great sense of excitement, knowing that they trusted and believed in her more than she did herself. It made her appreciate and respect them even more. The idea that she did it alone served as a reminder that she could practically do anything independently without the extra hand-holding. She just earned herself some more survival stripes, and she loved it.

CHAPTER 2

"*B*itchhhh! I can't believe you decided to go back to work." Xandra hollered through the Bluetooth speakers.

"What am I supposed to do? Just sit around and sulk in my sorrows for the rest of my life? It's been long enough, sis."

"Nahhh. I hear you, sis. I'm proud of you, that's all. You've come a long way and doing way better than anyone thought."

"Whattt?! Xandra? Is that you?" Royelle joked. "Are you getting all emotional on me?"

"Bitch! Not in your wildest." Xandra joked in return. "But just know, I'm on McKenzie's ass if she even blinks wrong."

Royelle laughed at the astronomical level of hate that Xandra had for McKenzie. Neither of them had seen McKenzie in months, so she had a hard time comprehending why Xandra turned into the spawn of Satan at the mere thought of McKenzie. Royelle was sure some underlined added hate was there, but she wasn't eager enough to figure out why. McKenzie was the last thing on Royelle's mind. She had too many other things to be concerned with, and McKenzie wasn't on those list of things.

She continued the ride to work listening to Xandra go on and on about McKenzie and how she would bash her up if she had the faintest notion that

McKenzie was trying Royelle on any level. So many times since the memorial service Xandra wanted to follow McKenzie in the hopes that she would lead her to Aruba's crib. But Royelle's up and down condition didn't allow her to be without supervision for long periods of time, considering all that had changed with her since her accident.

The meek, quiet, and reserved Royelle, was still present, but the new impulsive, offhand, incautious, sometimes hot-headed, and occasionally reckless Royelle showed its ugly face more often than not. All the changes in her attitude and how she handled people were new to everyone close to her. One day hot, one day cold, and always unpredictable as to what the trigger may or may not be for that day. It was eyebrow-raising for everyone, including tough-ass Xandra. Some days she wanted to choke the fuck out of Royelle. Other days she wanted to hug her, and recently she felt like they just needed to remake scenes from *Set It Off* with Royelle playing Cleo's role.

The more her memory came back, the more she moved on impulse. Anything she thought or felt was connected to Trevion; she got rid of. She sold her house and everything in it, downsizing to something smaller. She got rid of the clothes she felt came from him. Rather than get a new car after the wreck, she waited until she was well enough to drive and bought herself a Teal Blue Range Rover. She gave Chasity away to a child needing a friend at St. Jude's and bought herself a Teacup Yorkie. She wanted no remnants of him lingering with her into what she was trying to make of her new life.

She worked out excessively and religiously took Tai Chi, Yoga, and self-defense classes. Anything she could do to strengthen her mind and body to rid herself of Trevion once and for all, she did. When she and Xandra attempted to pawn her wedding ring, they learned it was faker than every addition of Barbie put together. She thought, how? She never took the ring off, and it never dimmed its shine or discolored her finger. She couldn't believe it.

She laughed obnoxiously when the pawnshop owner showed them a replica of her ring on one of his web pages. He explained that the ring she had looked eerily similar to the ones he sold from the Birkat Elyon line, and when she saw the catalog, she couldn't even be mad anymore. It was just more shit she was learning about her fake life with Trevion. Xandra, however, didn't share the same comical feeling. She knew about a lot of his dumb shit and wished she had known about it before all the fake ass shit he brought to the table, including the marriage.

Aside from all the things Royelle had done away with, the one thing she didn't change was her last name. Other than what the detectives had told her family, Royelle still had no proof that Trevion was truly married to someone else, and the memorial service didn't prove shit, at least not from Royelle's position. Xandra's stance on it was completely different and had been since the day of the service. Therefore, with some help and coercion from Xandra, Royelle decided to keep the last name.

As far as Xandra was concerned, Trevion might still have assets attached to him, and in keeping the name, Royelle would be able to attain all of them or at least fight for them once the dust settled. Ultimately, she had been with him for the last five years. Anything that was tied to him had to be linked to her in one way or another, and a great marital lawyer would make sure it did.

Despite working from home for months, going back to the office felt like the first day at a new job. An intense smile graced her face when she pulled into the parking lot. She was beyond nervous and excited to be back. The only thing on her mind was getting back to doing what she did best; research, investigate, analyze, and set Charlyn up for a win like she had done so many times in the past.

She grabbed her purse and stepped out of her truck, looking like something out of a Black Girl's Rock magazine. Her skin was flawless as usual, and her body was tight from all the hours of exercising. Looking for someone who had been experiencing trauma after trauma or diagnosed with amnesia was to be looking for a ghost in a crowd. It simply didn't exist. Royelle refused to let her misfortunes determine her outcomes, and it showed in everything she did and how she carried her appearance.

She gracefully walked into the building, catching the elevator to the third floor, shaky but ready. *'This is like riding a bike, remember that.'* She thought to herself. When the doors opened, she was startled. "Surpriseeeeeeeee!" The office staff yelled as she stepped off the elevator.

When the lights flickered back on, Royelle's eyes widened, and a smile formed as she took in all the smiling faces looking back at her. She was so grateful for the warm welcome. But given her traumatic experiences, she didn't care much for surprises anymore. Everything since the accident kept her on edge. If it wasn't planned or something she knew about; she wanted no parts. But in this instance, she had to play it off cool.

"Heyyyy sweetheart. Welcome back!" Charlyn walked over towards Royelle. Sooooo! How does it feel to be back?" Charlyn asked.

"It feels weird but good."

She didn't realize how much she missed being in the office until her chest vibrated from the clamor of the claps and the roars of voices welcoming her back. With the exception of McKenzie, whose hate could pierce the dead, everybody else in the office had chinky eyes from their hard-pressed smiles. The love Royelle received from them made McKenzie's disdain towards her null in void. She smiled as she looked around at all the flowers, balloons, and the largest edible arrangement she had ever seen. At that moment, she realized how much of an asset she was to them and how much they really cared about her and her hardships.

"Thank you for not giving up on me," Royelle whispered to Charlyn.

Charlyn grabbed Royelle's hands and looked her in the eyes.

"Royelle. Thanks is not needed. You've been family for a very long time now. And if I haven't told you before, I don't know what I'd do without you. You're the glue that keeps this place together. Now, are you sure that being here isn't too much for you?"

"Yes, Charlyn. I'm sure. I've worked from home long enough. I need some civilization in my life. If I weren't mentally unstable before, working from home any longer surely would've caused me to be."

Both women laughed.

As Royelle started to make her way to the office, the claps and voices got louder. To see her look so well put together after enduring so many tragedies and heartache was inspiring. She was the true definition of perseverance. Some staff wanted to hug her as a form of solace, but Charlyn had forewarned them against it, citing that Royelle was still extremely fragile and personal contact may not be good at this time. When Royelle reached her office, it was adorned with Sunflowers, her newfound favorite since the accident.

Later, she researched and was amazed to learn that the sunflower is regarded as a spiritual flower related to God's love, symbolizing adoration, longevity, true faith, and loyalty to something much bigger and brighter than oneself. So, she searched its biblical meaning and found Ephesians 5:9: " The fruit of the Spirit is in all goodness, justice, and truth. So, just as sunflowers produce oil, the believer who sets their sights on God shows the character of goodness, righteousness, and truth." Her eyes watered after she read it.

"Charlynnn." Royelle turned to her.

"Aht-Aht. I take no credit for what your colleagues did. This was all them."

Royelle was awestruck. The love was real. It brought her back to the memory of her mother telling her that if she did right by people, they'd do right by her, and it showed. She placed her purse down on her desk in awe at their kindness. It was unexpected and greatly appreciated. She was so glad she wasn't made to regret her decision.

"Well, I will let you get settled in. Take all the time you need, and if you need anything, anything at all, my office is still in the same place."

"Yes, ma'am." Royelle smiled.

"Well, get to work then! What are you waiting for?" Charlyn joked as she walked towards the door.

"Charlyn." Royelle subtly spoke.

Charlyn turned and looked at her.

"I love you so much. Seriously, thank you. I don't know what my family and I would've done without you." Royelle's eyes watered.

"Anytime beautiful. And before I forget, pull the drape off of that." Charlyn pointed at the wall and walked out, closing the door behind her.

Royelle walked over to the wall, unsure of what she might find. When she reached it, she slowly pulled down the covering, and affixed to the wall was a 28x40 canvas picture of Adala dressed in all White from the day of their family photoshoot. And just above that was a 72x18 rectangular canvas that read: *'Never forget your name.'*

Royelle gasped, placing both of her hands over her mouth, trying to hold in her screams. She was in complete amazement. She bumped into her desk as she staggered backward, trying to make it back to her chair without taking her eyes off the picture. A combination of happy and sad tears streamed from her eyes like falling droplets from a shower. She was blown away by what the office had done. When she finally reached her chair, she sat down, kept her eyes on the picture, and said, "Tell me what to do, momma? I feel so lost." She needed guidance and advice on how to move on with her new life. It was a struggle that no one in her immediate circle understood. Hell, some days, she didn't even understand it.

Charlyn, who was still standing on the outside of Royelle's door, waited until she thought it was the right time to go back into the office, and when she did, she found Royelle weeping into the palms of her hands. She walked up to her and gently rubbed her back as Royelle took all the time she needed to release her soul of some of the sorrow she was still experiencing. When Royelle finished, she stood and faced Charlyn.

"Don't say a word. Everyone here at the office thought it would be a great idea to help you remember who God put in charge of you and constantly reminded you of who you are. Never forget who you are and who God blessed you with. That woman there did a fine job raising you. She would be so proud of how you handled all you've gone through and conquered."

"You are a replica of everything she is. She loved you and still does. And know this— She can provide you with more protection now than she ever could when she was alive. Everywhere you are, she will be. No matter what you do, where you go, she will be there, constantly reminding you of her presence and that you are Royelle Amoire Blevins. I know you may have forgotten some things, but the meaning of your name, that woman there prided herself on making sure that you knew it and would never forget it, so don't! Today is a new day for you; make it count!"

CHAPTER 3

ood Morning Brain Diary,

I know it's been two days since I last wrote, but I just want to share my excitement and emotions this morning. Oh my goodness! First, you are not going to believe this. The day before yesterday, I was challenged by my family to confront Rayford, ALL BY MYSELF, and I didn't even know I was being challenged. I just did it! Here I thought my team didn't care or were too busy to come to the courthouse with me when the whole time, they were standing right outside the doors waiting to prove to me that I was much stronger than I thought.

I cannot lie, though. I was panicking and freaking out in that courthouse, but I did it, Brain Diary! I DID IT! And yesterday! Oh my goodness! I didn't get much done at work because I couldn't unglue my eyes from the picture of momma they presented me. It's huge brian diary! And every time I walk into that office, I am reminded of her beauty and who I am. And although I know she was gone long before she passed, it's still hard not being able to see her, hold her hand, or kiss her soft face. I wouldn't wish this type of loss and pain on my enemies. So, I appreciate the kind gesture and everything that everyone is doing to try and help me get through this. While it hasn't been easy, it's certainly been helpful.

Now last night, I had a dream about Trevion, and he was so perfect. Not a flaw in sight. He was everything that I dreamed of in a man. I hate that what I conjured up in my dream is in complete contrast to what I now know of him. Wishful thinking, right? I wish it was really that simple. I wish that what I had romanticized in my dream was my reality. I wish I was as blessed as the dream showed, blessed to have someone like him. But yet, here we are. Shattered and broken because of lies, betrayal, and deceit delivered by him. And thanks to him, no one will ever get to my heart like that again. That part of me is gone! But, enough about him, we all know how that story ends.

But today! Today is a new day, and I cannot wait to see what demons Dr. Angeli will drive out of me today! Nothing is ever easy when it comes to these therapy sessions, but they are so helpful and necessary.

Honestly, I just want to forget Trevion and everything about or connected to him. I want to go on with my life, not remembering anything about him. Things outside of him are great, and I would like to keep it that way. But, Dr. Angeli says that in order for me to live the life I deserve, I first have to fight these monsters so that I know how to maneuver my thoughts, and I guess she's right.

~ Royelle

Depending on the type of amnesia a person is suffering from will determine their level of memory. Unlike temporary episodes of forgetfulness, such as Lethologica, the inability to remember the right word, or Lethonomia, trying to remember the name of an actor, singer, or writer and can't, amnesia is the complete opposite of that and can be permanent. It's not like those moments you walk into a room to get something and have to backtrack your steps to remember what you were looking for in the first place.

A patient may experience a loss of self-identity, like Goldie Hawn in Overboard or Matt Damon in Jason Bourne. Luckily for Royelle, her dissociative amnesia is what some doctors refer to as situational, caused by the trauma or shock she experienced before and during the accident. And since Royelle's level of amnesia could be reversed with great therapy, she made sure to maintain her psychotherapy and hypnosis appointments with

Dr. Angeli.

While challenging, it was through those visits that Royelle managed to gradually regain parts of Trevion that she wished she hadn't. The way he looked, walked, kept his hair cut with the low fade tapered sides, his tattoos, and even the sound of his voice was rehashed. She could remember the scent of his favorite cologne Gucci Guilty for men, feel his touch, and how it made her feel when he whispered her name. It was a mind fuck for sure.

But, with time and therapy, things for Royelle had become a little easier. The more she could remember with ease, the more post-it notes she removed from her home. And by the time she was set to close on her new house, she was done with the post-it note era. It was like checking off an achieved goal from a vision board. But with every good thing was the bad. There were still things that Royelle had yet to uncover. And since Xandra told Dr. Angeli all there was to know about Trevion and Royelle's sexcapades, the doctor was confident a breakthrough with Royelle would soon be coming.

The problem was that Royelle's sexual visions came in pieces. What she could remember was limited and not being able to piece it all together bothered Royelle something fierce. However, Dr. Angeli promised to push her to all limits until she had an unearthing of sorts. There was a reason that the sex acts always manifested themselves in her sessions, and Dr. Angeli was as determined as Royelle to find out why.

When Royelle showed up for today's session, she was ready. She knew today wasn't going to be like all the other days in the past. She and Dr. Angeli agreed that today would be the no holds barred kind of day. She begged Dr. Angeli not to take her out of the hypnosis even if she looked like she needed rescue. Royelle wanted to get to the steak and potatoes surrounding Trevion and felt that an uninterrupted session had the potential of producing that.

"Royelle." Dr. Angeli signaled Royelle from the receptionist's desk. "How are you today?" She asked as they casually walked down to her office.

"I'm good, doctor. Ready for today, I know that." Royelle smiled.

When they made it to the office, Royelle sat her stuff down in the empty chair closest to the door, laid down on the Faux leather armless chaise lounge, and watched as Dr. Angeli switched from her desk chair to the chair on the side of the lounge chaise.

Like all the sessions before, they always started with Royelle detailing how her week had gone, the things she remembered, dreams she may have had that related to her visions, and her goals for the week. It was a way to get her thoughts flowing, keep her emotions in check, and for Dr. Angeli to analyze if Royelle was properly using her coping skill tools.

"Ok. You know the routine. All I need you to do is relax. Close your eyes, take several slow deep breaths, and relax." Dr. Angeli softly said.

Dr. Angeli got up and turned on the lamp at the foot of the chaise while Royelle began taking several deep breaths allowing her body to destress. The room was quiet, and the sounds from cars, trucks, or birds were non-existent. It was utter silence. The only thing that could be heard was the voice of Dr. Angeli and the sounds of Royelle's faint breathing.

"Ok. Slowly open your eyes, and when you do, I want you to focus on that lamp. And as you do, you'll feel that the LED lamp is quite bright. As you blink, you'll feel that it creates a black spot around your eyes that's quite harsh. I want you to fix your eyes on that for just a second. It's almost like you're glued to it, like you're in a trance."

Today they were trying the hypnosis in a different way, so it pleased Dr. Angeli to see the effects it was beginning to have on Royelle's body. It showed that Royelle was taking the process of the new hypnosis technique seriously while allowing her body to relax.

"As you stare at that light, listen to my voice and my voice only. What happens is, you stare at the light for so long that it almost has no more effect on you. I can see your eyes starting to go into a trance already. That's good. When you close your eyes, you'll start seeing flashing black spots, which is normal when you're staring at an object like that for so long. Just blink a couple of times, and you'll see that bright light come right back."

Royelle followed the instructions without a hitch.

"Ok. Now I want you to press down on the palm of my hand with yours, close your eyes, just relax and focus. Continue to press down, press down, and just sleep."

Dr. Angeli snapped her fingers, and immediately Royelle's head slumped over towards her shoulder.

"As you get yourself nice and comfortable, I want you to think of sleep. Just drift, float, and melt. And as you think of sleep, concentrate on your breathing. You're very relaxed and comfortable right now, and the more you drift and meltdown, the more in tune you're becoming with yourself. When I count to three, when you hear the word three, you'll sit up as best you can with your eyes open. One...two...and three." Dr. Angeli snapped her fingers again. "And now, raise your head while opening your eyes."

Royelle looked completely disheveled. However, Dr. Angeli could see the relaxed state Royelle was in. Her limbs were limp, and her eyes, while open, were low. It was exactly what Dr. Angeli needed to see to be sure that the hypnosis was working.

"Feels weird, doesn't it?" Dr. Angeli asked.

Royelle slowly nodded her head yes.

"You see, what happens, is the subconscious mind gets itself trained to understand simple instructions and directions. Now I just want you to focus and concentrate as I count down to ten. And as I count down, just focus on your breathing and just begin to relax."

"Ten, feeling better about yourself...nine, drifting, floating, melting...eight, the deeper you go, the better you feel, the better you feel, the deeper you go...seven, drifting, floating, melting....six....five, think of trends, think of sleep...four, drifting down all the way, feeling better about yourself, each and every day in every way...three, feeling more relaxed...two, nothing can disturb the peace you are feeling right now....and one, you are in complete relaxation, and the only sound you hear is the sound of my voice...you're completely melted just at peace with yourself."

"It's almost like, your body is loose and limp, like a rag doll. No tension, no stress, no aches, pains, no troubles, nothing in the world can disturb you in any way, shape, or form, just completely concentrated and relaxed, focused on your breathing. It's almost like you're asleep, but you can hear every word I say, and it sends you further down to where you are more relaxed. Every rhythm of my voice, everything I say just helps you relax."

Royelle's eyes were still closed, and her breathing was heavy. It was

26

almost as if she was asleep, but that was part of the hypnosis therapy. It was a trick of the mind, almost like mediation but with twice the power.

"Ok, Royelle. Let's go back to the day you went to Sapphire with Trevion. Tell me what you see."

Although Dr. Angeli always started the sessions with a scene at Club Sapphire, it wasn't the club that always came to mind first. It just opened the gate into that world. Club Sapphire, for Royelle, served as the gatekeeper of her thoughts because that is where her memories of having sex with other people began. Sometimes though, reconnecting with those memories involving Trevion felt like walking on bushes of thorns with no relief in sight.

"Where are you now?" Dr. Angeli asked.

"I'm lying down on my back in my bed." Royelle softly spoke.

"Who are you with, and what are you doing?"

Royelle paused for a second, heaving at the images in her head.

"I'm sucking on the other man's penis."

"Where's Trevion?"

Royelle's eyes squinted as she looked for him in her sights. But she couldn't spot him immediately. This reminded her of the many nights when they were having threesomes, and Trevion wasn't within her reach, forcing her to open her heavy eyes to see what he was doing until she couldn't open her eyes anymore. It was crazy to her. She could see Trevion making her drink, forcing her to guzzle it, and quickly making her another one. By the third drink, Trevion's image would appear behind whatever man was inside of Royelle at the time. That's when everything always became hazy to her.

It was like she knew she was having sex but had no control over the movement and could barely pry her eyes open to see who was sexing her. She attributed it to her being fucked up from the drinking, but she always felt there was more to it than that. And now, in hypnosis, she was experiencing the same exact visions.

"What position are you in right now?"

"On my back."

"Do you feel weird in the position you're in now?"

"Yes. I feel heavy. Like I can't move."

"Are you still having sex?" Dr. Angeli asked, confused at Royelle's response.

"Yes. The man is inside of me."

"Where's Trevion?" Dr. Angeli frowned.

"Behind him."

"What's he doing?"

Royelle tried very hard to pierce through the room's darkness to get a good look at Trevion, but she just couldn't. To her, he resembled the devil.

"Can you explain what's happening at this moment right now?"

"The man is on top of me. He feels very heavy."

"What's he doing, Royelle."

"Whispering in my ear while inside of me."

"What's he saying?"

"Worth every penny. He just keeps whispering my name and repeating worth every penny."

Dr. Angeli was growing concerned. With her expertise and the years that she treated patients, this sounded like a classic case of rape with a twist of prostitution.

"And Trevion? Where is he?"

"Still behind the man."

At this point, Dr. Angeli wanted to stop. She could see Royelle's discomfort and pleasure at the same time. It appeared as if Royelle was enjoying the sex very much, but not knowing Trevion's intentions or what he was doing behind the men made her experience less pleasurable. To try and help Royelle surge past the part of seeing Trevion but not really seeing him, Dr. Angeli decided to try one other tactic.

"Royelle, listen to my voice, and only my voice. I want you to calm your breathing. Take a few deep breaths, and as you release your breaths slowly, I want you to concentrate and focus only on Trevion. Forgetting about the weight, the man, and what he's doing. Instead, I want you to look past him and drill your eyes onto Trevion."

The more Dr. Angeli spoke, the more she could see Royelle's chest slow its beat down slightly. That meant Royelle was following instructions. It was a great thing.

"Now, the room may be dark, but our eyes, once adjusted to the darkness, can often see shapes, people, movement, and shadows. Bedrooms always have a little light in them. Look for yours, Royelle. Where's the little bit of light in your room?"

With her eyes closed, Royelle could see the street light that lightly pierced through the corners of her blinds.

"Did you find it?" Dr. Angeli asked after a few seconds.

"Yes."

"Ok. Now look at that light and back over at Trevion. What do you see?"

Dr. Angeli could see Royelle tighten her eyes as if squinting to see an object without glasses.

"He's just standing there," Royelle said.

"Try it again, Royelle. Focus."

Royelle did as she was told. But this time, her breathing was starting to get heavier again. That's when Dr. Angeli knew she was onto something.

"Royelle, what do you see?"

"I-I think his penis is inside the man." She stuttered.

Dr. Angeli's eyes opened wide, but she stayed professional.

"Look back at the light, Royelle." Dr. Angeli wanted Royelle to be sure of what she saw before bringing her back. "Now look back at Trevion. What's he doing, Royelle." Dr. Angeli asked in a whisper.

Royelle was breathing fast this time. It almost looked like she was hyperventilating.

"Royelle?"

"They're fucking!" She blurted out. "Trevion is fucking a man!"

On 5, you hear me and only me. On 4, you're slowing your breathing. On 3, you're calming your spirit. On 2, everything is peaceful. On 1, you wake." Dr. Angeli snapped her fingers, and Royelle jumped up from the chaise.

CHAPTER 4

Dear Brain Diary,

Yesterday's session was a complete shit show! It brought me to my knees. Do you know that the visions I've been having of other men while in therapy come from that bastard of a man Trevion having sex with men while they were having sex with me? Was it not enough that I was allowing him to have threesomes with me? Was it not enough that he was already married? Was it not enough that he was basically ruining my life right under my nose? He just had to go and drug me too, huh? He just had to have his way, no matter which way, huh?

The whispers of the man, "worth every penny," stick with me. I don't know why, but there's a reason. What did he mean by that? What was worth every penny? And why was he saying it to me? If it's in my stored away thoughts, then I had to have some sort of encounter with him. My visions don't lie.

In fact, they tell very vivid stories when they come together. And see, that's the downfall of this damn amnesia. Some days I remember, other days I don't. Some things are easy to retain; others just get lost until something else comes up. But, Dr. Angeli has always said, "if it sticks to you, then there's relevance." And since I know that to be true, I have to do some digging of my own. I know there's got to be something somewhere that will help me with this.

~ *Royelle*

"Hey girl, hey!" Xandra excitedly answered.

"Hey, sis." Royelle dryly responded.

"Ewww! What's wrong with you? You mad dry and shit." Xandra said, sensing the down mood.

"Sis, I didn't tell you this yet—

"Tell me what?!" Xandra cut Royelle off.

"Yesterday during therapy, I saw visions of Trevion having sex with a man while the man was having sex with me."

Right then and there, Xandra wanted to shit her pants. This was the day she was hoping wouldn't come too soon, but here it was. Royelle regaining parts of her lost memory was a good thing, but it was also concerning. It meant that Royelle would begin to ask more questions, and Xandra would have to include herself in the Trevion and Royelle fiasco, exposing that she was well aware of all of Trevion's dirt from the beginning. But to avoid any rising suspicions, Xandra engaged in the conversation as the concerned sister she had always been.

"Sis? What the hell are you talking about?"

"I'm talking about a man whispering worth every penny in my ear while he was having sex with me, and Trevion was having sex with him, or so it appeared."

Xandra gasped! "Sissss! Are you fucking serious?"

"Yes. Why?! Do you know something?!"

Xandra could never forget about him. She remembered him being the man who essentially exposed Trevion's sex schemes. But he never told Royelle anything about having sex with Trevion or why he dubbed her the name Worth Every Penny. Xandra explained to Royelle that the man she was referring to was someone she had spoken to before. She reminded her that he was what she and Xandra considered a paying customer to have sex with her. They didn't have any concrete evidence of it, but they assumed it to be true based on Royelle's conversation with him.

"Seriously?!" Royelle asked in disbelief. "Do you know if I have any information on him? Like a phone number or something?"

"The only thing I remember was an email you said he sent to your job.

Can you get to your emails right now?"

"Yes, I should be able to," Royelle responded. She hung Xandra up and quickly called her back through video chat. "How far back do you think I should go?" Royelle curiously asked.

"Sis, that was about a year ago. So you got some ways. Try typing in worth every penny in your search bar and see what comes up." Xandra said.

Royelle did just what Xandra suggested, and the screen jumped down to where the email was.

"I got it!" Royelle said excitedly. "Sis, you so smarttt!" Royelle joked.

"You knowww. Just a little razzle dazzle." Xandra joked in return. "What does it say?" She asked.

'Hello, Amorie,

I hope I spelled your name right. And since you never asked me mine, it's Ryan. The reason I am reaching out to you, has nothing to do with your 9-5 business. Please call me at (617) 436-3546. I'm sure you have some questions for me. I could tell from our last conversation.'

Royelle's brain faltered as she tried to process what she had just read. Every part of her paused as her thoughts caught up to what she was feeling at that moment. She was afflicted as she wrote his number down but hoped that maybe he could shed some light on the things she didn't have answers for. She told Xandra she would call him to see if he would still be up to a meeting and would call her back with the details. Royelle hung up the phone, gazing at the picture she and her mother took; then, suddenly, her thoughts took her into flashback mode.

"You know, darling, one day you will find the love you deserve." And when you do, you make sure to give him all of you."

"Ich Kenne Momma."

"Well, I'm glad you do know Royelle. I just don't want to see you get hurt, is all."

"Now, look at me. I didn't know anything then, and it seems like I know even less now. Girllll, if your momma saw what you've been through, been up to, and what you've been dealing with, she'd slap you into next year." Royelle said, coming out of her reverie.

The very thing that her mother was trying to school her about was the very thing causing her the most grief; now, it was time for her to get some real answers. There was much unfinished business with Trevion, and she realized that the truth would come in pieces and come from some unsuspecting places.

It was beginning to feel like she just couldn't catch a break. At every turn, she was faced with something new, something that would break her just a little more than the last situation. She was in a hurt state of mind. If anyone could see the mask under her perfect smile, they would find the pretense crumbling down and her raw emotions taking over everything inside her. Not to mention, the cry buried deep down beneath her soft subtle fictitious laughs was screaming to be released.

She paced around the house for a few minutes thinking up different ways to approach the situation, but she didn't know how much Ryan knew or didn't know. What she did know was that he was probably the only person she might be able to get some honest answers out of if she played her cards right. However, she was afraid that if she said too much or said the wrong thing, it would ruin her chances of finding out the truth. She was a smart girl, but this level of strategy required a different type of levelheaded, stay cool, calm, and collected type of thinking. And right now, Royelle wasn't any of those.

She gave herself time to cool down so she could think. Once she got herself together, she powered up the law firm's Hemisphere network and toggled in her mind about whether she should call or video chat with him. She grabbed a piece of paper, and as she began to write down notes, her heart began to twist and sink with nerves. Small sweat beads developed on her forehead and on the bridge of her nose. Her right leg started shaking, and her breaths came in sharp as she tried to regain her composure.

"Get it together, girl." She said, looking down at her clammy hands.

Mentally, she was in a strange place, but she knew that there was no better time than now to at least attempt to get some answers. After about five minutes of going back and forth in her mind about the video or phone, she decided that the phone was the better option. It was safer. For Royelle, it meant not having to explain her uninviting facial expressions. At least over the phone, she could manage her tone, mute it if she needed to, and make all the faces she wanted to without being detected.

"Hell, here goes nothing." She dialed the number, trying to remain calm.

"Hello. This is Ryan." He quickly answered.

"Hello, Ryan. This is Royelle King—"

"Ahh! Mrs. Kingsley!" He finished. "How are you? To what do I owe the pleasure?"

"I'm well, thank you. How about yourself?" She faintly answered.

Royelle had no recollection of who he was, but she kept the conversation as positive and friendly as possible.

"Well, I can't complain. Every day is a new challenge. But that's the business world for you, right? Every day it appears to be something." He chuckled. "But enough about me. How are you doing since everything?" He stopped himself from continuing the sentence.

"You know. I'm doing ok considering. I have to tie up many loose ends, but I'm better. Thank you for asking."

"I'm delighted to hear that. I remember the last time I reached out to you, a murder happened on your street, and I was hoping I wouldn't have to bail the Kingsley's out." He laughed.

"Bail us out? I didn't realize we were committing a crime." She joked.

"Yea. Well, I guess it all depends on who you ask, huh? He laughed.

"I guess so. But since we're on the subject, how did you learn about all the police activity that day? TV like everyone else, huh?"

"Actually, no. I don't watch much of it. A few of our mutual business partners told me about the heavy police activity going on over there, and I grew concerned."

"Mutual partners? Which ones? There's just so many." She laughed.

Royelle had absolutely no clue on what or who he was talking about, but this was the art of fishing for the information she was hoping to get more of.

"Ah!" He chuckled, "Just a few of the fellas. It's nothing, really. I later learned that it had nothing to do with you and everything to do with your neighbor."

"Well, I certainly do appreciate you for your concern on not just Mr.

Kingsley but also for me."

"How could I not? Worth every penny, remember?"

'Boo-yah!' Royelle thought, rolling her eyes to the back of her head. This was the opportunity she was waiting for. And now that it was given to her on a plater, she wasted no time jumping right on in.

"About that worth every penny."

"Yah! What about it?"

"Can you elaborate?"

"In what capacity, Amoire?"

"In that capacity." She shot right back.

"I'll tell ya what, Amoire. Let me take you to lunch, and I can tell you the meaning behind it and whatever else you want to know."

"Give me just a second to check my calendar." She said.

Royelle smacked her tongue and rolled her eyes to the back of her head when she heard him repeat her middle. She hated it! It was a sure indication that there had been a sexual encounter between them, and it made her sick to her stomach. But there was a goal. She thought about the lunch proposal he offered for a moment and decided to go for it. What harm could he do to her in public? She thought.

She unmuted the phone. "Ryan, you still there?" Royelle asked.

"I am."

"Would a late lunch at two work for you?"

"Absolutely!" He excitedly replied. "Do you like steak?"

"I do." She said.

"Wonderful! Let's meet at the Alba Restaurant."

"The Alba it is. I'll see you soon, Ryan."

Ryan hung up the phone, and Royelle quickly called Xandra to tell her the plan. She asked Royelle if she wanted her to go as backup, but Royelle declined. She wanted to handle it alone. Xandra was good with Royelle's decision but maintained that she would linger around The Alba

just in case anything was to shake the ground around Royelle. H/*er sister was doing good, but she refused to let her walk into any situation blind.

Royelle got showered and dressed and prepared for whatever Ryan might bring to the table. She was doing great with her memory, but things were a blur some days, so she had to plan things out on paper, in her head, and on her phone. As she drove to The Alba, she thought about the hypnosis session, and her vision of seeing Trevion with Ryan brutalized her insides. Her stomach got nauseous, and her mouth was watery as if she was getting ready to throw up. She had no issue with men being with other men; her issue was in the way these two men were with each other while she lay there, essentially getting raped. But, to get results, she was gonna have to suck it all up for a while.

She thought about how she was raised and how simpleminded she must've been to let her guard down and do everything under the sun that Trevion asked of her. And to not remember who Ryan was or what they actually did, made her feel disgusted and angry. She was mad at herself but held a ball of hate for Trevion for not protecting her through it all but rather engaging her.

When Royelle arrived at The Alba, nervous, anxious, and excited, Xandra was already parked across the street from it. She was far enough that Royelle couldn't see her but close enough that she could watch Royelle drive up to the valet and go inside the restaurant. She scoped out the area around the restaurant to see if there was anything suspicious or if anyone was moving around funny, but everything was calm. And when Royelle walked through the double doors, Ryan stood on the opposite side, waiting on her with a smile.

"Hello, Royelle." He greeted.

"Hello, Ryan." She cracked a small smile.

She couldn't remember what he looked like in her visions or on the video call that Xandra said they had nearly a year ago. So, she prayed that the man who greeted her was the man she was expecting to meet. The only thing that gave her some slight reassurance was the sound of his voice.

"Shall we?" He asked.

He began walking towards the hostess booth, and Royelle followed. "He's not a bad-looking White boy." She thought as they followed the waitress to their seats. Except for his slightly upturned nose, resembling Miss Piggy from Seasame Street, Ryan managed to capture Royelle's attention slightly. He stood about 5'7 or 5'8 with small narrow eyes, an oval-shaped head with a comb-over fade that gave his red hair some style. His beard and goatee connected with the fade perfectly, while his Olive looking skin complimented his Green eyes perfectly. And when he smiled, all his teeth were intact and White as snow. *'Veneers,'* Royelle thought.

She didn't pay much attention to the labels he was wearing, but his slim three-piece suit spoke volumes. He was a clean-cut guy in his mid 40's. Royelle was impressed and shocked at the same time, wondering what he could've ever wanted from Trevion or her, for that matter.

"Is this ok?" The waitress asked, pointing at the low-lit two-seater booth.

"Yes, this is fine, "Ryan responded.

Royelle nervously sat down across from him, picked up the menu, and began to falsely review its contents. It was her way of calming her nerves and avoiding eye contact with him, at least for the first few minutes.

"Good Afternoon. My name Is Jenna. Can I start you with something to drink?" The waitress asked, putting warm bread and butter down on the table.

Since they both had agendas as to why they were there, they each placed their drink and lunch orders just to get it out of the way.

"So, how was the rest of your afternoon," Ryan asked, cutting a slice of bread for them both.

"It was good. Busy, to say the least." She lied.

"Well, while we wait, why don't we get to why we're here."

"Yes! Lets." Royelle responded.

Royelle was feeling very awkward about the entire situation. But, here it was, the moment she knew she just might get some clarity on Trevion, and she was trying hard not to mess it up by showing her nervousness. She quickly gave herself a spiel to calm down and relax so Ryan could guide the conversation, something she quickly regretted doing. He asked more questions about the Benton murder than she cared to answer. She hoped he would catch a clue that she wasn't interested in that conversation by giving him short and dry responses, but it didn't work.

The more questions he asked about the things that had nothing to do with why she wanted to meet, the more anxious and irritated she became. And after about fifteen more minutes of repeated nothingness, she interjected the conversation.

"You know, you've asked me so many questions but have yet to get why we're here."

Ryan smirked. "By all means, ask away. The floor is yours." He said.

Royelle faked a smile to help her cut through the nerves.

"So did you, the man in Pharmaceuticals, and my husband, the man in Construction and Roofing, meet?" Royelle jumped right to it.

"Although we had different lines of work, many people from various industries know him. A lot of people liked Mr. Kingsley."

"Seems that way, doesn't it?"

"What, you don't believe it?" Ryan questioned.

"No, I do. It's just I didn't know how much until the memorial service, you know." Royelle put her head down, pretending to be somewhat sad.

"My apologies." Ryan grabbed her hand.

"It's ok. I've learned to deal with." She validated. "I just feel like I didn't get enough time with him, you know. We had businesses and things we were trying to build. It was short-lived."

"I understand. But I will say that the business you two ran was a bit risky."

"How so?" Royelle's eyebrows frowned in curiosity.

Royelle played it cool. They were finally getting somewhere. At least, she hoped. She had been in her profession long enough to know that if she remained calm, attentive, and let the other person do all the talking, she would soon get what she needed.

"Let me just say this. Mr. Kingsley was very lucky to have you. My wife would've never agreed to the things you did. Shit! I can barely get her to suck me off, never mind having threesomes, be it with a man or woman. She's a beautiful woman, but in the bedroom is where the magic lacks. But you and Mr. Kingsley! You guys ran a hell of an enterprise out of your home. That was a genius move. It was kept very low-key, with select customers, and since you both have lucrative jobs, the cops would've never suspected a thing as far as the money is concerned. It was brilliant! And

Amoire, as I told you before, you're worth every fucking penny."

Ryan placed his hand on top of Royelle's, and her immediate reaction was to snatch it from under his, but she knew she had to stay calm even though she was burning inside. She slightly smiled as he shifted the conversation back to what his wife was and wasn't doing. She couldn't have cared less. She heard him, but none of it was sticking. The only words she heard were *low-key, customers, and worth every fucking penny.*

She knew where he was going with it but wouldn't believe it until he actually said it or spelled it out for her. So, she did what she does best when helping Charlyn prepare for a winning case, put on her paralegal hat, and began her show. She slowly looked up at him seductively and said, "So tell me. What did that night do for you? What was so good about it that it was worth every fucking penny as you so eloquently put it?"

"Amoire. Everything you and Mr, Kinglsey did that night was worth the $600 I paid. For that kind of fucking, I'd do it again and again and again."

Royelle took a huge gulp of her water while simultaneously swallowing the knot in her throat, still trying to remain calm. "Well, I gather you enjoyed yourself, but I'm a details kind of girl, so tell me your favorite three parts." Here's where she was hoping the Lobster and Steak of the conversation would meet.

"Are you sure you wanna hear this? You might cream yah panties with the details."

Royelle giggled as she leaned in closer towards Ryan. "I don't have any on." She sat back and started to drink her water again. On the inside, emotionally, she was falling apart. But she was proud of herself for not folding and for being the girl Adala always knew her to be; strong and on her shit.

"Do you see that there?" Ryan chuckled

"See what?" Royelle blushed.

"That's part of the reason you have the clients you did or do have. The way you talk, your sassiness, and your level of seduction will bring joy to any unhappy married man." Ryan said with excitement. "But to answer your question, my top three would have to be when you were giving me a blow job, when I was riding Trevion, and when he was behind me."

Royelle died on the inside. Ryan had just confirmed what her visions were trying to show her. She was astonished at the revelation. Although her insides were crumbling, she showed no emotion, hoping it would keep Ryan talking. She was crushed, but she was a gluten for punishment. As if what she heard wasn't enough, she wanted to stretch her ear further to see what else Ryan would let escape. Therefore, she continued to play her game.

"Wheww! That last one of the three must've made you cum immensely, huh?" She asked.

"It sure did. But, I came a lot in general. Each time you touched me in any way, I made sure to be touching Mr. Kingsley, and each time he came, I came. It was a hell of a night. You two sure knew how to please your clients." Ryan ecstatically answered.

"We did try." She smirked.

"Oh, no! You didn't try; you both did."

"And your wife? I know you said she wasn't much to play with in the bed, but does she know you're bisexual?"

"Amoire. Come on now. You should know that the men who frequent Intensity are down-low brothers, who more than likely keep that secret from their wives. Honestly, you're probably the only wife that knows about her husband's status. That's what made the two of you so unique."

"Oh, I know, Ryan. But there are those exceptions."

"Well, my wife isn't one of them. She would take me for everything I got and probably chop my dick off in the process. But this is why most men frequented Intensity or went to your house. It was the level of privacy and confidentiality that both places provided."

Royelle was so deep into the conversation and engrossed by its contents that she never realized she was picking at her food that had been sitting in front of her for ten minutes. She was just praying that her phone was still recording inside her purse as it sat on top of the table in between her and Ryan. She had to keep going, though. She wasn't done.

"You know. One thing Mr. Kingsley never told me is how he went about his selection process. How did he select you or the others?"

Ryan chuckled. " He was a man of many secrets, wasn't he?"

"He sure was." Royelle giggled, raising her glass in a toasting motion.

"The vetting was really easy. Most of us came from Intensity, but it was his secretary, Ummm. What is that girl's name?" Ryan closed his eyes tight and snapped his fingers as he tried to remember her.

Royelle sat quiet and with the patience of a lion as she waited for his memory to serve him. She couldn't wait to hear the name of the bitch that solidified the guest list without her knowledge.

"It was like Mac something." He said, still struggling to get it out.

"McKenzie?" Royelle completed.

"Yes! Yes! McKenzie! How could I forget her name? The little wench was always so rude. I had to complain about her to Trevion on several occasions."

"Too bad you never told me. I would've set her straight long ago."

Ryan laughed. "Funny you should say that. I wanted to tell you and told Mr. Kingsley I was going to tell you, but he advised that I didn't. He said you would overreact. And given your response, he might've been right." Ryan smiled, taking another bite of his Chicken Cesar Salad.

"Well, in normal circumstances, I do not react. However, where there's money involved and my clients are at stake, that's a different ball game." Royelle lied, looking down at her watch. "Well, I hate to end this so abruptly, but I do have to get back to the office. Maybe I can call you up sometime?" Royelle continued to lie.

At this point, she felt like she had enough to move on with, and if she dared ask any more questions, she might create suspicion for Ryan regarding the entire enterprise, so she stopped.

"So, when will I see you again, Amoire?" He asked as Royelle stood up.

"I'm honestly not sure. My two worlds run on separate tracks these days. But I will keep in touch. You can bet your bottom dollar on that."

CHAPTER 5

oyelle couldn't wait to be done with Ryan. As soon as the valet brought her truck back, she got in and drove away down a quiet side street not too far from the restaurant, with Xandra following behind. As soon as she knew that she was out of the sight of others, she let all her emotions go and began screaming, crying, and banging her hands on the steering wheel. All Xandra could do was watch. Her eyes filled with tears knowing that the truth about Royelle's sex nights with Trevion included more than just sex had more than likely been exposed.

Royelle was dumbfounded. She had no idea how or what to feel. She felt heartbreak before, but this right here was beyond heartbreak—this was bone-crushing agony. Not only did Ryan confirm that she was sold for sex by the one person she was supposed to believe in, trust and confide in. But finding out he was gay, having sex with men under her nose, and McKenzie was the one making the connections killed her insides at a rapid pace. She began to question everything about herself. Every good thing she knew she was, she despised at that moment. She couldn't believe that what she perceived as her worst nightmare had just become torment from hell.

"Ahhh!"

Royelle screamed at the top of her lungs, sobbing profusely. It was the kind of cry that caused her breathing to pause, the kind where she had to stop crying for a moment just to catch her breath so she could continue. She couldn't believe that after all these years of not giving a man any part of her, she gave all of herself to him, only for him to do the one thing she feared the most; getting her heart torn apart. Royelle was completely enfeebled at this point. If he was deliberately trying to ruin her, he succeeded even from the grave.

Finally, after 20 minutes of unleashing her aches and trying to process everything that she had just heard, Royelle made it home in what seemed like 2.2 flat seconds, with Xandra right on her tail. She went into the family room and stood there looking around. She was trying to see if she could remember anything from those nights they spent with strangers; everything was simply a blur.

Ryan never said anything about them doing drugs, but it was the only thing that could validate why she couldn't remember any of the nights or the people. It only added up to one thing— date rape drugs. Total disbelief and shock was the only way to describe her feelings at this point. She looked down at her watch and saw that the office was still open. Rather than lay down as she had anticipated, she ran out of the house and jumped back in her truck.

"Where the fuck is she going?" Xandra said as she prepared to follow Royelle again.

As Royelle weaved in and out of the afternoon traffic, Xandra followed closely behind. At first, she had no clue where Royelle was going, but when they turned off near the Marina Bay sign, there was no question she was heading to the law offices. "What the hell?" Xandra said as Royelle pulled up into the small parking lot.

Royelle was relieved to see that all the reserved spaces for the law firm employees were empty. She got out of her truck and sprinted towards the front door, never noticing Xandra's truck parked on the corner. From the looks of Royelle's face, Xandra could see trouble brewing. Rather than staying seated in her truck, she decided to follow her inside.

When Royelle got off the elevator, she noticed that the floor was quiet. She checked every office space, and none of the attorneys or partners were there. The only one left was McKenzie, who was on the phone looking at Royelle crazy as she went office to office. "Girl, let me call you right back," McKenzie whispered to her friend on the other end, smiling as Royelle approached. "You good, Royelle?" She asked.

"Yup!"

Royelle took all the might she had in her right arm and punched the dog shit out of McKenzie. She landed the punch so hard on the bridge of her nose that it left McKenzie with a gash long enough to reach the inner corners of her eyes. But Royelle didn't stop there. Before McKenzie realized what was happening, Royelle was on top of her, wailing on her in full force. She delivered blow after blow after blow to McKenzie's head, face, and arms as she used them as a shield.

"Bitch! You knew all along! You were in on the shit this whole time! You filthy, grimey, stank ass bitch!"

Royelle continued to yell as she punched McKenzie, banging her head onto the floor. She was going so hard she never heard the elevator's ding as Xandra made it to the floor. When Xandra heard all the commotion, she ran towards them with her gun drawn, unsure of what was happening. When she saw Royelle on top of McKenize, she put her gun back on safety and into her waist. She tried to snatch Royelle up, but Royelle wasn't stopping. She continued to kick and throw punches in the air, trying to get at McKenzie.

"Get the fuck off me!" Royelle yelled, not realizing it was Xandra.

"Sisss! It's me! Chill! It's me!" Xandra hollered.

Hearing Xandra's voice didn't control the situation. Royelle was out for blood.

"This bitch knew, sis! She knew all along! She was the reason Trevion sold me for sex!" Royelle hollered.

Xandra had a muddled look. She couldn't believe what she was hearing. "What the fuck are you talking about?" She said with a crazed look.

"Ask this bitch! I'm gonna fucking kill her! Royelle attempted to reach McKenzie again as McKenzie stood up from the floor bruised, bleeding, and a mess.

"What the fuck is she talking about, McKenzie?" Xandra asked in a stern voice standing in between her and Royelle.

"I-I don't know." McKenzie cried.

Xandra smacked her in the face. "Lie to me again bitch! What the fuck is my sister talking about?"

"I don't—

Before she could finish her sentence, Royelle reached around Xandra and punched McKenzie in the face again.

"Bitch! You better be lucky my sister is protecting you. Cause she isn't here for me! Ooohhhh bitch! You just wait! Your ass is mine." Royelle promised.

"McKenzie, I'm only gonna ask one last time, and then it ain't my sister you gonna have to worry about. What the fuck is she talking about?"

"I swear I don't know."

Just then, Xandra pulled out her gun and pistol-whipped McKenzie.

"Where's your fucking car?" Xandra asked.

"It's in the shop." She stuttered through tears.

"How you getting home?"

"Uber."

"Nahhh! Yo ass coming with me," Xandra said.

Sis, get this shit cleaned up and go home."

"No! I'm coming with you!"

"Sis! You heard what the fuck I said! I'll call you. Go home!"

Xandra grabbed McKenzie by the arm and walked towards the elevator with her gun stuck into McKenzie's side.

"I swear to you. If you make one false move, I'll kill you where you stand. Do you understand me?" Xandra said subtly.

"Yes."McKenzie's voice trembled.

They walked out to Xandra's truck, and she let McKenzie in, making sure to put on the child safety lock so she wouldn't make an attempt to get out. "Put your seat belt on. Safety first." Xandra reached into the glove compartment, grabbed one of the unused cloths that she kept in her truck for cleaning purposes, and threw it at McKenzie. "Clean yourself up. You look a mess." Before pulling off, she texted Sion and told him she had a trash drop-off in about an hour.

"Where are you taking me?" McKenzie asked.

"Oh nahhh! You don't get to ask any muthafucking questions, Lil mama. That's all me."

McKenzie continued to cry, scared of what was coming next. She didn't have a phone or purse. She was hurt, bleeding, and in severe pain. Royelle spared no feeling as she beat on McKenzie. For every lie, every sting of pain and hurt, every betrayal, every wrong look, and every suspicion that Royelle ever felt, McKenzie felt it twice as hard.

She couldn't believe that the whole time McKenzie was working for Charlyn, she was also working undercover for whatever reason as Trevion's spy. Finding out about McKenzie's involvement all made sense now. It made it easier for Royelle to understand why McKenzie always gave her a hard time. But she wondered, *'How did they even know each other? When did it start? How could she have missed all of it? And why was she the target?'* She was beyond vexed at the thought of it all as she cleaned up the mess she had made.

She wished she knew where Xandra was going or what she was going to do so that she could take part in it. But, if she knew her sister like she believed she knew her, then McKenzie stood no chance with Xandra, and when it was all over, Xandra was gonna be the last one standing and would tell it all. So, when Royelle was done cleaning the mess, she hurried home to wait on Xandra's call. But, the wait wasn't easy at all. She paced the floors back and forth, biting on her nails again, anxious to hear what was happening or what was being said.

Since she knew it might be a while, she sat in her new rocking chair, closed her eyes, and began rocking herself in a slow, steady space. The idea was to calm herself down so that her thoughts could take her to some places that she felt might help her understand McKenzie's plight in her life. She knew that if she followed Dr. Angeli's directions on being self-sufficient in that area of her life, she would have no problem accomplishing the goal of remembering when McKenzie became a problem for her.

"Here we are, sweetheart."

McKenzie looked around, scared as hell. There were no cars, no houses, just a dark road with no street lights and a warehouse that looked abandoned, surrounded by high shrubs, untamed grass, and dim lights outside the building. It certainly wasn't a place for any woman to be, no matter how gangster they may have been.

Xandra opened the passenger door, grabbed McKenzie out, and walked her into the building with her gun poking into McKenzie's side. It was still dark inside but produced enough light to see where they were walking towards. They entered the open space where two chairs sat across from each other; one chair came complete with handcuffs already affixed to it. And by the way Xandra was guiding McKenzie, she could tell Xandra had been there and done this kind of low-level kidnapping before.

"Sit," Xandra demanded.

McKenzie followed Xandra's order without restraint. Xandra handcuffed McKenzie's hands behind her and pulled her chair up closer to McKenzie before taking her seat.

"Are you gonna kill me?"

Xandra smirked. "Girlll no! We just gonna have us a little girl chat. And you're gonna tell me everything I want to know. Cause if you don't, death is what you're gonna wish I gave you." Xandra cocked her gun and placed it on her lap.

McKenzie felt her blood flow reduce, her sweat glands perspire, heart palpitations grow, and her mouth got increasingly dry as Xandra spoke. She knew Xandra was about that life and not about to play any games with her. She vowed at that moment that she wanted to make it out alive, so she was going to answer every question as best as she could with only the truth.

"What do you want to know?" McKenzie nervously asked.

Girllll. Didn't I tell you I ask all the questions here? But you're right. Let's get to it since we are here to play Q & A, shall we? Let's start with what the fuck my sister was talking about?"

"I—

"Hold on." Xandra raised her index finger. "Before you say anything stupid like, I don't know. Let me remind you, my sister doesn't fight. So for her to whoop your ass like she did, you know something about something, and that's all I want to hear is what you know. Understood?"

McKenzie quickly nodded her head.

"Floors yours." Xandra pointed at the concrete.

"She didn't tell me what she was talking about, but I guess she might have found out that I know Trevion."

"Know him how?"

"Well, I worked for him."

"Bitch, you're playing with me. How?!" Xandra hollered.

"I was one of his escorts."

"Oh, like a hoe, you mean?" Xandra patronized.

McKenzie nodded her head in shame.

"Go on. When did y'all meet?"

"I've known Trevion for about seven years. I was the girl he was talking to when him and Royelle met. He asked me to stand there and pretend to be talking to him so he could get her attention. I was part of the plan from the beginning."

"Plan? What plan?"

"He wanted to get Royelle to work for him, but when he realized that she wasn't that type of girl, he decided to make her his one. But something changed a year into them being together because he made me get a job at her office to spy on her, get all her financial papers, and any information I could on her."

Xandra knew that McKenzie couldn't have been lying because a year after Trevion met Royelle, Adala told Royelle she would inherit a big lump sum, but she never said what. So maybe Trevion caught win to the amount Adala was leaving behind, and he wanted a piece of the pie. It was the only thing Xandra could think of at that moment.

"What else you know about him? Were y'all fucking?"

"Yes."

"Was he fucking them other bitches you came to the memorial service with too?"

"Yes."

"Who's his other fucking wife? You?"

"No. No. That's Aruba." McKenzie quickly redirected.

Xandra chuckled. "I fucking knew it." She said.

"So what information on Royelle did you give to Trevion and when?"

McKenzie paused for a moment. "I gave him everything that came in the mail or emails regarding her life insurance policies and the wills."

"How the fuck did you get into my sister's personal shit?"

"I saw her write her passwords down one day, and I memorized them. Trevion told me too."

"Tuh! Trevion, huh? Fuck that nigga!"

By now, McKenzie was a sweaty mess. She was nervous, scared, and anxious. She was trembling, and Xandra didn't just see the fear; she smelled it. Xandra knew there was more to the story, but McKenzie was nothing but a pawn in the game. If anyone was going to have any information for her, it was going to be Aruba, or maybe even Bella. Those were her next two targets.

Xandra continued asking questions about Bella and Aruba, and by the time she was done playing detective in the interrogation room, she had Bella and Aruba's addresses and their favorite hang-out spot. From A-Z, she learned about Aruba's shitshow of a plan to ruin Royelle and about her frequent trips to New York to see some dude. McKenzie left no stone unturned as she continued to spill the truth. And so far, she felt secure in knowing that her life was spared.

"Whew! You bitches were working hard, weren't y'all? But y'all didn't know that Royelle came with a one-woman army. I'll kill anybody behind my fucking sister. But you, today, you lucky. I ain't gonna kill you. You did good."

They walked side by side out of the warehouse, not saying a word, getting back into the truck. McKenzie grew nervous as they drove the city streets listening to R&B Coffee Shop music. She had no clue where they were going and was too afraid to say anything when they passed up her street. When they got to Cambridge, that's when she really started to panic. *"What the fuck are we doing out here?"* She thought to herself.

They pulled up to another abandoned building near the Lone Tree Hill trails, and there was a Black on Black Tahoe waiting with the engine running. Xandra parked her truck, opened McKenzie's door, and a dude with a black mask walked up to them with a black sack in his hands.

"How much?"

"Oh, nah. Let him know this one is on the house. She's used up.

49

Shouldn't be hard for her to get adjusted." Xandra looked over at McKenzie. "I told you I wasn't gonna kill you. But they might. Better do what they say. Toodles, sweetheart." Xandra smirked and waved her fingers in a rapid motion.

"No! Please! What the fuck are doing?! Where the fuck are they taking me?! Let me goooo!" McKenzie yelled and pleaded.

The dude covered McKenzie's face with a cloth full of propofol until she passed out. Once she was asleep, he covered her head with the sack and put her in the truck. As soon as they pulled off, Xandra called Royelle and gave her the 411 on everything except for what happened to McKenzie and who she gave her to. Royelle was distraught. But she needed closure so she could fully move on, and this was just one more step to being closer to closing this chapter in her life.

She was so tired from the fight and with everything she had been enduring in recent days and weeks that all she wanted to do was sleep her nightmare away. She went into her medicine cabinet, took two Ambien pills, got naked, pulled the sheets back, laid down, covered herself up, and closed her eyes.

"God, if you don't wake me from this slumber, I'm good with that. At least I know I'll be with you and my mother. I'm tired, Lord. I'm really tired."

CHAPTER 6

rain Diary,

  I have nothing for you today. I honestly do not know how to feel right now. Do you know, during hypnosis, I learned that the man who was supposed to love me for better or for worse was fucking a man in our bed, all while I was in the bed with them, and I had no damn clue?! I'm just now learning it! Not to mention, I met with the Worth Every Penny man Ryan, and he confirmed every vision I had during hypnosis. Anddddd, he told me that the bitch McKenzie who I knew had a problem with me, was part of the whole thing?!

  Am I really that slow? How did I not see that happening? It was happening right in front of me! I was a part of it! I was there! Dr. Angeli said that she believes the images I saw of Trevion making me something to drink may have been him poisoning me with something. Perhaps with the goal to inebriate me so I wouldn't remember anything after a certain point. And after talking to Ryan, I'm more than sure Dr. Angeli was right. I can't put together an entire night of a threesome we've ever had. Maybe the first few minutes once it started, but nothing after. Especially nothing that Ryan talked about.

  And McKenzie! That bitch deserves everything she gets and then some.

I knew I had seen that trash somewhere before. I just knew it! And she tried to make me think I was crazy! I only tried to help her raggedy ass. And the whole time, she was plotting with Trevion to destroy me. But why me?! Why is this happening to me?! What did I do to anyone to deserve such tragedy in my life. Men?! I could understand women, but men?! And why in our bed, in our house?! I'm sorry, brain diary. Today I woke up in the dumps. I just want to be left alone to sleep this torment away. Sometimes I wish I was still in the coma. I promise.

   ~ Roy

Rayford woke up the way he went to sleep…mad! The idea of his kids conspiring against him for anything was beyond him. Part of him understood Royelle's rebellion towards him, but he had zero understanding for Raymelle and Raylina's. Those two were always the closest to him, staying out the way and neutral, even when he and Royelle were at war. But now, they were dog meat just like Royelle. *'How could they?! Not those two. What has she done to them?'* He thought.

   Rayford couldn't fathom the idea that he was losing his power over them or that they might actually be seeing the real him as Royelle did some time ago. As far as he was concerned, it was all her fault that her siblings treated him the way they were. She had to be the one tainting their minds with venom. In no way did he associate their distance with his actions.

   He got out the bed thinking up ways to get in Royelle's good graces. And since the other two were also against him, he had to make it right with Royelle in order for things to get right between all of them. But the more he thought about it, the more it made him feel like he was kissing Royelle's ass, and that was a no for him. He was old school. She was the child; he was the parent. The idea of begging her to do what's right by him went against everything he believed in.

   "Ahuu duh shi tink shi a?" He mumbled in Patois as he walked towards the living room.

   The house was unbelievably disorganized. It looked like it did before Adala's passing and funeral. All the acting Rayford put on after Adala died was just that, a show. The house stayed clean for all but a few days. Within a week of people no longer coming over to pay their respects and show emotional or moral support, the house returned to what it looked like before; a pigsty.

Raymelle and Raylina, at this point, simply didn't give a fuck anymore. It wasn't that they didn't care about the house they grew up in; they just didn't want the argument anymore. And it made no sense to hire a cleaning crew when all he did was disrupt the peace that a clean house promotes. It was pointless. Therefore, to avoid any conflicts, they stayed away and haven't returned to the house since the second week of Adala's passing.

Rayford made it to the cluttered couch, pushed all the junk to one side, and plopped himself down, with money being the only thing on his mind. He figured if Adala had gone through all the trouble of hiring attorneys, paying for her own funeral, and hiding her insurance policies from him, she must've left a fortune behind for her children and was pegged on getting what he believed was rightfully his. If not all, at least a portion.

He sat for a while smoking cigarette butt after cigarette butt, not giving two shits that they were old and stale. Chain-smoking was his coping mechanism. It was his distraction to problems in a sense. And depending on the situation, it could also serve as motivation for resolving an issue.

"Ras Clawd!" He blurted out in Patois.

He got up off the couch, headed back towards his bedroom, gathered whatever clothes he could find scattered around the room, and headed towards the shower. Once he was done and fully dressed, he headed out the front door, into his raggedy car, and straight to Royelle's. On the drive there, rage kept building as he thought about how he would address or talk to her about the situation.

"Dis likkle gyal!" He banged on the sterring wheel. "She a guh gimme mi funds."

With the way he was raised in a strict home full of rules and the man always in control of the house, he couldn't make sense around the idea that what was happening between him and Royelle was happening in reverse. Since when did a child call the shots. That was unseen or unheard of in his day. It made him feel less of a man and father to have to go crawling on his knees for some shit he felt belonged to him from the get-go. Besides, he had been with Adala for nearly 40 years. So anything connected to her belonged to him, no matter their dysfunction. At least that's how he felt.

When he finally arrived at Royelle's house, he was surprised to see it was much smaller than the house she once shared with Trevion. As he exited the car, he stared at the small three-bedroom home with contempt in his eyes. It didn't look like anything Royelle would live in, giving her taste and the level of maintenance she liked to keep. And although she wasn't into name brands, Rayford knew she enjoyed looking nice, smelling good, and living comfortably. So to see her new living quarters was a bit awkward for him.

But his awkwardness or that of others phased Royelle none. It may not have had any of the amenities or the space that the last house was laced with, but for Royelle, it was perfect. It was just her and her new dog. Therefore, worries about space and accommodations for others were null in void. The less space she provided, the fewer people would be at her door.

He walked to her door boldly but with caution. He knew the situation between them was cavernous, but he was dead set on trying to make things right for the sake of whatever Adala may have left behind. He rang the bell and stepped to the center of the door, where he would be in clear view of the peephole, and anxiously waited for her to answer. Since he didn't know what he would get from Royelle and his unsolicited visit, he made sure to put enough distance between him and the door.

"Prowess, who could that be at the door, girl, huh? It's way too early for visitors, nor am I in the mood." Royelle said as she petted her dog.

Royelle was still sulking in her sorrows after learning about McKenzie and Trevion when Rayford rang the bell. The last two days with Dr. Angeli and Ryan were enough. Today, she just wanted to be left alone and was in no mood to deal with nobody else's bullshit. So to get to the door and see it was Rayford on the other side of it only added to the day's frustration.

She stood in place with both of her hands pressed up against the door, taking a deep breath. She couldn't believe that her father was standing on the opposite side, and suddenly all kinds of thoughts rushed through her. *'What does he want? Is this about the money? Does he really want to see how I'm doing? Why the hell is he here?'* She wondered. Not once has he ever popped up at the old house, let alone the new one. So, she began psyching herself up for whatever he was about to bring, good or bad. She stood quietly for a couple more minutes, pulled herself together, and opened the door.

"Good Morning." He greeted.

"Good Morning. It's a surprise to see you here." Royelle responded with a smile.

She looked him up and down, impressed at the way he looked and smelled. His appearance was the complete opposite of what she had heard from Raymelle and Raylina. She was amazed at his ability to clean up well. He almost looked like a different man, even better than what he looked like at court.

"Well, are you gonna welcome me in?" He asked, still standing on the step in front of the threshold.

Royelle didn't murmur a word. She opened the door a little further and extended her right arm and hand in the direction of the front room.

"You know this is my first time here. I'm not just gonna invite myself in." He said as he found his way to the living room.

"Can I get you something to drink?" She politely asked, trying to keep the peace.

"Coffee. I'll take that if you have it."

"It's early. What are you doing here?" She asked, walking to the kitchen.

Since the living room had an open concept, the dining room and kitchen could be seen without obscurities. Therefore, Rayford could stay where he was seated, and Royelle could keep her distance while still seeing and speaking to him.

"Well, I thought about what the judge said the other day, and she was right. So instead of asking everyone else, I wanted to see where you were living and how you were really doing. The judge made a lot of sense, and it hit me. So here I am."

Royelle looked in his eyes, looking for any sign of fuckery, and he showed none. *'Has he lost his rabbit ass mind,'* she thought. This display of affection was not in his DNA. Royelle was bewildered by his showmanship.

"Well, it's not much, but do you want to see the place.

"Sure. It's a lot smaller than what I'm used to seeing you in."

"Yes, well, it's just Prowess and me."

"Prow-what?" Rayford giggled. "What kind of name is that for a dog? Does it have a meaning?" He asked.

"Isaiah 28:6. It means strength. Your phone has google; utilize it. It'll teach you a lot."

Royelle giggled back, leaving out the part that Prowess was an emotional support dog. That was the last thing she needed Rayford to know. She knew that information would be a way for him to use it against her in another bullshit hearing. An emotional support dog for most people was a great thing. For people like Rayford, it meant crazy and incapable. She proceeded to walk him through the house, showing him each room and conducting small talk. When they made it back to the living room, he sat down on the loveseat facing away from Royelle.

"The house is small but nice."

He didn't quite know it yet, but he was wearing out his welcome, and that comment was speeding up the process. Royelle couldn't figure out his true intentions yet, but she knew it wasn't about checking up on her and was sure it was about money. Either way, she wasn't going to let him leave until she found out.

As she walked back towards him with her coffee in hand, it was hard for her to ignore his cat-daddy look. Although he looked like he took a turn back into the '70s with his Cream short-sleeve button-down and Brown flannel-style pants, he still looked nice. She handed him his coffee, grabbed her Orange juice, and joined him in the living room, sitting across from him. Bullshitting time was over. Now it was time to get down to the real reason he showed up before the cracking of the first egg.

"So, how are you, daddy, since momma?"

She tried to keep everything peaceful by calling him daddy instead of Rayford and speaking softly.

"Everything gud yuh kno."

"Are you sure? You don't have to lie to me, you know."

"Yah, mi sure. Mi nuh haffi lie tuh yah." He sucked his teeth.

Royelle was trying her hardest to talk about anything that did not

56

involve money. The subject always spurned bad blood between them, and she wanted to keep the peace. The problem was her mind wouldn't rest. At the onset of him showing up, her brain went into overdrive. It was like she was sitting in one of her hypnosis sessions, reliving her trauma with him. And although she was tougher in the physical sense, she was still shattered and torn mentally and emotionally.

She tried to shake the thoughts by taking him on the short tour, having small talk, and even making coffee. But him being in the house with her alone wasn't a good feeling. With every breath he took, she tensed up. She and Dr. Angeli discussed Rayford possibly being a trigger for Royelle, but now Royelle was certain. She had to hurry up and get him out of her house before she turned into the wicked witch of the west. But she wanted to do it with kindness.

"More coffee?" She asked, knowing he'd say no.

She grabbed his cup and hers and brought them into the kitchen. Prowess's eyes followed, watching Royelle's every move. She didn't skip a beat. Wherever Royelle went, she went. Her levels of protection for Royelle were at an all-time high.

When Royelle returned to the living room, she made sure to sit on the same couch before, creating ample space between them and a safe zone for her. Although. she didn't want to be the one to ask what the impromptu visit was about, the sudden silence was awkward. She gathered he was waiting on her like she was waiting on him. But something had to give, so she asked him again.

"So what really brought you here today, daddy?"

It was just the break Rayford was looking for. He figured since they shot the shit for a bit and the ice had melted, it would be a good time to get to the real reason he was sitting in her living room.

"Mi wa fi chat tuh yuh bout wah happened inna court."

"Bingo! Ding Ding Ding!" She exploded in her head.

There it was, the real intent. Royelle wasn't sure why she hoped the business of him being there was really about her, but she secretly wished it wasn't about her mother and the money. She hated that she was right about his real intentions. For once, she wanted him to be genuine about something.

Sadly, this wasn't it.

"What about the court?" She kept her tone down and her attitude in check.

"Wuh muss yuh challenge mi pan everything?"

Rayford, too, kept his tone down so as not to incite a hostile environment. He also wanted to keep the peace. After all, it was the only way he and Royelle might be able to come to some sort of understanding or agreement.

'I challenged you because you're greedy, self-centered, mean, cowardly, and don't deserve any of what momma left behind.' That's what she was thinking and really wanted to say, but the word peaceful kept floating around in her head. "Daddy, I wasn't challenging you. I believed that you needed help delegating everything, especially after momma got sick. But you wouldn't let me in, so I was forced to go the legal route."

Rayford wasn't buying any of the shit Royelle was selling. And even Royelle wasn't convinced of the shit she had just spewed out of her mouth. It sounded fraudulent as hell and felt that way too.

"Royelle, enuh dat a nuh chuu." He corrected.

"It may not be true for you, daddy, but it's my truth. You're entitled to yours as I am to mine." Her tone was still calm.

"Ow? Explain dat tuh mi."

Although Rayford tried to keep his cool, Royelle could sense some slight hostility accompanying the space. She maintained her chill but stayed guarded.

"Daddy, I'm not sure where you want to go with this conversation, but perhaps we should end it here while we are in good space."

Royelle gracefully tried to keep things in line, but by the way Rayford was shifting in his chair, she could tell things were about to start heating up.

"Royelle now is a good time to have this conversation. And since you seem to always want to be in control of everything. Let's talk."

Now there was no denying that Rayford was mad. Not only did he switch up his dialect, but he was also being cynical and taking jabs while Royelle was still trying to keep her cool and remember all of the coping skills she developed with Dr. Angeli.

"Daddy, please. I do not want this to turn into an argument." She pleaded.

"Well, it won't if you just answer my questions."

"What questions, daddy? I don't understand what it is you want to know."

Although Royelle attempted to stay calm, she was slowly starting to lose grip of her repose. She was fighting it, but the more Rayford spoke, the more the tone in his voice changed, the less at ease Royelle was becoming.

"It's not that hard to understand, Royelle. You have money that Adala should have shared with me. So, what is the share? That's what I want to know."

Royelle took a deep breath. "It's always been about the money with you. Never about the well-being of others. I actually wanted to believe that you came here for me. Just plain ole me. No hidden agendas, just to see about me. What was I thinking to believe that this visit would be different."

Royelle was trying so hard not to let Rayford get under her skin, but her efforts were beginning to slip from under her. It was like he didn't hear a word she said. He continued to talk about the money as if he had invested in it. And the more he spoke about the money and what was supposed to be his, the madder Royelle got.

With all the bitching he was doing, he didn't even give Royelle a chance to explain that she had no idea how much was left behind. And although her mother didn't leave anything for him, Royelle had every intention of going against her mother's wishes and giving him something. It was the right thing to do despite what her mother said. But the way he was acting and coming at her about it was causing her to have a complete change of heart.

"Daddy, listen." She said softly.

"No! You listen to me! We're gonna talk numbers. And since your mother put you in charge, I know you can make changes. Go get the papers." He said in a stern, aggressive tone.

Royelle got up to show him the door when he snatched her by her right arm. Instantly a raging ball of fire shot through her. She looked down at his tight grip wrapped around her right arm and, with fire-blazing eyes, glared back at him. Rayford was unfazed. All he saw was the girl who was always timid and meek. He refused to see the woman she had gracefully grown into. And he had yet to see the Royelle she had become since the accident.

"You know what's crazy." She said with dead-looking eyes while his grip was still tightened around her arm. "Here I was trying to give you the benefit of the doubt even when you showed me why I shouldn't; yet, I still wanted to believe different. But you're always gonna be the same egotistical, thoughtless, opportunistic, money-grubbing man I've known you to be. Oh, and let me not forget child molester."

At the release of her words, Rayford's left hand came clean across Royelle's left cheek, slapping her so hard it caused her face to turn. And when she turned back to look at him, there wasn't a tear in sight; not a single emotion or reaction was displayed. Immediately Rayford drew up a concern he had never had before and was smart enough to hide it behind his shadow.

"You will not disrespect me! I am your gawt damn father! You call yourself a woman of God and never follow the 5th commandment! Some child of God you are!"

Royelle looked at him with disparagement as he spoke. The raging fire that once burned inside her was now an inferno. In the bat of an eye, he had violated her in more ways than she cared to account for. Not only did he show up unannounced, he did so with no care for her and with no regard for her recovery or her mental state. He was talking shit, put his hands on her, and now was shaming her relationship with God, the one thing Adala told her children to never play about, and they didn't.

"Are you done?" She nonchalantly asked.

"No! Mi na finish!"

Royelle blankly stared.

"I'm the reason you're a part of this world, and I'll be damned if you speak to me as if I wasn't! Now go get the damn papers!" He released her arm in a shoving motion.

Royelle looked back down at her arm and then at him. The locked eyes between them spoke volumes. One hundred and one things ran through her mind of what she wanted to say, but she could barely pry her lips apart, let alone speak. The rage in her blocked her speaking gauges, And the greed in him only saw Green.

He sat on the couch with his left leg crossed over his right, mumbling all kinds of bullshit. Some that Royelle could hear and some that reflected Charlie Brown. But no matter the plight, at this point, there was no calming her.

The mutters of him calling her ugly, greedy, slow because of her memory loss, and dumb like her mother repeated in her head. All sense of calmness and rationality was nowhere to be found in Royelle. The vexation that had grown inside her was similar to that of a California wildfire in the forest. Quick, hot, and rapidly spreading with the incapability of cooling.

Knowing that neither of them could do shit with the papers, she grabbed them off the top of her nightstand in the hopes of getting him the fuck out of her house when he yelled, "Your mother was no good anyways. I took her from nothing and made her something, only for her to leave me high and dry. I don't fucking think so! I made her who she was! She was nothing!"

That was it. Royelle opened her nightstand drawer, grabbed the two syringes full of heroin from around the red scarf, and calmly walked back towards the living room. Since the sofa was facing away from her, Rayford had no way of knowing she was coming. With the acrimony built inside of her, she walked into the living room with the papers in her left hand and syringes in her right. She didn't say a word as she passed him the papers.

"It's about fucking time, hell!" He spat.

Royelle took a few steps back, giving him one last chance to leave, but when she saw the cunning smile grace his face, it took her completely over the edge. With his head buried in the documents, she casually walked behind the sofa, and before he could say another smart-ass remark, she jabbed both needles into the right side of his neck.

"Ahhh!" He shouted, dropping the papers.

He tried to grab his neck where the sting originated from, but it was too late. The effects of the drugs were already moving throughout his body. Royelle showed no concern as she stood behind him, watching his body go limp. She was expecting him to shake, foam from the mouth, do something, anything, but he didn't. She was really unsure of what to expect. Finally, he just nodded off and slumped over.

She came from behind the couch and could see his eyes closed and his rapidly beating chest slow down. To her, this was an indication that his heart was probably stopping. She was pleased. She sat on the same couch she was on before and watched him slowly meet the devil he so proudly danced for.

Before he took his final breath, she whispered, " I'm Royelle Amoire. Don't you ever forget my name." Then, when the dog started barking to be let outside, Royelle snapped out of her hypnotic state, realizing what she had just done.

CHAPTER 7

*R*oyelle stood frozen in disbelief, but not a single tear was shed. It was like her emotions had checked out. She looked at Rayford's dead body, flummoxing that she had just committed murder by way of lethal injection. Yet, she wasn't happy nor sad. She was just glad that the noise had been silenced.

Royelle knew she was in a lot of trouble, but there was no way she was calling the police. She knew she wouldn't be able to explain her father dying out of nowhere in her living room, and frankly, she didn't know how she'd be able to explain it to anyone but Xandra. And she wasn't sure about that either. Sure she trusted her with her life, but she had just taken someone else's, her father's, at that.

If nothing else, she knew for sure she had to get rid of the syringes. She wrapped them several times in paper towels, put them in a Walmart plastic bag, and threw them in her trash. She wasn't sure what to do, but she knew she had to think fast. She was left with the only trusted source she had; Xandra. She went into her room, grabbed her cell, and called.

"Please pick up. Please pick up." She nervously said.

Royelle was relieved when the phone stopped ringing after the second time.

"Bitch, this better be good. You call—

"I need you!" Royelle cut her off.

"What?"

Xandra was still half asleep, so her hearing wasn't fully ready for audibles, and her sight was still a bit blurred.

"I need you!" Royelled hollered.

"What's wrong?" Xandra asked, concerned.

"Sis! Just get here!"

Royelle hung up the phone leaving Xandra in suspense and questioning. She could hear the urgency in Royelle's voice and wondered if Royelle had learned about Trevion and Amadeo or worse. Could it be about what Xandra had done leading up to Trevion's death? She had no clue. And although she wasn't afraid to find out, she was a bit nervous.

While Royelle waited on Xandra, she sat in her room trying to think of all the lies she could dress up for the police, Raymelle, and Raylina. There was no way in hell they would understand her rage right before it happened. Hell, she didn't even understand it. Other than the ass whooping she handed McKenzie, this was the first time she ever reacted with such violence since the accident and coma. It was never her character. And although it frightened her, she was no longer operating off of emotion; she was now moving off adrenaline. Less than thirty minutes after the call to Xandra, the doorbell rang, causing the dog to bark, scaring the shit out of Royelle. She wanted to fling Prowess's ass clear across the house.

"Please be Xandra. Please be Xandra." She whispered, tip-toeing to the door.

She peeked through the peephole, relieved to see it was her, and cracked the door open.

"Bitch! What is —

"Shhh! Be quiet." Royelle said, snatching Xandra through the door.

Xandra was confused as hell. She looked at Royelle with a crazed look in her eye, trying to figure out if Royelle was having a mental breakdown, seeing ghosts, or having an epiphany of sorts. Nothing could have prepared her for a slumped, dead Rayford on the couch when she walked into the living room.

"Bitchhh! Is he deaddd?! She hollered.

"Shhh!" Royelle said again, covering Xandra's mouth.

Xandra quickly removed Royelle's hand. " Bitch shhh, for what?! Who else is here?"

"Just us."

"All right then! Stop fucking shushing me!" Xandra rolled her eyes. "What the fuck happened?!" She asked as the two stood beside each other, staring at Rayford.

"I killed him," Royelle responded in a low voice.

Xandra turned towards Royelle. "You did what?! Howww?!"

A part of her was in complete disbelief; the other part was jumping for joy on the inside. For so long, the job she had wanted to do was now officially written off her to-do list.

"What happened, Royelle?" Xandra's voice now had a tinge of concern.

Royelle began explaining all of the details to Xandra as they continued to stare at Rayford's lifeless body. Xandra could hear the shock in Royelle, but she also heard the sighs of relief from knowing that she no longer had to listen to Rayford's blathering or feel the effects of his disgust when he put his hands on her.

As Royelle continued to talk, Xandra looked her up and down, trying to figure out who the fuck she was standing next to. The way Royelle starred at Rayford and spoke about the incident let Xandra know her sister had checked out. Completely? She wasn't sure. But she definitely knew that a different Royelle had emerged, one who didn't seem affected by the fact that her own hands had just committed a murder.

"So what do I do now? How do I tell the other two?"

"Whoa! Whoa! Whoa! First of all, you don't tell the other two! Don't tell them shit about this. Second, we can't do shit until tonight. But for now, we need to get him out of this living room and into your garage. Do you still have the tarp from your truck?"

Royelle nodded yes.

"Go get it."

Royelle did as she was instructed and returned with two large Blue tarps, one belonging to the car that Trevion bought her a long time ago.

"We need duct tape too or some kind of strong tape."

Royelle went back to the garage and grabbed all the extra Gorilla tape she had from the move.

"Is this good?" She asked.

"We gon' see."

Xandra laid the tarps out side by side on the living room floor directly in front of Rayford and began tapping the middle where the tarps met, hoping to create one giant tarp. Royelle stood by, waiting on further instruction, periodically looking over at Rayford, still with no emotion. She wondered if he died a slow miserable death or if it was fast and painless. Either way, she was glad he stopped talking.

"Royelle!" Xandra snapped her fingers twice, taking Royelle out of her transfixion. "Pass me some more tape!"

It was official. Xandra now knew for a fact that Royelle was everywhere but there mentally. Like, she was with it, but she wasn't. Once Xandra was satisfied with the secureness of the tarps, she stood to her feet, facing Rayford.

"Now, listen to me. We're gonna move him to the floor and then roll him into a tight blunt. You get me?"

"I got you," Royelle responded.

She grabbed Rayford under his knees and Xandra under his arms. He was heavy, but they didn't have much distance to carry him. The moment they had a secure hold of him, it was easy for them to place him down onto the tarp.

"A'ight. We gotta move these couches a little to make some room." Xandra said.

Royelle quickly moved everything out of the way and rejoined Xandra on the floor as she began rolling Rayford cigarette tight. Once he was rolled him up with the tape secured all around him, they decided to take a break.

"That shit is tiring," Xandra heaved.

She knew Royelle was still in shock when she sat down next to her trying to catch her breath. What she had just done to her father hadn't fully hit her yet. This wasn't Royelle. And as soon as she realized it for herself, there was no telling how she was going to react. That being the case, Xandra wanted to be sure she'd be right there to catch Royelle when and if she fell.

"All right, sis. We need to get him to my truck."

"Your truck?" Royelle was confused.

"Yea! My truck! Do you think I'm gonna let you ride around with a dead body in yours?" Hell will freeze over before I ever let you be in a position where you and jail become friends. Now grab him."

Xandra was dead ass serious. Royelle wasn't jail material, and she'd be damned if she allowed her to be now. If anyone was going down for Rayford, it would be her before Royelle.

When they picked Rayford up, he felt a bit heavier than he did before the tarps. " Shit. I guess deadweight is a real thing." Xandra said as they walked towards the garage. Once they got to the truck, she pressed the trunk button on her remote, and they watched as the trunk took forever to lift, irritating the hell out of both of them.

"Damn, this shit is slow!" Xandra expressed.

Once it opened completely, the sisters pushed the body inside.

"Bring me a blanket," Xandra demanded.

Ultimately, Xandra was the brains of the operation. So when she gave Royelle orders, Royelle wasted no time following them. She went into her linen closet and grabbed the ugliest blanket she could find. She did not want the remnants of Rayford anywhere near her or anything she truly valued. As soon as Xandra had the blankets in her hands, she covered Rayford up real good, closed and locked all the doors, trunk included.

"Sis, where are the needles?" Xandra asked as they walked back into the house.

She watched as Royelle walked to the trash and pulled the bag out.

"Are you outta your fucking mind?! This could lead back to you, and where the fuck did you get this shit from anyway?"

Although reluctant to answer Xandra's question, Royelle had to say something.

"I'll explain it all to you later. But what do we do now?"

"Now, we wait. As soon as night falls, we leave."

Xandra had no idea Royelle knew anything about drugs, where to get them, how to use them, or that she even had suicidal ideations. However, she was slowly starting to learn new things about her sister, which caused a bit of an alarm.

While they waited for nightfall to approach, they straightened up the house, put all the furniture back, and made sure anything related to Rayford was non-existent. Royelle scrubbed the couch that Rayford was sitting on with the cleaning agent for so long that the fabric's color was beginning to change. She wanted no traces of him whatsoever. She even contemplated getting rid of the couch altogether.

Xandra was cool. She had no scruples about the situation. She hated him anyway. Good riddance is all she could say to herself, but she wouldn't dare say it out loud. At least not now. She had to get a feel for Royelle before she said anything that might trigger her again. Her anxiety was through the roof. In between the hours of waiting, she took a shower, tried to sleep, tried to eat, and none of it worked. Her nerves were bad. But relief was approaching, and she couldn't wait to be done with it all. Finally, after what seemed like an eternity, the time had arrived for them to make their next move, and Royelle couldn't wait.

"Let's go, sis. Be sure to grab your keys." Xandra directed.

Royelle hesitated. "Sis, what about his car?"

"Shit!"

Xandra had forgotten all about the car. And there was no way they could leave it at Royelle's house. One plus one equals two, and having Rayford's car at Royelle's house would've fucked up the equation.

"Ok, Listen. I'll drive his car, and you follow me. But try not to be too close. And make sure to follow all the rules of the road. The last thing we need are pigs pulling you over for some bullshit."

Royelle still didn't know where they were going or what they were about to do, but she trusted Xandra's judgment.

It was eerily quiet as they both drove the cleared-out streets at 1:30 am; no music and no phone conversations; just careful driving and focus. When they got off of the highway and drove onto Stoughton street, Royelle grew distressed. She didn't want anyone to see Xandra in Rayford's car, but Xandra was great at being a master of disguises.

Rayford's height and head size matched Xandra's perfectly, making it easy for her to conceal all of her hair under the hat he left in the car. And at the rate of speed Xandra was driving, If anyone looked into the semi-tinted 1989 Toyota Corolla, they would've easily assumed the driver was Rayford. Xandra knew exactly what she was doing.

"Sis. Where are you going?" Royelle said as if Xandra could hear her.

She continued following Xandra as she took every back street she could take, avoiding detection on the road. Finally, when they took the street that led to her parent's home, there was no question as to where they were heading. Royelle immediately panicked and called Xandra's cell.

"Sis! What are we going to momma's for?!" Royelle yelled when Xandra picked up.

"Royelle, just follow my lead. Do you trust me?" Xandra asked.

Royelle hesitated before responding yes.

"Then just follow my lead."

Royelle sighed and quickly hung up. She was nervous, but she knew Xandra had a plan. She always had a plan.

When they pulled up to the house, Xandra peeped the scene in the area before parking the car as Rayford would. She wiped everything down, got out, walked over to her truck's driver's side door, and instructed Royelle to move over. And like a pro, she backed the truck up onto the curve with the trunk end facing the stairs resembling a moving truck.

"Go open the door, and when you come back, we're gonna move him into the house like we're carrying a brand new carpet."

"But what if someone sees us?"

Now Royelle's shock and anxiety were turning into fear.

"Nobody's gonna see us. The medicaid's on this block be sleep by 8. Not in bed. Sleep! And you know that. Look around. All the lights in the houses are off, as usual. So, like I said, if it ever comes up, we're moving carpet. But it won't! Right?"

"Right," Royelle repeated.

Royelle got out of the truck, and when she opened the house doors, she immediately could smell the disgust coming from inside. But that was a worry for another time. She met Xandra back at the truck and began pulling Rayford out feet first. And when his head got closer to the end of the trunk,

Xandra grabbed a hold.

"Shit! This muthafucker done got heavier." Xandra whispered as they carried him up the three steps leading to the door.

Once they got him inside, they dropped him in the hallway.

"This shit is disgusting!" Royelle blurted out to Xandra, not realizing Xandra was already back at the truck, parking it the right way to avoid suspicion.

Royelle surveyed the immediate surroundings, mad at herself for doubting Raymelle and Raylina when they told her he was living like slum.

"Ok. Let's finish." Xandra said, closing and locking the doors behind her with the bag of syringes in her hand. "This muthafucker don't change, do he?" She said, looking at the pandemonium of a house.

"So, now what, sis? What's your plan?" Royelle asked sarcastically.

"Don't be fucking funny." Xandra snapped back. "We need to unwrap him and sit him on the couch."

Xandra found a dirty white shirt sitting on the couch beside him. She tore it, took one of the thinner pieces, and turned it into a tourniquet. Royelle watched as Xandra rolled Rayford's sleeve up and placed the shift-made tourniquet tightly around his arm.

"Get the needles out of the bag," Xandra ordered Royelle.

Royelle passed them to her and continued watching as Xandra staged the scene, leaving one syringe in his arm and another on the floor. Royelle was bemused and wondered how Xandra even knew how to do some shit like that. Once she was satisfied with how the scene looked, she ordered Royelle to roll the tarps up tightly and put them in a trash bag. Soon as she was done, she stood over by Xandra as they both looked at Rayford.

"Sis?" Royelle looked over at Xandra. "How did you know to do that? I mean, you got the details down to a science."

This was Xandra's moment of truth. The one she had wanted to share with Royelle for so many years. And now that they shared something in common other than sisterly love, there was no better time. Xandra looked back over at Rayford, looking like the common junkie. Her eyes were cold and full of empty emotion. It was a look that Royelle had never seen before. But she could tell that there was a story behind it.

"Once in Columbia Point," Xandra began. "There was a bitch named Rosalyn. She died of a drug overdose, as she should have. But it wasn't so simple. She didn't just die. She was cursed at, beat, and spit on until she finally died at the hands of her daughter Muneca. Muneca was so angry at Rosalyn for how she treated her, misused her, and sold her to men for sex, until one day she couldn't take it anymore and snapped. Muneca pinned Rosalyn down and injected Rosalyn's heroin-filled needles into her veins, causing her to overdose. That bitch is right where she needs to be, in hell. No one else knew about the story of Rosalyn and Muneca until just now."

Royelle didn't say shit. Surprisingly, she wasn't even shocked. She grabbed Xandra's hand, and they both turned towards each other, locking eyes.

"No Salt." They simultaneously said. Nothing left needed to be said. It was a mutual understanding that needed no explanation. If being sister's by love and not by blood didn't make them close, sharing a bond in murder did.

CHAPTER 8

For days, weeks, and months the detectives' Sean and Adam had been going in circles trying to solve Mrs. Benton's murder. But since Trevion was dead, there was nothing else to go on, witnesses to question, or other potential suspects to pull in. Therefore, the detectives pieced together the timing Trevion was seen on tape, in alliance with Mrs. Benton's reported time of death by the coroner's office, and decided that Trevion was good for the murder.

Xandra often waited for the day they would come knocking at her door, but it never happened. Now, she was no expert in policing, but she had watched enough crime shows to know that they didn't come banging her door down because they had absolutely nothing on her. However, it didn't keep her from wondering how they only saw Trevion on tape and not her. The way she saw it, at minimum, she should've at least been seen going into the house.

After so long, though, she gathered that when Trevion was in the house, he must've done something with the cameras forcing them to stop recording after he got inside. The problem for him was that he wasn't smart enough to take the tapes with him. And she was more than ok with that. His mistake was her rescue.

Trevion's murder, however, was very much active. No one was fully cleared of any wrongdoing, including those with solid alibis. The motto, everyone's a suspect until they're not, sang a very high tone in any case, whether it was murder or not. And Jayson continued to work the case night and day, looking for any kind of clue or loophole that would point him in the right direction. But, unfortunately, all the tailing he had done on Aruba and her girls led to nothing. It was almost as if they knew they were being watched, pulling a complete 360 since the day Aruba was questioned.

And as far as he could tell, they weren't seeing tricks either. Their moves were subtle and quite basic. Clothing stores here, grocery stores there, dinner spots here and there, but never anything to raise suspicion. None of that mattered, though. He was determined to stay on it until someone slipped.

With detective Presley now retired and working as a Private Investigator, he was able to listen in on any channel regardless of jurisdiction. There were no limits for him as an independent investigator. Tapping in as he did where other detectives couldn't was his way of landing gigs as a silent liaison for other detectives regardless of their district and for civilian families alike.

His old colleagues couldn't understand how he could be so lazy while on the force, but as a P.I. worked miracles around every case. And although no longer fully active in Trevion's murder, he still worked with Jayson on the side whenever he caught wind of anything new or there was something that needed another set of eyes. Subsequently, he immediately contacted Jayson when he heard Royelle's parents' house come across his police scanner.

"Hey, yah prick!" Thomas said when Jayson answered.

"Ya, momma! What the fuck do you want?" Jayson laughed.

When they worked as partners, Jayson couldn't tolerate him, but now that Thomas was gone, the two had formed a tighter bond. It seemed like for them to get along or get anything done, they had to do it apart from each other, and as such, it worked out well.

"Yah. A call just come through for your Nascar driver's parents' house."

Since Royelle's accident, Thomas had dubbed her the name and never called her anything else. He and the officers riding bandwagons were the only ones who found it funny, though.

"I know it's out of your juri, but I thought I'd let you know anyway."

"What's the call?" Jayson curiously asked.

"Sounds like the old man overdosed. But I'm gonna go check it out."

"What for if it sounds like an overdose?"

"My guy! Haven't you learned anything from me?! What it sounds like and what it really is are two different things. Especially since he's the father of one of your potential suspects."

Although Jayson wasn't 100% convinced that Thomas needed to impede, it did make sense as to why Thomas might've wanted to dot all his I's and cross his T's. What if it wasn't an overdose? What if it was something else like a revenge killing or maybe just poor health? Who knew without checking it out for themselves.

"Ok. Private eye. Well, let me know what you find when you get up there." Jayson said before hanging up.

When Thomas made it to the top of the hill, he witnessed a small crowd of people outside standing off to the right side of the house, crying and hugging each other. Most of them were the neighbors, but as he got closer, he saw Royelle and all of her siblings.

He pulled his car over, got out, and approached the uniformed officers standing off to the side of the ambulance. Since most, if not all, officers knew who he was, there was no need for him to show his ID or explain his credentials.

"Hey, boss." One of the officers greeted.

"How's it going, fellas? What we got here?"

"DOA. Looks like your typical overdose. He was found with a tourniquet around his arm, one syringe in him and another on the floor." The officer reported.

"Who found him?"

"The son. He's the one with the baseball cap on."

"Excuse me for a moment."

Thomas walked away from the officers and towards the crowd. When Royelle saw him, her eyes burned with revulsion. After a year of running through different scenarios and practices to help bring her memory back, he was one of the people she wanted to forget but couldn't.

After she got out of the hospital and was released to go back to work, Thomas made her life a living hell for months, calling and unexpectedly showing up to her home and office, with or without Jayson, to ask the same questions over and over only to get the same answers and results, and that level of disruption was simply too hard for her to forget.

As he approached, she stood like a lioness protecting her cub, warning of an aftermath if fucked with in the slightest way. She wondered what a Milton Police detective was doing in the Roxbury B2 jurisdiction. But before she could say anything to him, he quickly walked into the house. Like everyone else, his nose turned up at the stench when he walked in. And when he looked at the dysfunction around him, it had all the classic signs of a crackhead.

When he looked over at Rayford, he was just as the uniformed officer described. The only thing that struck him as odd was how clean Rayford appeared. He didn't look like the typical druggie he was used to seeing. The way he looked versus how the house looked didn't match. It wasn't impossible to see two stark differences, but it was extremely rare.

As he looked around the living room, he took note of all the pictures in the same manner he did the first time he entered Royelle's house. A few were of the three kids, some with their parents' some without, and some included Xandra in her teenage years. He stared at all the pictures as if he were replaying a moment in time in his head. The more pictures he looked at, the more his brain went into a state of extreme overload. Although a lazy bastard, his memory was sharp like a knife and full of information like an encyclopedia. He took his phone out and began taking pictures of the photos that contained Xandra. He wasn't quite sure why she interested him so much, but he was going to stop at nothing to figure it out.

"What are you doing here?" Royelle asked when Thomas stepped back outside.

Thomas pretended not to hear the question and continued walking toward his car.

"I asked you a question, sir!" Royelle spoke louder. "What are you doing here?" She repeated.

To avoid embarrassment or confrontation, Thomas turned around and decided to entertain Royelle with an answer.

"I'm investigating this situation."

"What situation?" Xandra jumped in. "The only situation here is him being dead, and it's obvious how."

'That voice.' Thomas thought. He wanted Xandra to keep on talking, hoping he'd be able to piece why he recognized it. "Muneca, is it?"

"It is. But you knew that."

"I'm following protocol."

"But see. That's just it, detective. This isn't your jurisdiction. So you being here makes no sense. You're harassing us." Royelle said.

"Well, I'm sorry you feel that way. But I can assure you that I am not harassing you. So that you know, I no longer work for MPD, and as a freelance Private Investigator, I have a right to be in any jurisdiction. So therefore, whenever a call comes in that needs inspecting, I'm the guy to do it."

Thomas waited for a response, but the look of shock, anger and surprise on Royelle and Xandra's faces said enough.

"If there's nothing else, please accept my deepest sympathy and condolences on your loss. I will leave you to be with your family." Thomas turned with a sly smirk gracing his face and walked away feeling like he had just hit the lottery.

"Hello." Aruba brashly answered.

"Hey, Aruba. It's Bella.

"I know who the fuck this is! What do you want?!"

Although Aruba had written Bella off long ago, and Bella could hear Aruba's annoyance because of the call, she had to swallow her response. She didn't want or feel like getting into it with Aruba over something so dumb. But Bella had no idea that the phone call alone was enough to ignite more negative blood from Aruba towards her. Bella took a deep breath and continued the conversation as calmly as she could.

"I just wanted to tell you that the streets are saying Royelle's father died."

"So?! What the fuck that gotta do with me? Fuck her and her father!"

Bella sighed. "Look! I'm just doing what you asked everybody to do. We been keeping our ears to the streets, and that's what the streets are saying."

"Yea, but that shit ain't useful. I didn't hear shit about no money."

"Yea. And you didn't say shit about only coming to you when it involved money."

It felt good to Bella snapping back as she had. She had gained some new fresh courage when she caught wind of Aruba's new drug habit. No one quite knew which drugs Aruba was on, but the way she slurred her words and stayed up for hours and days at a time, some folks thought Meth or heroin, while others said she was popping a gang of Ecstasy. No one really knew for sure, but whatever it was made her the weakest link in the game, and now, Bella was getting with her the way Aruba used to do her.

"Is that all? Did they say anything else?" Aruba asked.

"No. Just that he died. But on another note. Have you spoken to McKenzie? I've been trying to get in touch with her for days, and she ain't call me back yet. I asked some of the hoes on the block, but no one has seen or heard from her."

Aruba was a little stumped but not surprised. She hadn't heard from McKenzie either, but she thought it was because of work. But now that she knew others hadn't seen or spoken to her either raised some concern.

"Nah, I haven't heard from her. But when I speak to her, I'll let her know you're looking for her."

Aruba hung up thinking about what to do with the information Bella had just given her, wondering if it was even worth sharing. But then she felt that sharing the information would get her back in the gate with Da'Vegas. So she dialed his number, hoping he would answer.

When Da'Vegas saw her number come across his screen, his nose turned up. He hadn't been feeling her for quite some time, and when he learned that she was turning into the typical fiend, he completely lost all respect for her. He let the phone ring three more times before reluctantly answering.

"What up?" He dryly answered.

"Heyyyy Da'Vegas." She responded, trying to sound sexy.

Da'Vegas was the least impressed. "Man, what's up?" He responded.

Aruba, sensing the irritation, quickly got to it. "I was calling to tell you Royelle's father died today.

"Oh, for real? How'd you find out?" He said, uninterested in the conversation.

"Bella."

They both stayed silent on the phone, wondering if the other would say something until Aruba decided to speak.

"Can I ask you something?"

"What?" He snapped back.

"Why do you hate me so bad?"

"Oh boy! Here you go with that bullshit again!" Da'Vegas said, dismissing the question.

"I've been nothing but good to you. Never cheated, sold my ass for you, lied for you, kept all your secrets, and I do mean all of them. I gave and still give you whatever you want and ask of me, and you still treat me like shit. What did I ever do to you for you to treat me like you do?" Aruba whined.

She was genuinely hurt, though. Since the day they met, she had given Da'Vegas all of her, but the feelings were never reciprocated. She was hoping he wouldn't hit her with the typical, *it's me, not you* line, but what she got was worse.

"Look, I thought it was understood that this was always business. It was never supposed to be personal."

Aruba swallowed the knot in her throat. "What the fuck do you mean?!" She yelled.

"And this is why it can't be personal, because of shit like this!"

"Because of shit like what?!" Aruba continued to yell into the phone. "I've done more for you than any bitch you ever fucked with."

Da'Vegas chuckled.

"Oh, that's funny? It wouldn't be so funny if I decided to let these bitches know that you're alive and well, would it, Trevionnn." Aruba taunted.

Da'Vegas paused for a second and looked at his phone, wondering who the fuck she thought she was playing with. He took a moment to calm himself down before speaking his next set of words.

"Baby, look. I'm not saying it like it's a bad thing. What I was trying to say before you cut me off is that, yes, I see you as business because we are good business partners, and making it personal could ruin our chances of making it to that million we always be talking about."

Not only could Da'Vegas change his tone or talk someone out of their panties, but he also knew how to articulate his words to fit any situation or crowd. And every time he spoke in what Aruba would consider a loving voice, she melted for him all over again. Forgetting all about the negative shit he had ever done or how foul he has always treated her.

"But aye, look. It's been a minute since we linked. So come down next weekend, let's talk about the next move, and let daddy do what daddy does."

"You sure?" Aruba questioned.

"Fucking right I am. I'll see you soon, ma."

CHAPTER 9

The relationship between Ajah and Amadeo had the resemblance of distant roommates instead of a married couple. They had taken a downward spiral into nothingness. The communication was dull, and their sex life was none. Noting the apparent distance, Ajah asked Amadeo time and time again what was wrong? What could they do to fix the brokenness between them? But, rather than tell her the truth, Amadeo brushed it off, insisting that Ajah was bugging and they were fine. The fact was, Amadeo had completely checked out of the marriage and the love he once had for Ajah.

Not having Trevion in his life made him realize that it was because of Trevion that he stayed with Ajah for as long as he had. Being in relations with Trevion allowed him to be his true self while pretending to be someone else with Ajah. And since Trevion gave it to him regularly, it was easy for Amadeo to envision Trevion every time he had sex with Ajah. But now that Trevion was gone and there was no more sex between them, the visions he once was able to relive were vastly fading away and no longer had the same effect as before.

At this point, there was nothing Ajah could do or offer him that would rekindle the flame. He needed male affection in the worst way. And not just any male taste; He desired Trevion's. And since he couldn't get it, depression took a toll. His depression was so noticeable that it placed Ajah in an uncomfortable position in her own home. So much so that she began sneaking around in the hopes of getting some unanswered questions. Not so much because she wanted to make it work, but because women's intuition plagued her. She knew there was something else and was determined to find out just what or who it was.

"I'm making steak, asparagus cooked in garlic butter sauce, and baked potatoes. Do you want some?" She texted.

"Yea, that's cool," Amadeo responded.

The idea that she even had to ask him if he wanted dinner these days put her in an awkward space, but she was tired of cooking dinner for two when only one consumed it. Nevertheless, despite his consistent shadiness, she still took her time putting in the same amount of love into her cooking she always had.

The steak fell apart at the touch of the fork, and the asparagus was just right with a slight crunch and tinge of softness. And the potatoes were soft, loaded with finely shredded cheese, bacon bits, chives, and sour cream, just the way he liked it. By the time he made it home from work at 5:30, the house smelled delectable. To avoid giving off the idea that she wanted anything but a casual dinner, Ajah made no attempt to get dressed up in anything sexy. She kept her appearance simple with a pair of jeans, a cami, and her house slides.

"Hey, what's up?" He said, kissing her on the cheek before heading up the stairs.

"Not much. Just cooking dinner." She smirked.

Kissing her on the cheek became his thing now. Ajah couldn't remember the last time they kissed on the lips, and at this point, it no longer mattered. She had grown used to the *"two adults passing each other by"* scene.

While Amadeo showered, Ajah continued the finishing touches on dinner. In the past, she would serve his plate, he'd grab it and go watch television in another room. And depending on her mood, she would join him in whatever room he was in to try and keep some kind of normalcy in their marriage. But that gesture annoyed the hell out of Amadeo. He preferred that she left him to be in his thoughts but was never courageous enough to express it.

Today, she was playing it differently, though. She set the table up in an elegant way but avoided any type of romantic touch. And by the time he made it downstairs, she was placing the plates down on the table one at a time.

"This looks real good." He said as he walked closer to the table.

"Thank you. That one is yours." She pointed in the direction of his placement as she poured them glasses of juice. " Do you want a beer or something else before I sit down?" She asked.

"Nah, this is good."

She took her seat, reached her hand out to grab his, and quickly prayed over the food. She was grateful that he decided to sit with her, but she really didn't leave him with any other option. He was right where she wanted him to be. And to avoid the already awkward situation from continuing as such, she took the opportunity to spark up a conversation.

"So, how was your day?" She asked. "Anything interesting happen today?"

"Nah. Same ole, same ole. But what's up with you? Everything good on your end?" He asked, shocking the shit out of Ajah.

"Everything is good. Just working, working, working. I'm really sorry to hear that another company brought out the last of Trevion's projects today."

"Yea. Me too. It is what it is, though. I'll just have to partner up with other contractors and take it from there.

Ajah could tell Amadeo was really bothered by the situation. After all, the project in question was the one Amadeo had with Trevion. But, since Trevion was the primary on the account and had invested the majority of the money, there wasn't shit Amadeo could do to save it. His money wasn't as long as Trevion's; therefore, he took a hit. And everything Amadeo was hoping to gain died when Trevion did. For the next twenty minutes, they continued to talk about basic things, things that had no meaning, until AJ noticed Amadeo looking rather tired.

"Deo. You ok?" Ajah asked, noticing Amadeo's eyes getting heavy.

"Yea, I'm good. I'mma go watch some T.V."

"Ok. I got the kitchen. I'll see you in a minute."

Ajah watched as Amadeo slowly made his way to the family room. Once he was out of her view, she tip-toed towards the family room and saw him sitting in their Belleze Linen Lounge chair with his head leaned forward towards his chest.

"Deo." She called out.

When he didn't answer, she called his name out again, and he still didn't answer. Finally, she walked up closer and shoved his shoulder to make sure he was still alive. When he let out a slight groan, she was instantly relieved.

The same Ketamine, or liquid kitty as she called it, that she used on Trevion a while back, she had just used on Amadeo. But, this time, she used the powder version, integrating it into the garlic butter on his Asparagus. Again, the blend worked like a charm. Once she knew he'd be out cold for quite some time, she began to feel around the pockets of his cargo jogging pants until she found his phone. *'Yes!'* She thought as she sat down on the sofa across from him. She began trying to unlock it with all the numbers she thought he might use, but none of them worked.

"Think outside of the box Ajah. He's gotta be hiding something." She whispered.

She entered 0429, but that didn't work. She tried 042977, but that didn't work either. Finally, she entered 04291977, and whala! "Trevion's fucking birthday!?" She said. Just when she thought she was in the clear, the phone's two-step verification popped up requiring his thumbprint. "You got to be shitting me!" She chuckled.

She walked up to him, gently grabbed his right hand, and placed his thumb on the phone. "Bingo." She whispered. She sat back down on the sofa across from him and began scrolling through everything; call logs, pictures, emails, and text messages. And although everything appeared normal, that wasn't enough for her. Her woman's intuition was lit all the way up, and until she found out why, she wasn't stopping. She stopped scrolling and took a second to think. *'He doesn't carry a planner or a journal; his life is in this phone.'* She thought. Everything he had ever done or planned was on that phone, and she knew it.

"What am I missing?" She whispered.

She scrolled through everything once again, and nothing came of the search. So she decided to go through his apps. One by one, she started clicking and opening the apps, making sure that they were what they were supposed to be, and when she noticed he had not one but two calculator apps, she immediately knew one was a fake.

She wasn't sure which was which, and since they both had the same Samsung phones, finding out which was the authentic one wasn't going to be hard. She grabbed her phone, opened her finance folder, and saw that the calculator already programmed into their Samsung's was Green. The secondary calculator in Amadeo's phone was Black and Orange.

"Boo-yah!" She smiled sinisterly.

She knew she was getting closer to the truth. What truth? She wasn't sure yet, but she knew there was something. Otherwise, there would be no need for a fake app on the phone. To avoid locking herself out of the app and hoping to get some insight into the password, she clicked on the three tiny dots in the top right-hand corner. There were two options to choose from, theme and contact us. Unfortunately, the theme option didn't offer shit, and contact us was a bot answering generic questions. But she took a chance anyway.

She clicked theme, and all it showed were options on how to change the background screen and color. Then, she clicked on contact us, and the bot's automated system said, *"My name is Kaku. I'm a robot. I can speak English. What can I do for you?"* She quickly entered *"Forgot password"* in the message bar, and to her surprise, Kaku replied, *"Please enter 11223344 into Calculator and press = button."* She did as Kaku suggested, and it instantly opened up.

"That was too easy." She murmured.

As soon as she was granted access, she noticed three folders: Pictures, Personal Files, and Videos. Her heart started racing as she began opening the pictures file. She wanted to believe that Amadeo was always on the up and up with her. But her mind wouldn't release her of every doubt she felt. She knew that if her mind was controlling her heart, something was off. As soon as the pictures loaded, her eyes widened.

"Oh! You muthafucker! You low-down dirty muthafucker!" Ajah shouted. "I fucking knew it!"

She scrolled and scrolled, looking at pictures of men in various sexual positions and categories. And the more gay porn she saw, the more agitated she became. But, as soon as she opened the video and personal files folder, that's when she lost her shit.

All the messages of every rendezvous, meetup, or sexual encounter Trevion and Amadeo had was in the phone. And when she read the messages of Amadeo professing his love to him, she grew sick to her stomach. Everything he attempted to hide, including the naked pictures of Trevion, was now falling out of Amadeo's skeleton closet. She quickly screenshotted the messages and sent them to herself. Once she was done with that, she sent the video links of Amadeo having sex with the man in ATL to her phone.

Ajah was distraught. She knew something was happening behind her back, but not once in her wildest dreams did she think it involved men, let alone Trevion. Once she regained some composure, she got up and smacked the dog shit out of Amadeo, hurting herself more than she hurt him. She wanted so badly to call Royelle right then and there, but she still wasn't done with Amadeo yet. She was mad as hell at herself for giving him the amount of Ketamine that she did but took the opportunity to whoop his ass. She beat on him until she was completely out of breath, punching him in the face, chest, and stomach. She called him all kinds of names and even chopped off a bunch of his dreads. She had lost it, and couldn't wait for him to wake up, so he could feel the pain she was feeling and see the hurt and anger in her eyes.

Since he was out cold, she took the opportunity to go into every space he occupied, making trip after trip, gathering as much of his shit as she could, and piling it up in the middle of her backyard. As soon as she was done, she dowsed the pile down with Match Light charcoal fluid and set it ablaze. She stood by, watching as everything quickly burned to nothing. When she was satisfied knowing that nothing could be salvaged, she put the fire out with her extinguisher nearby. Next, she took the bag of unopened sugar from the pantry and emptied it into his gas tank. She started to key his car with obscene writings but decided against it.

She went back into the house, trying to think of other things she could destroy, but her mind was so overburdened that she couldn't function properly. But, one thing she knew for sure was that Amadeo was undeserving of anything in that house, and she was going to make sure he knew it too whenever he woke up.

A little over an hour after Ajah caused the havoc she did in her home and yard, she finally sat down to take in all that she had done. She stared at Amadeo with her nostrils flaring like a bull getting ready to attack. If she was the murdering kind, he would've been dead.

And even though she was a cheater and had been cheating for quite some time, she didn't see her level of cheating as a problem compared to Amadeo's. Indeed it was a double standard, but she didn't see it that way. For her, Amadeo's level of cheating was far worse. He was cheating with Trevion, the guy from Atlanta, and whoever else she didn't know about. This level of disrespect and betrayal was unfathomable and something she wouldn't soon forgive. It was a slap in the face, and she could no longer hold it. She had to tell Royelle.

"Hey, AJ," Royelle answered after the first ring.

"Hey, Royelle. I know you have a lot going on right now, but we really need to talk."

Royelle noted the concern in AJ's voice and now was the least bit concerned with her own issues. Truthfully, Royelle didn't want to be bothered with Rayford or the funeral plans. She was numb and unemotional about the whole situation. Besides, whatever AJ had going on, piqued Royelle's interest far more.

"What's going on, AJ? Is everything ok?" Royelle asked.

"No. Everything is not ok. Are you able to come over now? Like right now?!"

"Uhhh-yea." Royelle nervously answered.

"Ok. Please hurry."

Royelle threw on her White crop top shirt, a pair of Gray sweatpants, and her Gray and White J's. She called Xandra told her what happened with the call, and the two agreed to meet at AJ's. When Xandra stepped outside her door, she noticed something on her windshield. "The fuck?" She said as she walked towards her truck. When she picked it up, it was a picture of her and Royelle carrying Rayford's body from the truck to the house.

CHAPTER 10

$\mathcal{A}$ ttempting to hide the truth about Rayford's death, planning his funeral, and trying to keep Royelle's ass balanced was one thing. Trying to put the puzzle pieces together of who put the picture on her truck, who's been watching them, how long they've been watching, and what way they want to die was plenty 'nough for Xandra. Therefore, making her way to AJ's house for what sounded like more bullshit was the last thing she needed at the moment.

The idea of someone watching her and Royelle in that capacity did not sit well with Xandra. Immediately, she thought about Trevion, but there was no way; he was dead as far as she knew. She figured maybe it could've been one of the bitches from the memorial service, but they weren't smart enough. She didn't know anyone else that was close enough to Trevion to pull a stunt like that. She then tried to backtrack her thoughts to see if she could remember anyone on the block, and there was absolutely no one. She was sure of it.

The picture quality wasn't even all that great, but there was no denying it was her and Royelle carrying Rayford. But who could be watching them that hard she thought, and why? What the fuck were they looking to gain? Royelle was half alive most days, and Xandra had been real-real quiet since her return. But she swore the moment she had some time to start digging; she would.

As she drove to AJ's, she wondered what could be going on now? So many things ran through her mind, but whatever it was had better be good because time and bullshit were two things Xandra didn't have enough of, especially now that she knew someone was clocking her. When she pulled into AJ's driveway, Royelle was already there, standing outside her truck.

"About time." She softly said as Xandra exited her truck.

"I'm here, ain't I?" Xandra responded in the same tone.

"Shut up, stupid. Come on." Royelle clapped back.

When AJ heard voices coming from the driveway, she peeked out her window and panicked when she saw Xandra walking beside Royelle.

"Why the fuck did she call her?!" AJ whispered.

AJ thought Xandra was cool and all, but she knew Xandra brought heat wherever she landed, and it was the last thing she wanted or needed at this time. But there wasn't shit she could do about it now. Whatever was going to happen was going to happen right then and there. When the two reached the door, AJ opened it before either of them had the opportunity to knock or ring the bell.

"Hey, y'all." AJ greeted in a meek tone.

"Hey, AJ," Royelle said, surprised to see her unkempt. "What's going on? Ya look Verruckt."

AJ was in such a debilitated state that as she led them to the kitchen, away from the living room, she didn't notice that Royelle was speaking in German, which was one of her favorite things to hear come out of Royelle's mouth.

"Girl. What's up?! You're acting weird. What's going on?" Royelle asked again.

As much as Xandra wanted to know, too, she stayed quiet and observant. She didn't want anything she did or said to ruin the moment she felt was about to get really intense.

"Look. I'm sorry I wasn't more persistent."

"Persistent? Persistent about what?" Royelle asked.

"Remember a while back when I met you at Xandra's and told you I got smacked by Amadeo for accusing him and Trevion."

"Ummm, yeahhh." Royelle said, interested to hear what was coming next.

"Well, I should've stayed on it."

"Why? How so?" Royelle asked.

"I can show you better than I can tell you," AJ responded.

"Oh! This is about to get good!" Xandra thought still remaining quiet.

AJ grabbed Amadeo's phone and opened the file that contained all the messages between him and Trevion. When Xandra saw and read what Royelle was looking at, her heart jumped for joy. She was excited that she no longer had to find a way to explain to Royelle her involvement in the Trevion and Amadeo catastrophe.

Royelle continued reading the messages in utter disbelief and disgust, finding out that the man she was supposed to be married to was not only suspected of being married to someone else but was undoubtedly having an affair with Amadeo. Their secret meet-up places, dates, times, and their favorite spot, Intensity, were all outed. Much of what she wanted to learn about Trevion's life was in black and white on that phone. And when Xandra saw the affair between them went on a lot longer than she knew, it sent her into a frenzy.

"Wait! So where this nigga at now?" Xandra asked.

"He's in there sleeping." AJ pointed towards the living room.

"He's sleep? Like, sleep, sleep? Or dead sleep?" Xandra asked.

"Well, I guess you can say sleep, sleep," AJ said in a guilt-ridden tone.

"AJ, what the fuck does that mean?" Royelle asked as she walked towards the living room.

When they made it to the living room, AJ had his head titled towards the left arm of the chaise chair and appeared to be sleeping.

"Is he fucking dead, AJ?!" Xandra shouted.

"No, He's not dead. I checked on him a few times. He's just sleeping."

"What did you do to him, AJ?" Royelle worriedly asked.

AJ looked down to the floor in shame.

"AJ! What did you do?!" Royelle hollered.

AJ looked up at Royelle with sad eyes. "I drugged him with some

90

Ketamine."

Xandra laughed hysterically. "Oh! I see. You bitches been full of the shits lately!"

"How long has he been out?" Royelle asked.

"I don't know more than an hour, I guess."

Royelle sniffed the air. "AJ, what have you been up to? It smells like fire, and he looks horrible."

"Fuck him!" AJ blurted out.

She was tired of them asking questions about him as if he was the victim in all that was happening.

"So now what?" AJ asked.

"Now what, what?" Xandra responded. "We can't do shit with a man who's sleep. We gotta wait for his ass to get up to get some real answers."

Royelle couldn't believe that AJ had the guts to do something like that and be ok with it. And interestingly enough, AJ couldn't believe that Royelle wasn't more panicky or upset behind the problem. They each were expecting a different reaction from the other. And when they didn't see what they thought they should, they both began to see each other in a more menace kind of way.

Royelle sat on the love seat across from Amadeo while AJ and Xandra sat on the other couch. There were absolutely no words being spoken as they waited for Amadeo to wake up. And to pass the time, Royelle continued to read and re-read every single message Amadeo and Trevion exchanged.

She even saw the sneak pictures Amadeo took of Trevion as he lay naked asleep in the bed that Royelle and Trevion once shared. At that moment, she realized Amadeo might be the one responsible for the yellow post-it note that she had repeatedly seen in her visions during therapy. She took out her phone, found the picture of the post-it note she had taken a while back, and passed it to AJ.

"Does this handwriting look familiar to you?" Royelle asked her.

"It's his," AJ grunted.

"Wow. Just wow!" Royelle responded.

Royelle looked over at Xandra, who was fuming on the inside but cooled on the out. The only thing on Xandra's mind was how the night would end for Amadeo. Trevion already met his demise, but Amadeo being in the room with women scorned, well, that was a different kind of beast.

"AJ. Do you have anything I can tie him up with?" Royelle nonchalantly asked.

"For what?" AJ responded with an unhinged look.

"AJ! Do you have something? Yes or no?"

Xandra was impressed at the charge Royelle was taking, while AJ was surprised by it. To see Royelle behave in such a way concerned AJ a bit. She would've expected it from Xandra but never from Royelle. Nevertheless, she went into the closet that housed all the tools and miscellaneous supplies, grabbed an extension cord and the rope they used to tie down their outside tent.

"Here. This is all I have."

"This will do," Royelle responded.

Without instruction, Xandra walked over to Amadeo and began tying his hands with the rope.

"Wait! What are you all doing?!" AJ said.

"AJ, seriously. Shut up!" Royelle shouted. "Do you want to be on the receiving end of the fight this man is gonna wake up with?"

After bounding his hands, Xandra and Royelle began wrapping the extension cord around his ankles. AJ knew not to say anything else. Royelle was right. Amadeo was going to wake up dazed, confused, and on the defense. And if she wanted them all to survive the night, she had no choice but to follow Royelle's lead.

After hours of being frustrated and waiting for Amadeo to wake up, he finally started to murmur as he was fighting to come out of his sleep. And the more he grunted, the more worried AJ started to become. In all her years of knowing and being with Amadeo, this was the first time she had ever done something of this magnitude against him. But it was also the first time she had ever encountered this type of pain because of him. She was conflicted about it all.

"Mmm-hmm. Wake your ass up." Royelle said sinisterly.

Amadeo heard Royelle's voice but struggled to adjust to what was happening. He had a killer headache, and his face and body were sore from all the blows that AJ had handed him earlier while in his period of repose. He tried to sit up completely, but with his wrist and ankles bound, he was stiff.

"Here. Let me help you up." Royelle said calmly.

Royelle walked over to him, and with Xandra's help, the two of them pulled him up so he could sit up completely. His eyes were still closed as he tried to control the spinning going on in his head.

"What's going on, man?" His words slurred as he tried to open his eyes and adjust to the light.

"That's what we're here to find out," Royelle responded. "AJ, get him some water or something, please. I need this man's undivided attention." She continued.

AJ hated taking orders, but she invited them to the devil's playground, so she had to partake in the festivities. She brought back the glass of water with a straw and handed it to Royelle.

"Drink," Royelle aggressively said as she put the straw in his mouth.

Neither Xandra nor AJ knew what to make of Royelle or what her next step might be. The way she was treating Amadeo was confusing to them. One minute she was spazzing, the next, she was cool. She spoke calmly and treated him gently. It certainly wasn't the behavior they were expecting from a person who just found out that the person sitting before her was one of the people having an affair with the man said to be her husband.

"Go on, drink it up." She said as Amadeo attempted to guzzle the water.

AJ looked over at Xandra, and Xandra shrugged her shoulders. AJ was looking for an answer as to what was coming; only Xandra couldn't help because she didn't know either.

"Amadeo. Can you hear me, ok?" Royelle asked.

Amadeo nodded yes.

"That's good. I'm going to give you a few minutes to adjust your eyes and hearing so that I know you can understand me completely and see me clearly."

Amadeo looked around the room and judging from the look on his face, it was clear that worry and concern were starting to settle in. He looked down at his hands and feet when he felt the tight throbbing sensation.

"Wha-what's going on?" He fumbled his words.

"That's what I need you to tell me," Royelle responded.

As he became a bit more coherent, he stared back at Royelle with a confused look. He had an idea of where the conversation was heading, and as much as he hated to admit it to himself, fear coiled over him. Seeing the three of them gathered around as they were, meant that all the things he thought he kept in secret had officially met the tabletop. And to make matters worse, knowing that Ajah was a part of whatever was happening or about to happen threw him for a complete loop.

"Ajah. What's up? He asked with distressed eyes.

"She won't be answering any questions right now, Amadeo. However, I have questions, and if you don't tell me what I want to know or hear, I promise you this night is not going to end the way you think."

"Royelle," AJ spoke with a reasoning tone.

"Aht-Aht bitch! Don't you say shit!" Xandra cocked her 45 back and aimed it at AJ's head. "This shit needed to happen, and you're gonna let her have it."

AJ threw her hands up in defeat and took a few steps back.

"I want you to listen to me and listen to me good. The devil is in the details, and it's the details that I want. So, how this night goes solely depends on you, Amadeo."

Amadeo said nothing. Everyone in the room was astounded that the meek, timid, professional, and wholesome Royelle was the one sitting in front of him acting and sounding like some sort of crime boss who was about to torture her victim if she didn't get what she wanted.

Interestingly, that same meek, timid, professional, and wholesome Royelle was still before them. The difference now was that even though she was calm, didn't appear upset, spoke properly as she always had done, there was a sense of fright that she was giving off, and that was harrowing.

On the other hand, Xandra was getting used to the changes. Although Royelle was extremely unpredictable these days, the fact that she was beginning to hold her own made Xandra very happy. She was in awe at how Royelle was handling herself and the situation. This is what Xandra had wanted out of Royelle for years. She didn't want Royelle to be as thug as she appeared, but she definitely wanted her to have a backbone. And the more she watched and listened, the more life Royelle gave Xandra. It appeared that the days of people running over Royelle had met their end.

"First things first. How long, Amadeo?" Royelle asked.

"How long what?" He responded.

Royelle chuckled.

"Ok. I will let you make it this time because I understand that you just came out of a drug-induced slumber, and the question wasn't very clear. But the next one will not come with a free pass."

"Amadeo. How long?"

Royelle opened the phone, turned it towards Amadeo, and it showed the picture of a sprawled-out naked Trevion on her bed. He looked up at Royelle and then at Ajah.

"Mmm-hmm. All of it, Amadeo."

"Royelle," Amadeo spoke out.

Before speaking another word, Royelle slapped him in the face.

"I asked how long?"

Between knowing his wife drugged him, his secrets being revealed, and being trapped by three women, his blood was beyond crimson red. He didn't know about Ajah, but he knew the other two weren't playing. And since he knew that his back was against the wall and had no idea about what would happen next, he started talking.

"It started months before you saw me at the swingers club."

"Let me guess. You all met at Club Intensity? Right?

Amadeo nodded yes.

"So you mean to tell me you and Trevion have been having an affair while carrying on as business partners, husbands, and providers, leaving me to defend all the rumors that have been brought to the table. You slapped this woman because she brought your truth to you, and you tried to make her seem like she was crazy. You've been in my home, sat at my dinner table, ate my food, all while you were fucking — I'm sorry. Excuse my French. Having sex with my husband. Who approached who?"

"He approached me," Amadeo growled when a sharp pain hit his ribs.

"Not that it matters, but I needed to know for my closure."

As Amadeo prepared himself for the next set of questions or possibly another slap, he began to feel like a bitch for bowing down to Royelle. But he justified his feelings with the idea that since there was a 45 in the midst and he didn't have shit to back him up, not even his wife, he was going to sing like a canary. And singing is just what he did.

"What do you know about his other wife?"

Immediately Royelle could see the adjustment in Amadeo's facial features. It was clear to her, that he didn't know about Aruba, and she wasn't about to get into specifics regarding it.

"Forget about that. Was this you?" She showed Amadeo the picture of the yellow sticky note.

His eyes dropped to the floor.

"Where did this night happen?"

Amadeo swallowed the knot in his throat.

"At your house?" He answered with his head lowered.

"In my bed?" Royelle calmly asked.

"Yes."

"Hmph. Ok." Royelle sneered.

She got up, snatched the gun out of Xandra's hand, and shot him in the head before anyone could say anything else or stop her.

"Royelleee! What the fuck did you do!?!" Xandra hollered.

AJ stood in shock, staring at Royelle with fear, uncertainty, and contempt in her eyes. Here she was concerned that Xandra would make a scene or flip out, and it was Royelle she should've been concerned with. It bugged her out that the woman she was once in love with had just become a stranger. She didn't know what to do. She could hear Xandra's yelling, and it was all but clear. The high pitch ringing from the blast of the gun was still pinging in her ears as a million thoughts ran through her mind, none making any sense.

Xandra was pissed! It wasn't that she gave a fuck about Amadeo or that he was dead. It was the fact that she had just finished cleaning up Royelle's mess with Rayford, which still wasn't done. And now, she had to clean up another mess because of Royelle's impulses. Adding fuel to the fire was the fact that Royelle killed Amadeo in front of AJ, which made the possibility of killing AJ highly likely, meaning another mess to clean was soon to come. The idea of dead bodies popping up everywhere that are connected to Royelle's circle in one manner or another wasn't going to be a good look for anyone.

"Royelle! Snap the fuck out of it! Look at what the fuck you did!" She paused to get a response; there was nothing. "Royelle!" Xandra snapped her fingers.

She continued yelling, but that same blank stare and completely out-of-it look that Royelle displayed when she killed Rayford is what she was currently exhibiting, and it genuinely worried Xandra. There was no fear attached to Xandra's uneasy feeling; it was concern. *'Was this what she was going to have to deal with every time Royelle had a moment?'* Xandra thought. She needed answers because this side effect wasn't one of the ones listed on Royelle's discharge summary.

Xandra finally picked the gun up off of the floor and looked over at AJ, whose body was trembling with tears running down her face uncontrollably. For a moment, Xandra was feeling some sentiment but quickly reverted back to not giving a fuck. She had to get her head back in the game. She had her sister to protect, a mess to clean, and the possibility of having to kill AJ ran through her mind much more than she wanted it to.

AJ felt like shit. She wanted her revenge, but not to this degree. Had she known a call to Royelle would lead to Amadeo's murder and her being an accomplice, she would've never called. She reacted on an emotional impulse, and now she felt entirely responsible for the entire situation. It was way more than she had bargained for. As she placed her gun down on the end table, she took another look at AJ, who looked flushed, almost as if her soul had left her body.

"I need you to sit down." Xandra walked AJ over to the dining table and sat her down. "Just stay there. Don't move." Xandra ordered.

"Man. What the fuck did I get myself into?" Xandra questioned herself, walking back towards Royelle.

Both Royelle and AJ had checked out. Neither one of them was going to be any kind of help for Xandra. And seeing as how she was the only fully functioning one, she had to figure out how to be the brains of the operation again! When she went back into the living room, Royelle was still standing in front of Amadeo, with a crazed look, a sly sinister smile, and blood splatter all over her body, face, clothes, and hair.

"Royelle!"

Royelle turned to look at Xandra when she heard her name.

"What the fuck is so funny?! You done killed this man in this woman's house! What the fuck are we supposed to do now?! How are we gonna explain this shit?!" Xandra continued to holler.

Royelle shrugged her shoulders. "Fuck him." She calmly said. "If he and his gay boyfriend wanted to be together, they could've just said that and left me and AJ out of it. I did everyone a favor. Now they can meet in hell." She said, spitting on Amadeo.

"Bitch! Do you even hear yourself?! Now that you did that, what are we supposed to do with him?!" Xandra questioned.

"The same thing we did—"

Xandra covered Royelle's mouth. "Shut the fuck up! You getting careless bitch. Shut up!" She released her hand from around Royelle's mouth.

"Ok. Well, now what?" Royelle asked, minding her tone.

"I don't know, killer. What, you ain't got no fucking ideas now? You thought of everything the fuck else."

Royelle cut her eyes over at Xandra. She was in no mood for the sarcasm, and cynicism Xandra was giving off. Royelle found it unamusing, and Xandra didn't care.

"I'm not afraid of you bitch! I'm trying to help your muthafucking ass! So don't give me that fucking look!" Xandra stormed off. "AJ, where are your tools, towels, blankets, anything?" She asked, walking back into the dining room.

"Up-up-upstairs." AJ managed to say through her stutters.

"Stay here. We'll be right back down. Do you hear me?"

AJ nodded yes.

"You come with me." Xandra pointed at Royelle.

The two went upstairs with no direction. They scavenged through all the closets looking for any and everything they could find to help clean the mess. In the meantime, AJ made her way back into the living room, where her husband lay dead.

She slowly walked in and sat across from him, in disbelief that this was now her new reality. *'What did I do?'* She thought to herself. The fact that they were all there because of her discovery of Amadeo and Trevion's affair meant nothing to her anymore. Amadeo was dead now, and she blamed herself. But she had to think fast. Between loud sobs and a runny nose, she opened her phone and texted Royelle, and began deleting messages and numbers out of her call log. Anything that might offer any sort of implication she got rid of.

When she was done with her phone, she released Amadeo of all his bondages and placed them on the end table. And when she heard what she thought was Xandra and Royelle getting ready to come downstairs, she looked over at the gun, grabbed it, and wiped it clean. She walked back over to Amadeo and kissed him on the lips. "I love you, Amadeo. And God, please forgive me!" She said before pulling the trigger.

Both Xandra and Royelle froze at the sound of the pop.

"Bitch! What the fuck was that?!" Xandra said.

"No! No! No!" Royelle said in hysterics running down the stairs. When she got to the living room, she liked to have died at that moment. "Nooo!!!" She screamed at the top of her lungs when she saw AJ laid out at Amadeo's feet with a gunshot wound to her right temple.

"Oh fuck!" Xandra said when she saw what had taken place.

Xandra was outdone. So much had happened in such a short period of time that it put her in a place of affliction, something that never happened. But being the Xandra she was, she thought quickly on her feet. And although the situation was fucked up, she saw her and Royelle's way out of the chaos.

"Royelle! We gotta get the fuck out of here! But first, we gotta put all that shit back we just moved, get you cleaned up and something else to wear. You can't walk out of the house like that."

Royelle heard what Xandra was saying, but she couldn't respond. She starkly stared at both Amdeo and AJ as they lay bleeding profusely. Royelle had seen death before, even been the reason for it, but this was massive. She had never seen anything to this disagree. She was in shock.

"Nowww, Royelle!" Xandra hollered, grabbing a plastic bag out of the kitchen.

Royelle catching the drift, followed her sister's lead upstairs. While Xandra went to find Royelle some clothes, Royelle went into the bathroom, wiped her sneakers down, and carefully removed the clothes she had on, placing them in the plastic bag Xandra gave her. Soon as she was done with that, she quickly washed her face, got dressed in a shirt and pair of jeans that belonged to AJ, and put her sneakers back on.

"Don't touch shit else, and everything we did touch, we need to wipe clean and fast!"

Royelle continued to follow Xandra's instructions, and once they were done upstairs, they made their way back downstairs and followed the same wiping techniques they had completed upstairs, making sure not to a miss a thing.

"Sis, what about your gun?" Royelle asked.

"Uh-Uh bitch! She can keep it."

"But what if—"

"Nahhh, sis. No serial numbers, no body's and ain't shit coming back to me. Grab all that shit from around homeboy, though. The last thing we need is any of that shit tracing back to either of us. And Royelle—

Royelle turned back towards Xandra with a serious look.

"When we walk out of this house, walk out as if everything is cool. We don't know what nosey-ass neighbor might've heard the gunshots, wondering about what the fuck they just heard. So, when we walk up out of here, we need to be laughing and joking. Do you hear me?"

Royelle nodded her head in agreement. She looked back over at AJ and blew her a kiss. "I'm so so sorry." She said. Royelle quickly wiped the tears running down her face and followed Xandra's lead, who was already standing at the front door. Xandra opened the door with her sleeve and directed Royelle to lock the door using the same method. As soon as they stepped outside, they faked and joked their way into their vehicles. The minute they got away from AJ's house, Royelle's phone rang.

"Hello." She answered sadly.

"Sis, meet me at my house," Xandra said before quickly hanging up.

Xandra was in no mood for Royelle's baby-fied bullshit. And as soon Xandra got to her house, she wasted no time going inside, leaving Royelle outside, something she never did.

"Yup! She's pissed," Royelle said as she hit the alarm to her truck. "I know what you're going to say," Royelle said, closing the door behind her.

Xandra sharply cut her eyes towards Royelle.

"You don't know shit of what I'm about to say! What the fuck is up with you?! Since when did killing for fun become a fucking thing for you?!"

"It was an accident," Royelle responded in a defenseless tone.

"Look. Don't give me none of that baby soft bullshit. When a minute ago, you were looking and acting like a straight-up killer!"

Xandra was not feeling or hearing none of what Royelle was talking about. Although a killer herself, she always did it with a purpose and a plan. None of what Royelle had done in the last few days was strategic or thought out. Everything was on impulse based on emotion, and those kinds of movements caused unwanted mistakes, something Xandra prided herself on not making in situations like these.

"Look. I know how you felt about AJ, and I'm sorry you're hurt, but even in a moment like this, she thought about you."

"How?" Royelle shot back.

"She left us with a perfect alibi in case we might need one."

"How?" She asked again.

"Bitch she set the stage for a murder-suicide. Once they find the phone with all that shit in it, they're gonna assume she found out and killed him before she killed herself. Think!"

"But, how do you know that?"

"I don't know that, sis. But the bullet in him matches the one in her, and the gun is lying right beside her. So for now, we don't say shit; we don't know shit. If the cops come knocking, we have to say we were there earlier in the day in case a nosey-ass neighbor saw us. But as far as the murders, we don't know shit! Do you hear me?!"

"Now, sis, you got a lot of shit going on, and I know you've been purposely avoiding your therapist. But I need you to stay in line with that shit. You can't fall off of routine now. It's gonna look funny. And with the way you been acting, you need that shit right about now." Xandra paused, waiting on a response from Royelle, whose face was looking down into her phone. "Earth to Royelle. Do you hear meee?" Xandra snapped her fingers as a stream of tears ran down Royelle's face.

"By the time you read this text, I'll be gone. I'm sorry, Royelle. I couldn't let you find out about Amadeo and Trevion. But so you know, I was right along; they were having an affair. I found out about all of their dirty little secrets in Amadeo's phone when he was in the shower."

"And not only was he sleeping with Trevion, but he was also sleeping with others outside of Massachusetts. Our husbands were pigs! I know you wanted to believe the best in Trevion, but he and Amadeo had been lying to the both of us for a very long time. This I cannot live with. The shock of knowing everything I now know is a bit more than I am willing to deal with. It's embarrassing, humiliating, and shameful! But believe me, I made him feel all the pain he's ever caused me and any he might have caused you.

"Just know that before killing myself, I killed him too. He doesn't deserve the slap on the wrist you would've given him, and I refuse to live with this level of disgrace for the rest of my life. Thank you for being an amazing woman and friend. I hope you can learn to forgive me someday. And I pray I see you on the brightest of the other side. Ajah!"

"What the fuck is it, sis?" Xandra asked.

"It's a text from AJ." Royelle sighed.

"Let me see that!" Xandra grabbed the phone out of Royelle's hand and was floored. She couldn't believe how much AJ had just saved not only Royelle but her too. "Oh, yea! She played that shit well. She's a mutherfucking G for that for real!"

"What do you mean?" Royelle sounded agitated.

"Bitch, I mean just that. She gave you an out. Only a real G would do the shit she did. Honestly, sis, she's your muthafucking savior. She made it to where all you need to do is call the cops right fucking now and tell them you need them to do a wellness check. Now!"

CHAPTER 11

*A*s Royelle began the drive back home, Xandra's words were the only thing replaying in her head. Calling the police was the furthest thing from her mind. And now that she had a moment to think, she was too afraid to do anything. There was just too much heat around her—Trevion, Mrs. Benton, her father, and now Amadeo and AJ. She was shook, so she called Xandra back, hoping to get some advice that didn't include calling the police.

"Royelle? What did they say?" Xandra asked when she answered.

"Nothing. I haven't called."

"Royelle. If you don't fucking call them, they're gonna find her phone, see that she texted you, and question why you didn't call them. So you need to get ahead of this."

"But I don't know what to say."

"Royelle!" Xandra grew irritated. "I told you what to say. Call them and tell them your friend texted you and said she was gonna kill herself and her husband, and you need them to do a wellness check. That's it!"

"You make it sound so simple. What if they want to ask me questions? Then what?"

"Bitch! Now you have all these muthafucking questions! You should've thought of this shit before you became Kill Bill!"

Royelle didn't say anything else. She just cried. Her heart was already shattered, and Xandra talking to her like she was simple didn't make matters any better.

"Man, sis, my fault," Xandra said, noticing the silence. " I ain't trying to be a bitch. I'm really just trying to help you. So please just do what I'm telling you to do.

Xandra felt bad for Royelle. She had to take a second to remember that the Royelle who was afraid and asking all the questions was the same Royelle she knew from before the accident. The Royelle who was killing people for fun, her brain had been rewired and wasn't her sister at all. She just had to remember that the two Royelle's she now knew weren't exactly the same.

"And sis. They probably will send the police over to ask you questions about what you know and don't know about their relationship."

"But that's just it, sis. That's what I'm trying to avoid."

"Listen. You got one over everybody. You got amnesia. You better use that shit to your advantage. Besides, it's routine for them to ask questions. It's part of their job."

Just then, a lightbulb emerged over Royelle. This was the first time that using her mental instability as an escape had ever been thought of, but it made sense. No one knew just how much she had remembered about Trevion or that her outburst directly resulted from those memories. No one knew. Not Xandra, not Dr. Angeli, no one. And she liked it that way.

"Look. I'm heading over there. Please Royelle. Listen to me when I say you need to call the police now. I'm gonna help you through the rest."

"Ok, sis." Royelle hesitantly responded.

She took a big sigh before hanging up and then dialed out the emergency services.

"911. What is your emergency?"

"Yes. I'd like to request a wellness check for a friend."

"What's your friend's name?"

"Ajah Corey."

"And what is your name?"

"Royelle Kingsley."

Royelle, when's the last time you or anyone else has seen or spoken to her?"

"She sent me a text stating that she was going to kill herself and her husband."

"Ma'am?" The dispatcher said, unsure of what she had just heard. "Did you say she was going to—

"Yes, ma'am! Please send someone right away to 4513 Quincy Lane."

Royelle quickly disconnected the call before the dispatcher could ask any more questions and sat in her living room anxiously waiting for Xandra to arrive. As a paralegal, she knew all the right things to do and say, but lately, with the shit she had been doing, all her training wasn't worth a damn.—She did more worrying and less critical thinking.

She balled as she embraced her body that was apparelled in AJ's clothing. She took deep whiffs of the shirt, hoping to grab AJ's scent, but all she could smell was Downy. It mattered none. The clothes belonged to AJ, and that was plenty for her. While she sat, tense feelings began to emerge as she replayed all the shit she had done. She couldn't believe or understand who she was becoming.

In her moments of menace, she couldn't feel a thing, not her heartbeat, not a pulsation of her veins, not a sweat, not a tremble or fear. She felt nothing. Even the devil showed feeling when he and his minions created havoc onto others; negative feelings perhaps, but feelings nonetheless. Royelle, well, she was mentally paralyzed. Becoming a killer was never in her DNA. So, numbness was the best way to describe her absence from the mess she was creating.

When the uniformed officers finally busted Ajah's door down and got inside the house, they walked into a gruesome scene. They found AJ and Amadeo exactly how Royelle and Xandra left them and instantly became sick at the sight of all the blood and brain matter everywhere.

"This is unit 210. Get a bus, homicide, and forensics down here to 4513 Quincy Lane. We have Two DOA's." One of the officers radioed out to dispatch.

When Thomas heard the dispatchers call on the scanner, he grew excited. It had been a while since he stepped foot onto a murder scene, so he was eager to poke his nose all up in this one. As he got closer to the scene, he could see that it was pretty active from afar. When he pulled up, he noticed police from different departments and teams everywhere, some he knew, some he didn't.

But since he never worked with the Quincy Police Department, he kept a low profile and stayed out of the way. He didn't ask any questions but kept his ears open for any conversation that would give him more insight as to what happened and why. When he walked into the living room, he and the other officers could tell without compromising the scene that it appeared to be a murder-suicide. The two bodies lay near each other and were completely unrecognizable. The trajectory of the bullets damn near split their wigs in half. Having an open casket for either of them would require a miracle on the mortician's part.

"Hey! Who did they say called this in?" One of the detectives asked the other.

"A woman by the name of Royelle Kingsley," the detective answered, reading from his notes.

Thomas was dumbfounded when he heard Royelle's name. He couldn't believe that it was her who kept coming up in almost every murder or death notification he was a part of. But, it was happening too often for it to be ignored. At this point, his suspicions about Royelle were beyond repose. He quickly left out the house and called Jayson.

"Thomasss! How's it going?!" Jayson happily answered.

"You're not gonna believe this shit!" Thomas said, disregarding the greeting.

"What shit?"

"Nascar Driver's name came up again and this time in a double murder."

"What!" Jayson yelled into the phone. "You have got to be fucking kidding me!"

"I'm telling you, son; there is something with that woman. Every time we turn around, it's her name that comes up."

"Are they saying she's a suspect?"

"No. She's the one who reported it."

"Who got the case?"

"Quincy. But you know I'm trailing."

"Well, let me know what you find out." Jayson sighed.

"Listen. I know you want to think the best about her, but something's not right about that woman. Death seems to follow her every which way she turns."

"Nah. I hear you, brother. Just call me when you find out more."

Jayson didn't want to see Royelle as a killer of any kind. After all his investigations, all he heard about her were great things. To think that she might be responsible for the deaths of anyone was beyond him. But, despite his personal views on Royelle, he had to admit Thomas was right; something strange was going on. So, he took heed to Thomas's words and swore to be on the lookout for any suspicions surrounding Royelle.

When Thomas pulled up to Royelle's house, he sat in his car for a moment. His relationship with Royelle wasn't the best, and he was prying into almost every investigation she was mentioned in. So, he knew him popping up was going to be a problem. Therefore, he took a moment to mentally prepare himself for the challenge he knew he was about to face. Finally, when he got to her door, he sighed before ringing her bell.

"What now?!" Royelle said, frustrated that she had an unexpected visitor.

"Sis, it's probably the police. You need to calm down," Xandra said while drinking her Patron on the couch.

"I am calm." Royelle barked.

Xandra rolled her eyes and let Royelle be. She noticed that Royelle was becoming a real hothead, and experience would have to show her why she needed to gain control of her attitude and emotions because talking to her wasn't working.

"Sir. What do you want?" Royelle snapped when she saw Thomas standing in front of her door.

Xandra noticing the change in Royelle's tone quickly walked over to the front door to find out what was happening. When she saw it was Thomas at the door, her attitude quickly changed too. She crossed her arms and stood beside Royelle with a murderous look as she grilled Thomas.

"Hello, ladies. I'm here to ask you a few questions about your call regarding the wellness check." He gently said.

"I know you didn't come to ask me any questions. You're not a detective, you don't work for the Quincy police department, and honestly, at this point, you're getting on my last damn nerve." Royelle snarled. "Anything you want to know, go to them."

"I'm sorry you feel that way, but this is an independent investigation."

"Then independently take your ass down to Quincy and talk to them! You know. You've been a problem since the day we met. You've never been considerate to any of my impasses. Not that I'm asking you to be, but you have no damn compassion. Yet, you keep popping up, flashing your badge and gun, taking your notes on your pad during the most inopportune times wanting me to be a friend when it's best for you.

"You're heartless and inconsiderate. Maybe if you tried being nice sometimes, you'd catch the bees that you've been hoping for. But, respectfully, since that isn't you, get your ass off my doorstep and go private investigate someone who needs it because I'm not it." Royelle slammed the door leaving Thomas empty-handed.

CHAPTER 12

Dear Brain Diary,

I know I've been neglecting you, and I'm sorry. But so much has happened; I don't even know where to start. My dad died of an apparent drug overdose, one of Trevion's business associates, Amadeo, and his wife Ajah, who happens to be a dear friend of mines, has also passed away. They say it was a murder-suicide.

You wouldn't believe that she found evidence in Amadeo's phone of him having an affair with Trevion?! Yup! You heard me right! My so-called husband and her husband were having a damn affair! And that's what took her to her breaking point. But can you blame her? I mean, I don't know what she found, but I'm sure it couldn't have been good.

Lately, it seems like my life is just falling apart. I still don't know what I've done to deserve the level of heartache I've been facing. Was my past life that bad? I've been nothing but great to people, so why does it seem like everything and everyone is against me.

The way my life has been unfolding lately is bizarre. It's like I'm in a nightmare that I won't soon be waking up from. If I could just go to sleep and not wake back up until my life is back to where it was before the accident, that would be perfect! I just want to go back to the place where my life was simple and normal. No heartache, no pain, no confusion, and for damn sure no deaths!

~ Royelle

Royelle looked at herself in the mirror affixed behind her bedroom door, and it was hard for her to see the beautiful half Jamaican, half German woman born to Adala, who had beautiful hair, a radiant smile, and smooth skin. The same girl who's a Suffolk University student, the dopest paralegal for the Premier Law office, and one of the most amazing women that anyone had the pleasure of meeting.

She couldn't find the image of the wholesome girl Adala had raised to become a worthy woman who valued her name and reputation. The depiction of virtuousness was no longer manifesting itself. It had dissipated, vanished, been wiped clean of all that was Royelle. She no longer saw herself in the same light others did.

When she looked In the mirror, the vision of a lost, confused, uncivil, and odious woman is what she saw as her reflection. There was nothing pretty, warm, or smart about the woman everyone saw her as, or so she thought. Royelle was struggling. The rendition she saw of herself was garbage, and she reveled in it.

She tried not to take pity on herself, but it was hard not to. She had done and been through so much that defeatism was easy to embrace. She hoped that today's visit with Dr. Angeli would help her see the beauty in herself that everyone else saw.

When she finally got herself together and made it to Dr. Angeli's office, Dr. Angeli took one look at her and knew today was going to be a visit of talking, not one of hypnosis. Dr. Angeli could tell that hell had paid Royelle a visit. She looked a hot mess, something Dr. Angeli had never seen in Royelle since she's been a patient.

When she called out Royelle's name, Dr. Angeli watched as Royelle dragged her feet walking towards her office. It seemed as though Royelle was carrying the weight of the world on her shoulders and then some.

"Royelle. Dare I ask how you're feeling, or should I just ask what happened?" Dr. Angeli said as she took her seat.

Royelle looked up at her with her red eyes and looked back down towards the floor.

"You haven't been here in over a week, and it's clear something is wrong. We have a two-hour block. So we can sit here in silence, or we can talk about what's been going on, channel through it, and try to come up with solutions on how to deal with whatever it is moving forward. You decide."

Royelle took a deep breath and looked back up at the doctor. But before the words could come out, the tears fell, and Royelle began to sob uncontrollably. Still unaware of all that Royelle had been through and done, Dr. Angeli was taken aback by her breakdown. She grabbed the box of Kleenex off her desk and placed it on the side of Royelle.

"Royelle, what's happening right now? What is causing this emotion?" Dr. Angeli gently asked.

Royelle continued to sob. She couldn't stop. It was as if she was rinsing her soul of all the dirt and shame she had acquired over the last few days. After about ten minutes of her wailings and Dr. Angeli rubbing her back, Royelle was finally ready to talk.

"Are you ready and ok to speak now?" Dr. Angeli asked.

"Yes, ma'am," Royelle responded softly.

"OK. Can you tell me what's going on? What caused your emotional outburst?"

Royelle heavily sighed again. "Everybody's dying around me?" She said.

" How so?" Dr. Angeli asked, unaware of Royelle's current circumstances.

"My dad is gone, and a very good friend of mine committed suicide and killed her husband," Royelle said before crying again.

Dr. Angeli was shocked. She wasn't expecting that type of blowback. *'This isn't good,'* she thought. Royelle was already suffering from so much trauma, including the loss of her mother. To be enduring more loss and trauma was for sure going to set Royelle back from all the progress she had attained while working with Dr. Angeli thought.

"Royelle, I am so so sorry to hear about this. My deepest condolences to you, your family, and the other families as well."

Dr. Angeli was at a loss for words, but she couldn't express that to

Royelle; she was her therapist, after all. She gave Royelle a few more minutes to compose herself and then reconvened the session.

"Look at this."

Royelle passed Dr. Angeli her phone, and as Dr. Angeli read the message from AJ to Royelle, Royelle could see Dr. Angeli's facial expressions change from one extreme to the next.

"That's a lot to digest, Royelle. Do you feel at fault for any of this?"

Royelle shrugged her shoulders to indicate she didn't know.

"Well, I'm telling you you're not. Sometimes people have emotional breakdowns that cause them to snap in the heat of the moment."

"Dr. Do you think that those breakdowns cause people to have blackouts before they cause harm to another?" Royelle was intentional with her question.

"Absolutely, Royelle. People handle traumas differently. And someone blacking out after finding out something of that magnitude is not uncommon. Do you think that's what happened to your friend? Do you think she blacked out and snapped?"

Royelle sighed. "That's the only thing that makes sense. I mean, she's never had a mean streak in her. On the contrary, she was always nice, professional, helpful, and respectful towards everyone she met. I'm just trying to understand what went wrong."

"Royelle several things could've happened, and you had no way of preventing it. When people snap like that, it's hard to talk them off of the 80th-floor ledge."

Dr. Angeli had no idea that Royelle was describing herself when she spoke about AJ, nor did she know that the advice she was offering Royelle was for Royelle's benefit. Royelle played her part and played it well while soaking up whatever information she could get from Dr. Angeli.

"Dr. Angeli, what's it like for a person who blacks out? Does it happen to normal people or just people with mental health issues?"

Dr. Angeli chuckled. "Royelle, it can happen to anyone at any given time. Blackouts are a temporary loss of consciousness and have different variables to them. In your friend's case, she more than likely lost touch with reality and her surroundings when she read and saw all that she did.

Everything Royelle did in the session was strategic. She took heed to every direction Xandra had given her in the days leading up to her therapy session, and it was working like a charm. She continued to listen as the doctor gave descriptions and scenarios of people who have blacked out in the past and how it may or may not have affected them.

And although the client/Dr privilege protected her, she couldn't be sure about anything. And since she knew every session was documented on paper or recorded on tape, she played the role of the grieving friend, daughter, wife, and amnesia patient like a true Hollywood actress and made sure to ask all the right questions and say all the right things just in case the police came snooping around.

By the end of the session, Dr. Angeli was still confident that her patient could only remember the things of Trevion that the two of them uncovered together and that she was still suffering other Trevion-based traumas immensely. She had no idea that the Royelle sitting before her was now a murderer, times two, and the things that she remembered about Trevvion were beyond the scope of anyone's knowledge, Xandra included.

CHAPTER 13

*A*ruba woke up excited about her trip to New York. The whole week she had been bragging to others about how she had her boy toy tightly wrapped up by the balls. She never told them who she was talking about, but she couldn't stop talking about how. However, she was so strung out most days that any tale she told was considered *"just talk."* Nobody ever took her seriously enough or gave a fuck. If she didn't have any proof, then there was no action.

Since she knew the real side of Da'Vegas, she knew that going to him looking like trash wasn't going to cut it. Therefore, she made an appointment at Carolyn's Hair Salon with Bernice, the biggest mouth in town and was the most ghetto transexual anyone knew. And although she was the baddest in the hair game, she couldn't stay out of drama or other people's business to save her life. So, Trevion introducing Royelle, Bella, and Aruba to Bernice was not the thing to do; whether she knew their connection or not remained to be seen. But her loose lips sunk ships all throughout the hood. If she knew the business, no matter how big or small, so didn't the community.

She was the source of marriages breaking up, bitches fighting in the stores, in the streets, and sometimes in the church. She was the reason some men didn't have to go to Club Intensity. All they had to do was pay for her service through Trevion's business Xclusive, and it was on from there. Hell, even he and Amadeo had their share of her. She was dangerous in more ways than anyone could count. And not cause she could fight, but because her mouth was a weapon.

"Good afternoon Aruba. How are you doing today?" The receptionist, Lorraine, asked.

"I'm good."

"I'll let Bernice know you're here. Are you ok, though? You look overwhelmed," Lorraine asked in a concerned manner.

Although Lorraine knew what kind of female Aruba was and what she was into, she still treated her with respect, even if Aruba didn't do the same. Aruba turned around and looked in the mirror behind her, fixed her hat, turned from left to right, and started surveying her face to make sure she didn't miss something when she took a shower, but she saw nothing.

"Lorraine girl, I'm fine. I might just look a little crazy, but I'm good." Aruba fakely smiled before sitting down.

Although Aruba was more of a hip-hop and rap kind of woman, she closed her eyes and effortlessly embraced the sounds of the smooth jazz music playing in the background. It was perfect. She felt so good and at peace. The only thing on her mind was the meeting with Da'Vegas. The curiosity to see what he looked, liked, felt like, and smelled like this time was intense. She couldn't release her mind from it and slightly smiled with every thought as she felt her pussy get moist by the second.

"What you smiling about, girl! You don't hear me calling you?" Bernice chuckled.

"What's up, girl?" Aruba smiled back at her. "I wasn't smiling. I was just thinking."

"Well, whatever you were thinking about, had you out of there. Care to share?"

"Chile, there's nothing to share."

"Mmm-hmm. Come on here." Bernice ordered.

They walked to the shampoo bowl, and as Aruba sat and got comfortable, she knew she was in the right hands with Bernice. So, there was no need to explain what she wanted done. She closed her eyes and began to enjoy the gentleness that Bernice took with her. Despite Aruba being who she was, her money was green like everybody else's, and she was one that Trevion had referred. His absence didn't stop the money; it just made things weird. After a good five-minute wash, Bernice gently pushed Aruba back into an upright seating position. She blotted her hair dry and walked with her back to her styling station.

"Bernice, Royelle's on the phone," Lorraine yelled across the floor.

Instantly, Aruba became hot. *'Royelle!'* She thought. *'Don't tell me that bitch is a client here too. What the fuck?!'* Aruba continued in her thoughts. She watched Bernice through the mounted square-shaped mirrors as she grabbed the cordless phone and walked back to her station.

"Heyyy Royelle! How have you been, darling? It's been a while, my love."

Aruba hated all the excitement in Bernice's voice. It was clear to her that, like many others, she had high regard and respect for Royelle, and Aruba did not like that. Nevertheless, she stayed quiet with her eyes in her phone, pretending not to listen to the conversation. She couldn't believe that they went to the same salon and were seen by the same stylist. Sure, Boston was small, but hair salons were everywhere. There was no way it was a coincidence. Aruba surmised Trevion was the reason for the combo.

"Here you go, Lorriane," Bernice yelled out.

"It's been a while since she's been here. How she doing, B?" Lorraine asked, walking over to grab the phone.

"She's gonna be all right. You know she was in that accident, was in a coma, her husband died, mother and father died, she got that amnesia shit, and I heard that the murder-suicide that just happened was Trevion's people's."

"People's? What do you mean people's? Like family?" Lorraine questioned.

"No, girl! His business partners."

"Whattt! You don't say."

"Mmm-Hmm. They say the wife smoked the husband for having affairs with men and shit."

"Bitchhh! I know you lying! What men?"

"If I'm lying, I'm flying." Bernice laughed. "And that ain't for me to say. I ain't about to put these men on blast. Their wives will find out on their own, honey."

"Berniceee!"

"What chile?! Lorraine, you ain't about to get me to spill no names. They out there, though." Bernice laughed again.

Lorraine smacked her lips. "You crazy! Anyway, I just feel bad for her cause she's been going through it."

"Yea, she has been. But that girl is a beast! She stays holding her own. I don't care what nobody says. I don't think the devil himself can get with her." Bernice chuckled.

"Hmph! I'm sure." Lorraine said.

As long as Bernice talked about Royelle's misfortunes, Aruba was content, but her attitude changed the minute Bernice began to praise Royelle for her strengths. Typical like a hater. They love to see you down, hate to see you up.

"So, do you think she knew the business associates?" Lorraine asked.

"Had to girl. How couldn't she? Her and Trevion were inseparable. She had to know them."

"Inseparable? What about those rumors about him having another wife? Can't be too damn inseparable if he was doing all of that." Lorraine joked.

Aruba kept her head slightly down but stayed listening attentively.

"Now see that there, that gotta be a lie. Cause how? When did he ever have the time to see someone else? Him and Royelle were tight. Girl, you saw he kept her. If there was somebody else, I'm sure she was getting all the sloppy seconds and hand-me-downs. Chile, please." Bernice snickered.

Aruba boiled on the inside as the women continued to talk. And the fact that she couldn't say anything about their curiosities didn't make the situation any better. It was apparent to her that the only people who ever knew she existed in Trevion's life were Trevion and the girls who worked for him. It seemed like every time she turned around, her place in his life had become less relevant.

"But honestly, who knows. A nigga like Trevion was probably only with Royelle because the girl got money." Bernice continued.

"Bernice, how do you know that?" Lorraine asked.

Bernice sucked her teeth. "Come on, Lorraine. This is me you talking to. How could I not know?"

Everybody in the salon laughed.

"You sho'right about that," Lorraine responded.

Once Bernice was done roller setting Aruba's hair, she placed her under the hairdryer and set the timer for 60 minutes. It was enough time for her to think about everything she wanted to say to Da'Vegas when she got to him. She felt so low and disregarded that the visit she was so excited to have, turned into regret. She started thinking about her life and all it had turned into.

Her mother was to blame for much of it. Showing her how to sell herself at such an early age did nothing but introduce her to the likes of men like Trevion. But she saw him as different. She thought he would rescue her. Take her from the confines of being a sex slave to men for pennies on a dollar. She knew she was worth more than she gave, but her mind wasn't so convinced.

She was led to believe that fucking with Trevion would create a better life for her, but when she went to jail, Trevion left her for dead. She was useless to him at that point. Even getting money on her books was a thing she had to beg for, and she couldn't understand why. The lies he told about the streets being dry and him folding is what he led with and what she believed. He was such a charmer it was hard to believe anything less.

All she ever wanted from him was the good life he promised her. She saw how he treated Bella and heard all the things he did for Royelle, and none of it matched the way he treated her. She couldn't understand what she had done so wrong to get the '*bottom of the barrel*' treatment from him.

Now here she was strung out, lost, still having sex for pennies, and Trevion left her with shit. Besides D-Rock, she was the only one who knew he was still alive, knew his true identity, knew where he lived, and all the scams he had pulled on other women over the years. But she never gave him up. She stayed committed to his every move. And yet he showed her she

118

wasn't worthy enough. Deep in her heart, she wanted to believe that he wasn't the asshole he had been presenting himself as, but it was hard not to see it. Trevion getting shot changed the game significantly; his behaviors were one.

"Come on, Aruba!" Bernice shouted from across the room when she heard the dryer go off. "Are you combing your curls out today?" She asked as Aruba took her seat.

"No, just take them out, give me a good massage, and were good.

"So, where you going today? Anywhere special?"

"Nahhh, just needed to get it done, you know. But I might hit New York sometime this weekend."

"New York?! What's out there? You got people's in New York?"

"No nosey. Since when do we ever need people's in New York to go out there."

"I guess." Bernice smacked her lips.

Aruba wished she would've never opened her mouth. The little bit she did tell Bernice was about to be made into a big production in later conversation for no reason.

"All right, girl. You good to go. Now get ya ass out my chair." Bernice laughed.

"Girl give me the check, so I can get out of here," Aruba said, snatching the check out of Bernice's right hand.

Aruba handed Bernice a ten-dollar tip and walked the check up to Lorraine.

"Byeeeee Aruba!" Bernice teased.

"Girl, bye!" Aruba smiled.

"Why you looking like that, Bernice? Lorraine asked.

"Cause that girl a gawt damn lie."

"Ah lie? What she lied about?"

"Her ass going to New York to see some nigga named Da'Vegas who lives in Brooklyn."

"How do you even know thattt?!" Lorraine laughed.

"Girlll, I read her text messages."

"Berniceee! How is any of that your businesss?" Lorraine simpered.

"Girl, please! Cause it is. If you sit in my chair with your phone open, your business is my business. We sharing!"

CHAPTER 14

ongratulations! You have a son!" The doctor yelled as he gently pulled the baby out of Bessie Pennington's swollen vagina.

"Get him out of here!" She yelled, looking away as the doctor attempted to bring the baby closer. "Please! Just get him out of here!" She continued as the baby cried.

Confused, the doctor ordered the nurses to clean the baby up quickly and take him down to the nursery to be cared for.

"Mrs. Pennington. Are you ok?" The doctor asked.

Bessie didn't answer. She continued to look away from the doctor as the tears from her left eye slowly moved across the bridge of her nose, joining the tears releasing from her right eye.

"Mrs. Pennington, the nurses are going to get you all cleaned up and then give you some time to rest. But, we'll be back to check in on you in a bit." The doctor said as he removed his gloves and gown.

Bessie didn't say a word. She let the nurses take their time cleaning her from the waist down, changing her johnny, and replacing the soaked chucks with some clean, dry ones. Finally, they got her nice and comfortable, placed a jug of ice and water on her food tray table, and let her be. The entire time they worked, she cried. She didn't speak or contest any of the help; she just cried.

They assumed that she was experiencing some postpartum as they had seen time and time again with new mothers, but that was far from it.

Three days into being in the hospital, Bessie was still disconnected from the baby. So much so, she refused to name him, see him, change or feed him. She wanted absolutely nothing to do with him. When the social workers offered her some support and services, she declined and announced that she wanted to relinquish her rights and put him up for adoption.

No one understood the reason behind her disconnect or decision, but they couldn't force her hand to be something she wasn't ready to become. After four days of recovering from the long hours of labor and twenty-two stitches sewing her vagina back together, Bessie was set to be released.

"Mrs. Pennington, before you completely sign over your rights and we deliver the baby to a family, are you sure you don't want to take advantage of the honor in naming him?" The social worker asked.

Bessie sighed heavily.

"You know, it's hard to love a child that was made on a dark, stormy night when all the streets were clear of people, even animals. Especially when all you could think about was going home to enjoy a night's rest after working sixteen long hours. Instead, you were running for your life from five wolves, who would later catch you, tearing you to shreds and eating away at your pure flesh—leaving you to lie still in a pool of your own blood and tears.

"No one to hear your screams or care if they did. Each wolf taking its pleasure in roughing you up in every position and angle unimaginable, leaving you with no fight left other than to lie there and die.

"To keep that child is to say that I must forget despite being misused and bitten by snakes. Ma'am, my mind and body are still feeling the stings of the piercing through my skin and the venom entering my bloodstream from that fateful night nine months ago.

" I can't love that child. That baby is the bastard son of satan. I hope you live long enough to see that he's going to be a problem for many. I can feel it in my spirit. So lets him call him Malachi, Lucifer's son."

Bessie grabbed the pen out of the social worker's hand, signing the documents and birth certificate, placing Malachi Lucifer Pennington as his legal birth name.

"Please don't ever try to contact me about this child. I don't want to know anything about him. Ever!"

The social worker was left speechless as Bessie walked toward the elevator doors. She couldn't believe that she had even suggested it. And sadly, there wasn't anything she could do about it either. The baby's birth name was given to the child by the biological mother, and altering the documents was illegal. It was also a violation of the HIPPA laws and grounds for imprisonment and termination.

In her thirteen years of being in social work, she had never experienced anything quite like the spectacle she had just been a part of. And after what she had just heard and seen, she was glad Bessie decided to pass up motherhood. The fear of her hurting the baby would've been very likely had she decided to keep him.

Once the social worker was done completing the necessary transition paperwork, she wrapped the baby up and delivered him to the family, who would later adopt him and change his name from Malachi Lucifer Pennington to Trevion Da'Vegas Kingsley.

Tracy and Tony Kingsley, or TNT as their friends called them, were hardworking, easy-going, everyday people. Tracy worked as a registered nurse, and Tony drove 18 Wheelers for a living, traveling locally and nationally. Neither of them did any drugs or abused alcohol. They might've had a drink here and there, but certainly nothing they couldn't handle.

Married for seven years at the time, they tried extensively to get pregnant. Tracy read all kinds of literature detailing in Black and White all the sexual positions that could work to get the sperm to meet the egg. They went as far as to have sex on different days and hours and even included the moon's schedule in their efforts; but they all failed.

For a long time, Tracy struggled with the idea that maybe Tony was no longer attracted to her, making it difficult for him to perform at his maximum capacity. He reassured her that wasn't the case and suggested they see a doctor to get some answers. After researching for several weeks, they found Dr. Zahir, a fertility specialist who performed test after test with no results. After many efforts, the only conclusion Dr. Zahir could come to was that Tracy was barren and that crushed everything inside of her, knowing she'd never be able to bear children for Tony.

She was afraid she would die alone with no one to care for her or Tony when they got old, but Tony wouldn't hear of it. Having children was of the utmost importance for Tracy, and Tony saw to it being done. He researched adoption agencies, and when he found the one he felt was the right fit for them, he let Tracy know what he had been up to. She was beyond ecstatic at his caring gesture and enthralled at how he cared for her heart. It was the confirmation she needed to know that Tony still loved her and wanted to see her wishes come true.

A few months later, DaKari, became a part of their life when he was three months old. His mother was young, in the streets, doing drugs, with no intentions of getting pregnant or becoming a mother, ever. She never received prenatal care or bothered seeing a doctor unless she was trying to get pain medications. And as soon as she learned pregnant women could only take Tylenol, she stopped going to the doctor's altogether and found the drugs another way. And on the day her water broke, she walked into the hospital, gave birth, and bailed when she got up enough rest and strength. No one has seen her since. She abandoned baby DaKari, leaving the hospital to decide on what to do next.

Nine months later, after Tracy and Tony saw how fast DaKari was progressing and growing, they decided they wanted another child, a boy preferably, to accompany and grow with DaKari. TNT were both the only child born to their parents and remembered how lonely times could get when they weren't around other kids. They didn't want the same for DaKari, so they reached back out to the same adoption agency they used before, and four months later, Malachi, later renamed Trevion, was presented to them.

As children, both were respectful, loving boys, always well behaved at home, as well as at school. And since they had each other and needed absolutely nothing, Tracy rarely let them hang outside or with other children. Instead, like most mothers, she wanted to protect and shield them from the corrupted streets they were conceived in. And in doing so, she sheltered them tremendously.

Over the years, the boys flourished through the first eight years of school. But when they got to high school, things changed. They got their first piece of ass, smoked weed for the first time, and learned about the drug game. Although the brothers quickly learned how to make fast money by selling weed to other students, it was the ability to get a girl to do anything they asked of them that fascinated Trevion the most. And by the time he made it to the Twelfth grade, with his smooth-talking, charismatic, and charming self, he had girls buying his clothes, sneakers, jewelry, paying his phone bill, giving him money and sex whenever he wanted.

DaKari, on the other hand, was well on his way to starting his drug empire. But first, they had to finish school. Tracy was on their ass. She always said, *"I don't care how dark your days may be, remember, education is always first. Knowledge is power if you apply it well. In this house, graduating from high school is not optional; it's a requirement!"* She said it so much that she even wrote it on paper and put it up on the fridge held by magnets so that they would always see it as a reminder. And each time the paper got old, she'd write it again and again until they finally crossed that stage with a diploma in hand.

A few months after graduating, Tony left Tracy and the boys high and dry. The rumor was he was having an affair with a woman he met while on the road. Rumor or not, the way Tony was moving before leaving let her know that the rumor had some truth to it. What kind of man just up and leaves his ill wife and family unless he got some pussy somewhere else, none! That's what kind. Tracy wasted no time filing for divorce and moving on without him, but not before seeing him in court one last time, where she was awarded $8,750 a month in alimony.

The boys didn't know, but Tracy was sick. She had a brain tumor that she and Tony were sure would take her out one day soon. She refused surgery or treatment of any kind and asked God to spare her so that she could at least see her boys graduate from high school. And he did. Not only did he give her plenty of time to bank the money she was getting every month from Tony, but she was blessed long enough to see DaKari become an amazing father to twin girls and two boys who were a year apart. On the day the girls made it to the first grade, she passed.

If Tracy was alive to see all the shit her sons had been up to, they'd have hell to pay the captain. They weren't raised to be the no-good sons of bitches they had become in their adult years. But, the impact of Tony's sudden absence during a time his wife and children needed him played a major part in what would become the foulness of DaKari and Trevion's adult lives.

Although an amazing father to four beautiful children, fatherhood didn't stop DaKari from being one of the most respected and hated drug kingpins in the hood. When no one else from other sets could enter projects like Orchard Park, Mission Hill, Lenox, Columbia Point, and Heath Street without getting jumped or killed, DaKari walked through them like a God. He feared no one and had the manpower and ammunition to back it all up.

Trevion was different. He could sell dope like his brother and even helped him with some runs from time to time, but that wasn't his style. Judging by the expensive cars, nice clothes, and fancy jewelry DaKari had, it showed that the drug game provided a great payout, but it didn't come without a cost. Trevion witnessed too many murders, robberies, and niggas getting locked up, and that was enough for him to know that the drug hustle wasn't his kind of hustle.

His moneymaker came from the women; it always had. He saw easy money in them and knew how to get it. Trevion had a gift for gab and used it well. He was so damn good; he could sell snow cones to a snowman. And as he perfected it over the years, he realized he could get women to do two things; sell ass and buy his love and attention.

His only job was to make sure the ones he had working on the street and the ones taking private calls through his escort service were protected. Those who didn't want anything to do with the sex for money business had to pay what they weighed to be around him, and they were paying heavy. He expected nothing but the finest in clothes, jewelry, and cars. And if the cops ever questioned him about any of it, he had his start-up construction and roofing business and the payout from his mother's insurance policy to use as a backup.

By the time Trevion met Lyra, he was ocean deep in the pimps and hoes game. She tried to use the fact that she was a madam before so he could see her as a top bitch, but her lack of hoes and money said otherwise.

Therefore, he started her at the bottom to see what she could do. For the first two years, she delivered paper after paper in weight. She never gave him less than four to five thousand a week.

The money was flowing good and always accounted for. So, to keep the hoes in check, Trevion decided to let all of them know that he and Lyra were now married. It not only gave Lyra instant respect, but it also gave her rank in his life and over the others. And although the marriage was false, the two of them were the only ones who knew it and saw it as legal. And the moment Trevion declared her position, she changed her name from Lyra to Aruba, which meant, *"Loves her husband."* But, she let the title "wife" get to her head.

Everything was good until she turned her feelings on for love instead of maintaining them as a business. She constantly blamed her emotions on the fact that they were always fucking. But it was no different from the rest of the girls he fucked on their team. He made his rounds amongst the girls, and none of them acted like her. Even Bella, who he brought in a year after Aruba, acted accordingly, and she spent way more time with Trevion than Aruba would ever know.

Trevion was still pissed off at Aruba for letting Bella and McKenzie get involved with Jayson. Honestly, he couldn't care less if McKenize got hit by a truck or jumped off the Zakim or Charles River bridge; he washed his hands of her. Everything he asked her to do, no matter how small the assignment, never produced any results. Bella was his one, though. He knew that had she known the truth about Jayson, she would've never walked into that wall with McKenzie. Above all else, she would've protected them both from the bullshit. Instead, Aruba set Bella up for a trap, which was a no for him. He had some deciding to do, and he knew just who to call to get it done quickly.

CHAPTER 15

*A*ruba took her time making it through the city streets, trying to get to the Mass Pike. "What was the rush," she thought. She knew she would be with Trevion all weekend, and besides, she had liquor and weed in the car. The last thing she wanted to do was get pulled over and locked up on her way to see her husband.

As she passed up the South Bay Correctional Center on meth mile, she started going through the motions. She didn't miss that part of her life. But she knew if she didn't slow down on the drugs and the tricking, she'd be looking like everyone on that block or be right back inside of South Bay or at the Framingham Women's Prison; she didn't miss or desire either.

Every time she took the drive to New York, she wondered what would be the best way to talk to Trevion about everything that was bothering her. She didn't want to seem like she was pressing him, but she was. She really loved him, but the feeling wasn't mutual. She tried and tried and tried to understand how she could be better for him without asking him, but it never worked. So, she concluded that being his top bitch was just for the money, never for the love. It was Bella he wanted; it was always Bella as far as she could tell.

As she drove down 93 North making it onto the Mass Pike, the tunes of Keyshia Cole's Woman to Woman featuring Ashanti played through her speakers from her Apple music shuffle. And every word the two of them sang Aruba related to. When K.C. said, *"You got me like the feds, checking on evidence,"* she felt that. She did feel like the feds. Only they had no qualms about asking questions; she did. But when Ashanti sang, *"He told me I was his one and only,"* it broke her. Trevion had told her she was his one and only almost every time they fucked or when they discussed business, and it stuck to her like glue. She may have been a hoe, poor in education, with a rap sheet the length of a scroll, but she was still a woman. And women, no matter their age, profession, race, height, or weight, are driven by emotion, and if played with, it could lead to so many unfortunate circumstances.

When Trevion met Royelle and learned about everything she stood to inherit, a million dollars to be exact, he wanted in. Aruba and the others were just going to have to fall in line and follow his lead. The plan was for him to marry her, do what husbands do for a little while, and then create an unfortunate incident causing her life to end. But a few things got in the way of that and what should've been a big payout.

One, Aruba got locked up. So now he had to find two hoe's; one who could bring in the money like her and another he could trust to collect the money from others when he wasn't around. Two, Royelle having a sister like Xandra wasn't easy for anybody. From the beginning, he should've known she was the one to watch, but he never took her seriously enough. And three, him getting caught up with Amadeo and all his other schemes was surely going to get him off of her papers, and it did.

The papers he claimed he was looking for the day she busted him going through her stuff were old. He never knew that a copy with changes was at the same lawyer's office her mother used for her estates. The only ones that stood to get any of her inheritance were her siblings. Royelle was naïve in a lot of ways, but her mother didn't raise no fool. The moment she caught wind of the funny business and felt uneasy about Trevion, she ran down to the lawyer's office, assigning them as Power of Attorney over her policies, and made her three best friends, as she called them, her beneficiaries. Trevion had lost a long time ago and didn't even know it.

Aruba looked in the rearview mirror to make sure her hair was still looking good as the song changed to K. Michelle's, Cry. "Awww shit!" She said, turning the volume all the way up. The switch between feelings was instantaneous. She went from being hurt with Keyshia Cole to being brutal with K. Michelle.

"Nobodies off limits, not even your friends
I'm about to go in, about to go in
I'm gon' do something I never do
I'mma try and hurt you too."

"But you wouldn't even care cause you have no heart, Trev-i-onnn! I've been nothing but good to you. Being good in return is the least you could fucking do! You assholeee!"

"You gon' suffer, you gone suffer
For everything you did."

She continued to sing in a high-pitched voice, feeling each verse K. Michelle sung. It was like her shuffle knew what she was feeling and played on that emotion. It made no sense that song after song had everything to do with what she was feeling about Trevion and what she was going through.

After four hours and thirty minutes of straight driving, Aruba had finally arrived at 1825. She took a deep breath as she pulled into the same spot she parked in the last time she was there. A mix of emotions ran through her as she gathered all of her belongings. While excited to be there, she needed real answers about Royelle and wanted to know how he would rid himself of Bella. She had never given him ultimatums before, but he was gonna have to choose this weekend. He was either going to get on board or jump ship, but he had to choose either way. She didn't see it any other way.

She grabbed her weekend bag out of the backseat of her car and headed for the front lobby. She smiled when she walked in and saw that the building was lit. It was nothing like the last time she was there. This time, a mixed crowd of Black, White, Hispanic, and Asian descent men and women gathered with Red and Blue cups in their hands. Most were in the common areas talking, some were in the entertainment room shooting pool, while others watched the game. It had a sports bar & grill feel to it without the bar and kitchen.

She smiled as she got on the elevator, overjoyed at all the activity. She wanted the weekend to be about more than just sex. She wanted it to have meaning and wondered if Trevion would be all interested in a game of pool or something. After everything that happened and all that he had gone through, she wanted and needed to re-learn him, and she figured getting him out of his apartment would be a great way to start.

When she reached the door, it was already cracked open. She smiled when she caught a whiff of a sweet floral fragrance coming from the inside. *"He's been waiting for me."* She thought. When she walked inside, she choked up. She put her bags down, and with both hands over her chest, she slowly surveyed the room. She couldn't believe her eyes. For the first time in all the years of knowing and sexing each other, Trevion had never taken the time to serenade her in any way.

She carefully stepped onto the bed of Light Pink and White Roses that were sprawled out from the front door leading to the living room. There were so many she could barely see the floor. Everywhere she looked, there were Roses. If they weren't on the floor, they sat atop a counter or table in various vases. She couldn't believe her eyes. Her heart fluttered. This made her feel beyond anything she had ever felt. She felt loved, appreciated, wanted, and extremely beautiful at this moment. The idea of going to shoot pool had long escaped her. Any ill feelings she had about him before arriving, gone! She just wanted him, but there was more.

As she approached the coffee table in the living room, she noticed an envelope propped up against one of the many lit candles, surrounded by more rose petals, with her name written on it. When she picked it up, she closed her eyes to take a whiff of the men's Chanel cologne that he had sprayed it with.

"Mmm." She said, delighted by the scent.

She slowly opened it, unsure of what to expect, but there was only a piece of paper folded in tri-fold.

"Welcome to The Abyss, baby. Go into the bathroom and do what women do. There's something in there for you. But before you do, take the pills, and drink both glasses of the Red Devil that I made for you. Wait 30 minutes before you come into the room. I'll be waiting for you."

She folded the letter back up and put it in her pocket. That was her safe keep, her later memory of what today was all about. She picked the pills up, unsure of what they were, but judging from the color, size, and shape; she was almost sure they were ecstasy. She wasted no time doing what the note said and headed into the bathroom.

Tears streamed down her face when she walked in to find more roses on the floor and inside the already prepared scented bubble bath. When she closed the door and turned around, a Red see-through negligee and G-String with open-toed red heels match graced her vision. She was bewildered. No one had ever taken out so much time with or for her. For once, she felt valued.

Before she did anything else, she wrapped her hair and put her scarf on. The last thing she wanted was for her hair to get wet before Trevion could see it or sweat it out. Her jaw hurt from all the smiling as she stepped into the hot to the feet, warm to the body water. She still couldn't believe this was all for her. She knew she was on his shit list, so she wondered what it was that she had done to deserve such a thing. Maybe this was his way of saying he was sorry and that he forgave her. She didn't know, but she damn sure wasn't going to ask. Ruining a moment like this would just be plain ol' suicide.

After a little over an hour of her indulging herself in the bubble bath and then taking a thorough shower, she was finally dressed and ready to enter the room. She had on the lingerie Trevion had given her, and her body was lotioned down with a combination of Nivea's 24hr moisture release and her Gucci Bamboo lotion. She always combined the two—Nivea to keep her body from being ashy and Bamboo for the scent. High-end products such as Gucci didn't serve a skin moisturizing purpose, but the scent was undeniable. She combed her hair down, swooping the front bang to the left behind her ear and pulling the hair on the right side behind her right ear. She made sure not to comb it out too hard or fast; she wanted to keep as much of the curl as possible. Once she liked what she saw, she made her way to his room.

To add some effect to the already mounting suspicion, rather than opening the door suddenly and fast, she slowly turned the knob and began opening the door without haste. When she walked in, she found Trevion

132

standing in front of his bed, with his dick lodged inside Bella's mouth and his right hand gripping her head.

"What the fuck!" She hollered.

Aruba was in shock. She couldn't move. Her body wanted to react. She wanted to attack, but her feet remained pegged to the floor as she continued to watch the motions of Bella's mouth deep throat Trevion. As soon as the initial shock released itself from her, she took a limitless breath.

"Trevion! What the fuck is this shit?! This is why you wanted me here?! Why is this bitch here?!"

Through all the yelling and name-calling, Bella never moved. On the contrary, she enjoyed every bit of Aruba's pain and confusion. If there were two things she knew about Aruba, her love for Trevion ran deep, and her jealousy towards her because of Trevion was deeper. And because of that, for every name, every slap, every hair pull, every bit of disrespect that Aruba ever showed Bella, she gave it to her in return, by sucking Trevion off, in a way that Aruba never could. She continued sucking until Trevion busted all his inches in her mouth, and she still didn't stop. She swallowed and kept going, and he let her. It pissed Aruba off, knowing that Bella was being facetious.

"I'm getting the fuck outta here!" Bella turned to walk away.

"Don't you fucking move! You don't move until I say you move. Now watch!" Trevion gave her the death stare.

He ordered Bella to her feet and told her to turn around, so he could hit it from the back. He quickly slid inside of her and began stroking. And Bella being Bella, knowing how Aruba was feeling, overexerted her moans. Trevion wasn't even hard enough for her to feel her walls swell, but she was going to put on an undeniable act for her audience.

Aruba couldn't do shit. She had to do what she was told or suffer the consequences. A few things ran through her mind as she stood there speechless. First, when did Trevion get out of his wheelchair, and why didn't he ever tell her? Second, why did Bella have on the exact same thing she did? Third, how the fuck did she know about Trevion, how long had she known, and when did she get to New York? Last, she promised herself she would kill Bella when this was all over. After several minutes of watching

Trevion fuck her nemesis, he called her over.

"Shhh! Now see, this could've been you, but you talk too much. Now kiss me."

Like Bella, Trevion, too, was making Aruba pay for her fuck ups. He knew what it was between the two girls; he always knew. But, Aruba being jealous of Bella, to the point of trying to destroy her, only intensified Trevion's revenge on Aruba. He enjoyed watching her suffer the pain of seeing him with Bella. He wanted her to feel all the emotions of euphoria before walking into the room just so that it could all be taken away. He knew Aruba seeing Bella on her knees with the man they both loved would make Aruba feel like shit. And it worked. He needed her to feel that way and to know that he was the man and still in control, not her.

While still up in Bella, Trevion tongued Aruba down and fondled her pussy. He didn't know if her wetness derived from everything she first walked into when she got there, from the E-pills she took, or if she was truly turned on by watching Bella, and she just pretended to be mad. Whatever it was didn't matter. She was right where he wanted her to be.

"Bella, get up on the bed."He ordered.

She did as she was told, making direct eye contact with Aruba. This was her way of saying, *"Yea bitch! Payback! I'm here! In your face, fucking the man you thought was yours!"*

Bella knew her position in Trevion's life and knew Aruba could never match the status. So, when she got the visit from DaKari, who detailed A—Z to her about Trevion, she was confounded and full of mixed emotions. She couldn't believe that the man she loved, and the one she knew loved her too, was still alive. It took her a while to process it all, but when DaKari called Trevion and she heard his voice for the first time in over a year, there was no denying the truth. She cried for several minutes from the joy of knowing he was still with her but quickly pulled it together when he told her he had a plan that he needed her to be a part of. And when she learned it had everything to do with fucking with Aruba's emotions, she was all over it.

DaKari purchased her flight to arrive in New York a day before Aruba was set to make it and arranged for a driver to pick her up from the airport. When she arrived at 1825 and saw Trevion's face for the first time, she gasped. She knew it was him, but the impact from the bullet and all the reconstructive surgery altered many of his previous features. He was still fly, though, with a curly hair taper fade that connected to his full beard, mustache, and goatee, something he didn't have before. In addition, he now wore glasses that resembled the ones Malcolm X wore, and he was much thinner. Bella was bemused by his sexiness and new appearance.

She listened attentively as they talked for hours about everything ranging from the day he met Royelle, the day he got shot, down to the reason why Royelle was so important to his bank account. The only thing that he didn't share was the name of the person who shot him and that he was born Malachi Lucifer Pennington —that secret he was going to hold. And while everything he told her was intriguing, she honestly didn't give a shit. She was just happy to see and be with him.

That night leading to the morning, they drank, smoked some weed, popped a few pills, and fucked like old times, going hard and non-stop, minus the rush out of the backdoor that they both laughed at when Bella brought it up. And once it was time to set the scene for Aruba, Bella was ready. The look of *"aww, hell nah,"* that she was sure Aruba would display, Bella couldn't wait to see.

When Bella climbed the bed, he ordered Aruba to do the same and dive in-between Bella's legs to eat her nectar. Everything he demanded her to do, he knew she hated. He knew that eating Bella out was the last thing she wanted to do, but he was gonna disgrace her until she got comfortable.

"And you better eat that shit like you want it!" He commanded as he slid underneath her, reaching for Peach.

Both ladies hated the idea of the other being there, but this was Trevion; they had better listen and act accordingly, or else. Aruba slightly jerked the moment Trevion's warm lips and wet tongue touched her clit. She couldn't remember the last time she sat on his face, but it felt so good to her. He sucked gently, making love to her feline, periodically inserting two fingers to feel her wetness. He got hard knowing that two of his bitches who were at odds were now like conjoining twins.

He slipped from under Aruba, pulled her ass cheeks apart, and softly licked her anus. Her moans got louder while her mouth stayed mounted around Bella. And judging from the looks on Bella's face and her grip on Aruba's freshly done hair, Trevion could tell Aruba was doing as she was told. By now, the E-pills everyone had taken were in full effect. Everyone was rolling, horny, and on go-mode. They fucked from sundown to sun up, well into the afternoon. There was so much heat in the room that the two ladies had forgotten there was tension between them. They were into each other as if they were in love, and Trevion loved it as he continued to bang them like the jackrabbit he resembled.

Finally, after several hours of procreating, no sleep in between, and drinking lots of water, Trevion decided to make everyone a drink. The ladies sat up in the bed, still feeling on each other, while they waited for Trevion to bring back their drinks.

"What's this?" Bella asked, reaching for hers.

"Cranberry and Orange juice with some Vodka. I call it the Abyss." He responded.

Bella chuckled. "After all that we just did. I could see why."

"Drink up, ladies. We ain't done yet. The grand finale is next." He gave a half-smile and raised his glass in a toasting motion. After a few minutes of drinking and joking around, Trevion slipped two of his fingers back inside of Aruba. "Mmm. That pussy juicy. I just wanted to feel it one last time." He smiled.

Just as Aruba looked up at him to respond, she collapsed, spilling her drink all over the bed.

"Ohhh shit! What the fuck?! Aruba!" Bella yelled.

She shook Aruba to see if she would wake up, and she didn't. She checked for air in her lungs and a pulse on her wrist; there was nothing. She looked over at Trevion for some sort of guidance and instantly noticed the nonchalant look he had as he stared at Aruba with dark eyes taking sips of his drink.

"Trevion! Do something!" She hollered.

"Shhh." He put his finger over his mouth. "You're yelling too loud." He whispered with a crazed look in his eyes.

Bella stared back in shock. She expected him to care and do something, but he never budged, which changed her worry to fear.

136

"Come er'." He summoned her over to the chair where he sat. "Ride me backward, facing her. And don't you dare close your eyes."

The idea was to build fear in Bella. Trevion might've loved her, but Malachi was the part of him that didn't give a shit about her feelings. He needed to remind her that he was then, as he is now, and always will be in charge of her and any other bitch that he crossed paths with. That part of him of being abandoned by his biological mother and being named after Satan himself never left Trevion. No matter how amazing of a mother Tracy had always been to him, Bessie and the evil ass men who raped her that night was who ran through his bloodline. And consequently, Bella was inadvertently witnessing Trevion's other personality, Malachi, firsthand.

Feeling Bella tremble and sensing her fear as she straddled him enticed the hell out of him. Sure killing Aruba was the end goal for him, but placing that torment inside of Bella was also necessary. He needed Bella on his side, but the only way to keep her at bay was to place the fear of the devil in her heart.

"Tragic isn't it? Dying from potassium cyanide. I put so much in her drink that I'm sure it stopped her heart quick." He snapped his fingers. "She didn't suffer long or feel a thing. Trust me. And she's the first of many that are in line. That bitch sister of Royelle's, she next. Don't make yourself the target after her."

"Trevion." Bella's voice shook as she continued to ride him.

"Shhh…" He said, grabbing her by the throat when he noticed her speed change.

"Ride that mutherfucker like you mean it, and don't stop until I cum or until I tell you to. Do you hear me?!" He yanked her hair.

Bella was frightened. She had never met this side of Trevion, and she didn't know shit about the Malachi side to even begin to understand. She tried to process all of what he said about Xandra being the next target, but she was so traumatized by what was happening she couldn't even think straight and continued to do as she was told.

"See." He began to speak in a slow, eerie whisper. " I did a little research on roses and learned that the light pink ones are given to a person when they are experiencing some difficulty in their life. Check!" He used his index finger to outline a checkmark in the air. "And those white ones, everybody thinks they're meant for weddings or some spiritual bullshit, some sort of goodness. Nahhh. Those are for people who have a heart unacquainted with love. Check!" He used his index finger again.

"You see her. I tried to make her the charge bitch, but she crossed me and threatened to expose me. I can't have that. There were two who knew about me; now, there's only one. Don't let this be you."

He pushed Bella onto the bed in a doggy-style position facing Aruba and made her look directly at her as he bust' nut after nut after nut. Finally, after an hour of forcing her to look at Aruba's corpse while he copulated her, he was satisfied with what he thought he had achieved.

CHAPTER 16

$\mathcal{L}$ ess than 24 hours after Trevion poisoned Aruba, Bella was already back in Boston. She no longer had the spirit of joy over her. Instead, seeing Trevion now had a negative connotation to it. She couldn't stop thinking about all that had transpired within the last few days. The fact that Trevion took out the time to set the scene of love and passion only to turn it into redrum took her for a complete loop.

Aside from that, knowing that he threatened her with murder if word got about him was astonishing. He never threatened or treated her with violence. He didn't know what to think or how to feel about any of it. One thing she did know, though, was that if she even as so much sneezed the wrong way, Trevion would be on that ass.

She recognized that the Trevion she once knew was not the Trevion she left back in New York. This Trevion was a loose cannon out for blood, and she wanted nothing else to do with him, but she had to play it smart. The idea of him thinking he placed fear in her heart so she wouldn't cross him took the opposite effect. As much as Bella hated Aruba, she strongly felt that Aruba didn't deserve what she got. And threatening to kill her next was out of the question too.

One thing about Bella, she didn't kindly to threats no matter who they came from. She may have played soft, dumb, and naïve, but she always got her revenge in the end. And now that she had so much information on him, including the plan to take Royelle out financially and physically, she promised herself to play her cards right and do whatever was necessary to survive.

All the excitement she had from the day she learned about his existence was gone. Everything she once loved about him vanished the moment he showed no reaction to Aruba's collapse. His cold-hearted ways, dead eyes, and lack of emotion were all but fake.

She sat on her bed, recapping the day she arrived in New York, and not once did he show a sign of a killer. While Aruba got the ride from the airport, the roses, the lingerie, and a bubble bath, Bella got the roses, a promise ring he bought when he took her to NYC Diamond District store, a helicopter ride of the five boroughs, and dinner at La Bernardin. She never paid $370.00 for some lobster and wine. And had it not been for Trevion paying the ticket, it would still be on her bucket list of expensive shit she wanted to try.

She looked down at the ring placed on her ring finger, twirling it from left to right, wondering about its significance. Did the ring mean she and Trevion were consummated in marriage now that Aruba was gone? Did it put her in charge of whatever he was trying to build next? Was it his way of saying sorry for the year he made her believe he was dead? Her list of questions ran long.

In the years that she had known him, she only saw the good in him. Malachi never reared his ugly face, and she still knew nothing about that side of him, so she never had a reason for concern. Had she seen that side of him before, it would've been a deal-breaker for Bella. She came from a place of abuse, and sadly, Trevion had now put her in the mindset of her mother.

Most mothers have a profound bond with their children. It's sacred, a place of love, nurturing, and respect. It's where mothers teach their daughters about respecting their bodies, being mindful of boys, and taking care of themselves in the future. It's also the same place fathers teach their sons about being a man, a provider, and respecting women. It's where most parents do their best to be better than their parents were to them. It's where losing their child in any capacity is the greatest pain to a parent's soul. And sadly, it's also the place where none of these things exist. The same place of love and nurture is the same place of chaos and misfortune. It's the same place where your soul is built up, only to be torn down.

Growing up, Bella's mother always told her that on her 10th birthday, she would be crowned queen. That there would be a massive party in her honor, a coronation of sorts. Bella imagined she'd have a Princes themed party dressed in a white ball gown with friends dressed the same, kind of like the Disney Princesses. She pictured a horse and carriage pulling up to her house to take her on a tour around the city, as she waved at all the onlookers who were in awe of her majesty. And for ten years, Bella couldn't wait to see what being crowned a beautiful queen would look and feel like.

Finally, the day had arrived! It was Bella's 10th birthday, and she was ecstatic! She couldn't wait to see what her mother had planned outside of her bedroom door. It was the birthday that her mother told her was going to be the birthday of all birthdays to remember. The one no other birthday could match. She made Bella shower and when she came out, she sat Bella at her vanity facing away from the mirror.

She took her time doing her hair and make-up, reminding her of how beautiful she was; one of the most beautiful girls this earth had ever seen, with her beautiful brown curly hair, hazel eyes, and dimples that radiated her smile. Once her mother was done, she got Bella all dressed and added the final touch of some Red lipstick. When she turned Bella around to look at herself in the mirror, she didn't even recognize who she was. And she looked far from a princess and more like a prostitute.

Over the years, as Bella got older, her mother saw the beauty that Bella possessed and what it could bring when the time was right. Sadly, everything beautiful she saw in her daughter had money attached to it. So, while she was preparing Bella for what Bella thought would be the time of her life, she was also lining up Bella's clientele. And thirty days before Bella's 10th birthday, she had a long list of clients willing to pay the $100 fee to be with the young, tender, innocent named Isabel.

For ten years, she was made to feel loved, special, and beautiful, only for it to be ripped away from her in a flash. Her place of solitude, her sanctuary, and carefree world where she believed in her dreams had been shattered, turned into a dark cave where only bats hung to escape the light. Every childhood memory she had leading up to her 10th birthday completely vanished. The magic of youth life existed no more.

Instead of a Pink and Purple Princess party, complete with balloons, cake, ice cream, and other guests dressed as Princesses, what she got was a grown-ass man who could've easily been her father. To the innocent eyes of Bella, he looked like a dirty street mechanic. He was White, about six feet tall, wearing dark blue rugged jeans and a flannel shirt with a gray t-shirt underneath. His hair was long at the top, shorter on the sides, oily and stringy from not having been washed in weeks. His teeth were yellow, underneath his nails were dirty, and it wasn't until he got closer that she realized how bad his breath smelled.

The first time was the worst. She was scared, a virgin, and completely broken. But no one cared; not her mother or the men that paid her mother for her innocence. For every stroke the mechanic hit her with, a sense of herself became extinct. She no longer saw the beautiful girl her mother had always described her to be, and for the next five years, two hundred and forty weekends to be exact, Bella no longer identified herself as Bella, the queen; she was now Bella, the whore in her eyes.

The day a Latina girl turns 15 is one of the most anticipated days in her life. She gets to pick out this huge, something out of a fairytale ball gown while her parents spend thousands of dollars in preparation for their daughter's Quinceanera Party, the Hispanic tradition of celebrating their daughter's coming of age. Sadly for Bella, she was no longer a virgin; the tradition no longer applied to her. Her coming of age happened five years prior. Today she was preparing for more of the same shit she did every weekend—having sex with grown men. And today, on her 15th birthday, grease monkey, the mechanic, was set to be her first client of the day.

Since he knew it was a special day for Bella, he felt the need to be first in line to the not-so-welcoming party. He paid his $100 and was escorted by Bella's mother to Bella's castle, now turned dungeon. She went back to the kitchen to finish washing the dishes, and in less than five minutes after walking away from the room, she heard a howling scream. She ran back into the room to find Bella in the corner, crouched up with a frightened look, holding her knees to her chest with blood all over her mouth. The mechanic was screaming and holding his penis. Bella had bitten him so hard she pierced through the skin in several places.

While her mother tended to the mechanic, trying to console him, Bella ran out of the room to the kitchen, grabbed a kitchen knife, and hid. When the mechanic came out of the room going about the house screaming her name, she came out of hiding, stabbing him repeatedly in both of his legs. He finally got up enough strength to kick her in the face knocking her to the floor, giving him the chance to get away, and he did.

When her mother asked her why she stabbed him, Bella plunged the knife into her mother's chest, killing her instantly. She didn't run from it or try to hide. Instead, she called the police and waited for them to take her into custody. For six long hours, Bella left no stone unturned for the detectives. She explained her ordeal in detail from the age of 10 until the moment she was sitting before them. Her story was so tragic it broke the detectives down. It was the first time both detectives had ever experienced such a case.

At trial, the judge considered her age, statement, and diary, which corroborated what she told the detectives and ruled the homicide as justifiable. Bella was ordered to a group home until she turned 21, with mandatory intense therapy sessions three times a week. The mechanic was arrested and sentenced to 60 years to life.

By the time Trevion met Bella, the choice to stick beside him was easy because he didn't remind her of the mechanic. He didn't strip her of her crown. Trevion, although her pimp in so many words, was gentle, kind, always loving, and never abusive. He made her feel something no man had since the age of ten—safe! But now, with what he had just pulled, she knew safety was off the table, as was her life. And just like the mechanic and her mother, if she wanted to survive, she would have to make Trevion disappear for good this time by enlisting the help of a few unlikely people.

CHAPTER 17

Dear Brain Diary,

They say a bad parent is nothing but a traumatized child suffering from their own iniquities. Maybe that's true. Growing up, all I wanted was to have the kind of father every little girl envied. The kind that showed up at his daughter's recitals, basketball games, track meets, and cheer competitions. Instead, I was no better than the fatherless girls, and I lived in a two-parent home. My father exhibited the same attributes of every absent father in and out of the hood. How could a child have parents and still feel like they don't exist? Was there something wrong with the child? Or was it the parent all along?

Above all of that, how could a child fear the one person who's supposed to protect them at all times? You know, the kind of protector who would break a boy's arm for mistreating his daughter. The kind who would hem up a boy for even looking at his daughter a certain kind of way or speaking to her with bass in his voice. It's sad when you quickly learn that your protector is your predator.

He's the one who needs his arm broken, or better yet, his thing cut off. He is the one violating his daughter while he points the finger at everyone else. His penis is the first one she had ever laid eyes on. He's the one that fondled her first, even taught her what a blow job was. It's because of him she knows sex as well as she does. He is her first impression of a protector and predator walking in the exact same shoes every day joined together.

So how does she begin to forgive a person who saw no wrong in their actions? She doesn't, that's how. She goes on with her life and tries not to let her childhood trauma become her adulthood curse. She goes to school every day, staying late hours attending different activities to avoid him. And when that doesn't work, she gets a job or makes excuses as to why she has to go to a friend's house. She does everything she possibly can to escape the reality waiting for at home. Some days it worked. And on the days that it didn't, she braced for brutality and promised herself that one day when she had children, she would become the parent she needed rather than the one she had. With that said, today, we bury our father. And that's all I have to say about that.

~ Royelle

Thanks to Xandra, the funeral plans for Rayford were done. If not for her, none of them or the guest sitting behind and beside them would be at J.B. Johnson's ghetto ass funeral home. The four siblings sat in the front row as guest after guest paid their respects, shaking their hands, offering their condolences, and hugging them. If anyone was looking for emotion out of Royelle, then they had attended the wrong funeral.

She sat quietly, pretending to be in mourning with her black dress, black slingback stilettos, and dark-colored shades. The same feeling and emotion she had when she killed him was the same one presenting itself now. She honestly couldn't care less about being there. But to keep any fingers from pointing at her, she had to do what every killer does—Show up! Xandra knew the vibe. The other two just thought she was numb. And she was—

The entire time she sat staring at her father and greeting guests, all she thought about was AJ. The vision of AJ on the floor swimming in her own blood taunted Royelle. She felt absolutely guilty. She was having blackouts with no clue on how to manage them. And because of that, it was causing people their lives. Apart from that, what feared her the most, was her lack of emotion after the fact. She searched her heart for feeling after what she did to Rayford and Amadeo and found none. It bled in pain for AJ. Was this her new norm, or would this too pass, she wondered?

"On behalf of the Blevins family, I want to take this opportunity to say thank you all for being here. This family has endured so much in such a short time. First Mrs. Adala and now their wonderful father Rayford." The minister spoke.

"Aint shit wonderful." Royelle thought as she sat with a bare look on her face while the minister performed the Eulogy.

The minister was sermonizing on things he had absolutely no fundamental knowledge of. As far as Royelle knew, the man had never met her father. The information he was dishing out to the attendees had to come from Rayford's drunken friends and his other two children. *'The Rayford I know and the one he's talking about aren't one and the same.'* She thought to herself.

"You good, sis?" Xandra asked as they slowly walked behind the pallbearers who carefully escorted the casket out the front door.

"I'm just tired," Royelle responded in a hushed tone.

Xandra knew part of that was true, but AJ was on the other side of that wariness. Rumor had it that AJ's family was taking her back to North Carolina for her services and final resting place. And each time Royelle tried to get any information from AJ's family and friends, she was shunned. They knew about the text messages and Amadeo's affair with Trevion and somehow placed the blame on Royelle, saying that she wasn't a good enough woman to keep her husband in line, which is why he cheated on her with men and women. Not once did they consider that Amadeo did what he did because he wanted to.

Royelle didn't care about the rumors. However, it killed her to know that her final goodbye, her final visual of AJ, happened at the feet of Amadeo. It wasn't fair. Shattered was an understatement; debilitating was more like it. The one person she had a connection to romantically, emotionally, and mentally was now gone.

She regretted not telling AJ that she remembered more about her than anyone suspected. From her sessions with Dr. Angeli, she remembered the first time she and AJ had sex and how well AJ took care of her sexually, showing that she was nothing like Trevion. And that her soft touch, gentle smile, and the way she soothed Royelle on her laborious days were way better and more significant than Trevion could have ever known.

From time to time, Royelle would read the last text AJ sent, and her eyes instantly bested up. It suffocated her mind to know that she could never repay the ultimate sacrifice of love that AJ last gave to her. She wished that she could have told her that she forgave her for the $500.00 payout she took from Trevion. After the memory of her and AJ meeting at the bar resurfaced, it didn't take much time to figure out why AJ was so pressed on giving her that money. Once she learned about the people paying Trevion to have sex with her, it only made sense that Trevion would pay AJ not just for the favor but also as hush money.

Royelle put the pieces together and couldn't even be mad at AJ when she put two and two together. When AJ gave Royelle back the money, Royelle knew that AJ was after her heart and nothing else. And it sucked that all of it was just gone in a blink of an eye. The money never mattered; AJ's life did.

"You sure you good, sis?" Xandra asked, noticing Royelle wipe her tears as they drove onto the Oak Lawn cemetery grounds.

"I'm good." Royelle cracked a smile.

"This is me, sis. You can be honest."

"I know, sis. I promise I'm good. Just thinking too much is all."

"Well, I'm right here, sis. I'm right here." Xandra reassured. "It's always no salt. Remember that." Xandra continued.

"I know, sis," Royelle responded.

She placed her hand over Xandra's and turned her attention back to looking out the passenger side window. She didn't give a shit about Rayford's funeral and never inquired about Amadeo's. All Royelle wanted was AJ, and her soul was crushed knowing that everything AJ ever made her feel would never come back. This was final. And all Royelle wanted was her Ajah back.

For days Bella paced around her apartment, freaked the fuck out. She was so traumatized by the recent events. She wouldn't even leave her place. Making money was the last thing on her mind. For nights, she couldn't sleep, and when she would try, the image of Aruba lying dead while she was getting fucked from behind replayed. Shit was so bad she couldn't even masturbate. Each time she closed her eyes to touch herself, Aruba reappeared. At this point, she was convinced Aruba's ghost was haunting her. Aruba hated her while she was alive; she was sure Aruba still hated her in death.

She wanted to tell someone so bad about what had happened, but she didn't trust anyone. And since she couldn't speak about that, she just wanted to talk to someone about anything that would help her mind focus on something other than Trevion, Aruba, and that day. She had been calling McKenzie for days to see if she had heard anything in the streets about Aruba, but each time she called, the call went straight to voicemail, making Bella feel like McKenzie had blocked her. McKenzie being trafficked was the furthest thing from her mind.

Something had to give, though. She had to find a way of keeping her ears to the streets without actually being in them and had to try to stay one step ahead of Trevion. She thought about moving outside of the state, but she didn't have the means, and she knew Trevion would hunt her until he found her.

She considered staying with family, but that was a wasted idea too. For one, they didn't fuck with her like that, and for two, if Trevion wanted her dead, he would kill everything moving, children included and she wouldn't dare put them in that position. She didn't know what to do. But one thing was for certain, if she had any chance of making Trevion disappear, she knew Royelle would be the best person to partner with. She figured if she told Royelle what she now knew and came correct with a proposition, Royelle wouldn't be able to resist.

She took into account all that Trevion had lied about and all that Royelle had been through. She surmised that it would be enough to send Royelle into a roaring rage of revenge against Trevion rather than on her. Of course, it wasn't every day that the mistress of a cheating husband reached out to the wife to try and team up with her, intending to conspire against the husband. But Bella paced her floors, biting on her nails, trying to determine the best way to approach Royelle with the dose of calamity she wanted to serve her. She called McKenzie again to get Royelle's phone number, but the call went straight to voicemail again.

"Fuck McKenzie!" She spat while dialing out the other number she had for her.

"Thank you for calling Premier Law Offices. This is Claudia. How may I direct your call?" Claudia greeted.

Bella was surprised by the greeting. "Yes. May I please speak with McKenzie?" She asked in a professional manner.

"I apologize, ma'am, but McKenzie is no longer employed here," Claudia responded.

"Really? Since when?"

"I'm sorry, ma'am. But I am not at liberty to say. Is there something someone else can assist you with?"

"No. No. That's fine. Thank you."

"Ok. Well—"

"You know what. Yes. Please transfer me to Royelle." Bella built up the courage to say.

"Mrs. Kingsley is out today. Would you like her voicemail instead?"

"Yes, please. Thank you."

Bella released a prostrated sigh. She was drained, nervous, and confused. Her emotions had her exhausted. While she listened to Royelle's voicemail greeting, she rehearsed in her mind what she was going to say. When the greeting stopped, she sighed again. *"Hello, Royelle. This Bella. We met at Trevion's memorial service. Please give me a call back at 617-265-4361. I'd like to talk to you about some things."* Bella hung up the phone inhaling through her nose and releasing it through her mouth. "It's either do or die from here." She said, finally sitting down.

CHAPTER 18

Although they missed their mother, walking into their childhood home without Rayford there to cause a scene felt so good. It was theirs! No one could take it from them, tell them when to get out, or destroy what they believed their mother single-handily put her heart and soul into. Sure Rayford had his hands in it, but the truth was, Adala's love is what brought life to the home. But the destruction that Rayford brought to it stained the walls, every corner, crevice, and room. His remnants were massive. And now, they had to find a way to restore it.

Waiting on the life insurance policies to pass clearance was like waiting on money trees to fall out of the sky, and Royelle couldn't understand why, but she didn't fuss. There was plenty of money in the other accounts that Adala left behind, which Royelle had full access to. And with that money, she decided to give the house a complete makeover.

The pangs of embarrassment rang through Royelle's mind as she looked around the house at everything that needed to be done. Every time she saw the house looking as it was, it made her sick to her stomach. But this was the last time that she would ever see it in this condition again. So before bringing anyone else into the home, the four of them cleaned the house from top to bottom, getting rid of pretty much everything.

Once they completed that daunting task, Royelle brought in pest control to get rid of the roach problem that they never should've had to begin with. Shortly after, she hired painters to repaint all the walls, hoping that it would remove the yellow stains off the walls and the stench of the Winston 100's Rayford smoked religiously.

They went furniture shopping replacing their parents' brown leather couches with a plush microfiber gray sectional, which came complete with dark gray and white pillows, white end tables to match, two modern gray lamps, and a gray and white marble top coffee table. Royelle, with her eye for interior decorating, completed the look with a yellow, gray, and white area rug and abstract canvas art to fill up the walls. The living room looked like something out of a Pinterest photo by the time she was done with it. She purchased a 5-piece dining set and bedroom sets for each room, allowing Raylina and Raymelle to decide on theirs.

Since Royelle and Xandra already had homes, they had no need for space at the house. So Raymelle took their parents' room, Raylina took Royelle's old room, Raymelle's old room became the guest suite, and Raylina's old room was now the office-workout setup. They smiled as each room smoothly took on a transformation of its own. La Loma was home to them, and it was officially starting to feel that way again.

The final piece to it all was going through Adala's personal things once and for all. It was the one thing Royelle had avoided since she woke up from the coma. For Royelle, everything that she did on behalf of her mother since her passing was a reminder that finality was absolute, and she hated the reality of that. In her mind, if she avoided the things that reminded her of her mother's absence, then her mother truly being gone wouldn't be real for her. And although she wanted everyone to believe her strong exterior, she was struggling with the acceptance of her mother's demise. But the job was hers to handle, and there was no other way to do it other than to just do it.

She went down into the basement and located Adala's box of things that Rayford deemed as junk and brought it back upstairs to what used to be her room. She began carefully removing and reviewing each item, noting its content. She wasn't sure what she would find and didn't want to mistreat or discard anything of value. She pulled out of the box item after item, mad that Rayford didn't even consider storing or caring for some of the nic-nacks that Adala loved and her charms. If not for nothing else, at least for safe keep, a momentum of sorts.

As she continued going through Adala's things, she stumbled upon her mother's journal. When she opened it up and began reading it, it was almost as if Adala knew Royelle would find it one day and decided to write specifically for Royelle. Besides that, Royelle could sense the liberty Adala expressed in her writing. She wrote without judgment or conviction. It was her freedom from Rayford. Everything that she felt she couldn't say to him directly, she said in her journal. It made Royelle smile to see that she and her mother were freeing themselves in similar ways. *'How ironic?'* she thought as she continued to read.

"Although a homemaker practically my entire life, living most of it church, if not at home, I was always very smart, moving like a snake but attacking like an eagle. And since I never wanted to take my kids away from a two-parent home environment, I made sure to give them everything Rayford never did, including a fake marriage.

Was I wrong for that, maybe? But at least my kids can see what not to become and who not to choose in the future. See Rayford; he never knew what he was up against messing with me. He always wrote me off as a meek, quiet pushover, but he never, not once, thought I would turn into a silent slayer. Not with swords or weapons, not even with my words, but with my financnes, which is what he was always after.

And interestingly enough, it's also something that I think that boy is after with my Royelle. She is much like her mother. We attract the guys who look good, sound good, and even pretend well, but there is always darkness behind them. Some hidden secrets, a dark place they live outside of their primary home.

That boy and Rayford favor each other in a lot of ways. I see him in Rayford and Rayford in that boy. I don't know how, but he knows my daughter stands to inherit a lot when I pass. He's after my daughter's money like Rayford is after mine. But I will not interrupt my daughter's heart. When my mother did it to me against Rayford, I felt like she was being judgmental and rebelled anyway. I don't want to do the same to my daughter. But, I've raised her well. She'll know what to do when she senses or feels what I do. And when she does, she'll set her plan in motion just like I did. I've raised her well."

Royelle's eyes were wide. She couldn't believe her mother had semi-predicted what type of person Trevion would turn out to be. She continued to read on, hoping to read more of her mother's thoughts on Trevion, but it was more of the same. She simply didn't trust him. Her spirit of discernment concerning him was always uneasy. She didn't like his movements, how smooth he talked, or how perfect he always tried to be around them. She also hated the idea of not truly knowing his family or background. She knew all about fucked up family dynamics far too well and spoke about them often, but Trevion avoided the subject at all cost, and Royelle always defended it.

There was something about him. Adala's heart jumped, her hair stood up, and a discomposed feeling overcame her every time he was around. And as bad as she wanted to tell Royelle to put him on her watch list, she couldn't. Love is a crazy place, and when you stand against it, that's when the person is most attracted to it. But when you stay quiet and out of the way, the visions of fake love become extremely clear. She had to let Royelle see it on her own

Royelle chuckled a bit when she read that their long-time neighbor Mrs. Lupe gave Adala the drop on Rayford's infidelities. Adala secretly learned the names of the other women, the dates he was with them, the locations of his hangouts, including his creeping places. All the times that Rayford thought Adala was at church, she was following him to gain as much information as she could to present when it was time to file for a divorce; sadly, that day never came. Glory came first.

Royelle was very surprised by her mother's knowledge regarding Rosalyn and Muneca. Adala spoke with her words as if she knew Muneca had killed Rosalyn. Her words resembled that of a protective mother who understood the confines of a child like Muneca. So, when the young uniformed officer brought Muneca to Adala, she didn't hesitate telling officer Presley that she'd take Muneca in. Royelle bugged out when she read the detective's name turned P.I. in her mother's journal.

Adala's account of Detective Presley's reservations about releasing Muneca to her was even more bizarre. She recalled that while he never verbally said he felt Muneca was responsible for the murder, his actions implied it. Moreover, according to Adala, by the look in officer Presley's eyes, he appeared to have an infatuation with the young Muneca, which scared Adala. Xandra was her dauhgter now. So, she remained vigilant about him over the years and kept tabs on him, making sure he stayed as far away from Muneca as possible. For all she knew, he was a pedophile in a cops uniform.

"Xan! Come here right quick!" Royelle yelled down the hall.

"What's up?" Xandra responded, walking into the room.

"Girl, look at this."

She handed Xandra the journal and pointed to where she wanted her to read. Royelle watched as Xandra's eyes went from being carefree to, oh shit! When she read about Detective Presley, now she knew for sure that he remembered her from so many years prior. His tone and the way he looked at her the day they found Rayford dead and when she approached him in front of Royelle's house, all made sense now.

"Sis. You gotta get rid of this shit. No one else can read or see it." Xandra whispered.

"I know," Royelle whispered back, taking the journal out of Xandra's hands. "So, what are we going to do? Do you think he really remembers you? I mean, do you even remember him."

"Nah, sis. I don't remember his fat ass. I'm guessing he looked a lot different back then. But, I don't know, sis. I mean shit, he might remember me. The way he looked at me and talked to me makes me believe he does. But I don't know. Let me think about how to handle this. This is fucked. I knew that muthafucker was up to no good." Xandra continued to whisper.

Both girls were shook. It meant that if Presley remembered Xandra, then he for sure was trying to piece together how one or both of them were connected to all the murders attached to Royelle's name. Royelle was never the one to brainstorm killer plots, but she could help administratively. Since she was a paralegal, she could search databases and documents on just about anyone; police officers were no exception. Royelle let Xandra know that she would run searches on Presley and get her all the information she could on him, leaving Xandra to handle it from there; Xandra agreed.

CHAPTER 19

With the exception of remodeling the house, everything that could go wrong over the last few weeks and days did, and Royelle wondered if going back to work at a time like this was even worth it. The idea of being focused on court cases seemed to escape her more regularly these days. But she knew she had to keep things looking ordinary by going to therapy and showing up for work. Not to mention, she had some private investigating of her own she had to do.

On her drive in, she thought about the fight with McKenzie and wondered what she might've told Charlyn. The thought of not knowing what she would have to deal with when she walked in made her cringe a bit, but to her surprise, when she got off the elevator, Claudia was sitting at McKenzie's desk.

"Good Morning, Claudia." Royelle greeted. "McKenzie out today?" She quickly asked.

"Good Morning, Royelle. McKenzie hasn't been here in days."

"Really? Is she ok?" Royelle genuinely asked.

"Honestly, I don't know. You'll have to ask Charlyn."

"Is she here yet?"

"Yes. She's in her office." Claudia politely responded.

As Royelle walked away towards Charlyn's office, so many thoughts ran through her head. First, she wondered if McKenzie had been skipping work because of the fight? Did she tell Charyln what happened and how much did Charlyn know? Did McKenzie get fired, and was she next? But instantly, the thought of Charlyn knowing about the fight was dead. She knew if Charlyn knew about the fight, Charlyn would've been on the phone the same day she found out about it. Something like that, Charlyn wouldn't have delayed in responding to.

As soon as the thought of Charlyn knowing about the fight dismissed itself, her mind quickly reverted to Xandra. She wondered what really happened to McKenzie after Xandra took her. All she knew were the details McKenzie shared about her dealings with Trevion; outside of that, she knew nothing else. But she swore to herself that today, Xandra would have to stop sheltering her. She knew the protection and love Xandra had for her, but it hindered Royelle from a lot of things and put her in positions she wasn't sure how to defend herself from if she needed to. Royelle nervously knocked on Charlyn's office, unsure of what reactions she might get. But when she heard Charlyn's calm voice welcome her in, she was instantly relieved.

"Good morning, Royelle." Charlyn greeted with a smile. "Glad to have you back. It's been a zoo around here." She chuckled.

Royelle wanted to say, "Glad to be back." But she wasn't. Royelle was going with the motions of trying to keep things routine. "Is McKenzie ok?" she asked, quickly shifting the conversation. "Claudia told me she hasn't been here."

"I couldn't tell you, honey. She's been a no-call, no-show for days. And now she can add no-employment to the list of no's attached to her name."

They both laughed.

"I'm sorry to hear that, Charlyn."

"Chile, I'm not. I have to learn to stop trying to save everyone. Besides, that girl brought more problems than I was willing to deal with. I was just trying to do good, you know. Show her that life has beauty to it. But, only a handful of people can appreciate it, while countless others never get it. That's neither here nor there, though. Claudia has agreed to be the Administrative Assistant for the entire office now. So, there will be no hiring of anyone new. But enough about that. How are you and the family doing?"

After hearing that McKenzie was a no-call, no-show, the look of confusion and worry graced Royelle's beautiful face. She had grown numb, and panic settled in. She was convinced that Xandra had everything to do with McKenzie's disappearing act, and it showed all over her face. Sadly, there was no chance of fixing her distinction. Charlyn was too quick on the draw.

"Royelle? Are you ok? You look flushed all of a sudden." Charlyn concernedly asked.

Royelle snapped out of her fog. "Oh, yes, I'm fine." She smiled. "Daydreaming is all. I tend to do that a lot these days without realizing it." She lied.

"In the middle of a conversation?" Charlyn giggled. "Get you some coffee or something chile. I need you on your game like always."

"Yes, ma'am." Royelle laughed. "I have a question, though. I know you said you were helping McKenzie, but where did you meet her? I guess what I'm asking is, how do you find or select the people you do?"

Royelle hoped Charlyn might unwillingly give her just enough information to work with. She already knew McKenzie was from Mattapan, had siblings, and her mother was still alive. But, she needed to get a little deeper in case she might have to lay down some spike strips on the movement of others because of McKenzie's disappearance.

"To be completely honest, most of the women I've employed were either prostitutes or young girls lost in the streets needing some guidance, someone who could get them to see that there was another way, that they weren't wasted away like the streets would have them to believe. But with McKenzie, we kind of found each other."

"Oh? How so?" Royelle asked, taking a seat.

"Had I not known better, I would've believed that she was stalking me. It was like she knew about me and what I had done for others. It seemed like she knew my day-to-day routine and schedules. She managed to be at every court hearing I had in Quincy, looking desolate. She never asked for money just for food, and I obliged each time. Finally, it got to the point where she didn't even have to ask me anymore, I would just buy something before I got to the courthouse, and like clockwork, there she was.

"Over time, we talked more and more about her life goals and family history. And that's when I learned that her family wanted no parts of her since she became a street worker. When they kicked her out, that's when she started staying in abandoned warehouses, taking bird baths wherever she could, and getting food using whatever means necessary. Now whether her story is true or not remains to be seen. But who am I to question? My only responsibility was to follow and be obedient to my spirit.

"One day, she caught me completely off guard. She was in front of the courthouse, looking really good, clean, and well dressed. She mentioned that a male friend of hers brought her some new clothes, put her up in an apartment, and paid the rent for three months, but she needed to find a job to manage the expenses, and that's when I offered her a position here to become a part of the firm. I often wondered if this male friend of hers was her pimp or something, but I never asked."

Royelle took an exhausted breath. "Whewww! That's a lot, Charlyn."

"Tell me about it." Charlyn rolled her eyes to the back of her head. "But hey. I did my part. The rest was up to her."

"I completely get it. Have you tried reaching out to her or to anyone from her emergency contact list to ensure she's alright? I mean, giving her background and all." Royelle inquired.

"I haven't. Didn't even think to."Her eyebrows frowned. "I have a commitment to this firm to show up, be on time, and be the best leader I can be. Likewise, the same expectation my team has of me, I have for those who I employ. It is not my responsibility to hunt down employees who already know my expectations." Charlyn scowled. "But I guess you're right. The least I can do is make sure she's ok." She digressed.

She opened her file drawer attached to her desk and shuffled for McKenzie's file. "Before it gets too busy, would you mind reaching out to whoever's listed and make sure she's ok, please? But as always—"

"Try the employee first." Royelle smiled, finishing the sentence.

"That-ah-girl." Charlyn smiled back. "Let me know if you're able to make contact. And remember, we're just checking in; we're not offering her job back. That's done! And whoever you reach out to, let them know we'll mail out her last check and belongings. She is not to step foot back on these premises. Understood?"

"Yes, ma'am. You got it."

Royelle eagerly walked back to her office with McKenzie's file on hand. She sat down at her desk for a moment to process everything that Charlyn had told her about McKenzie's consistency at Quincy court. She went back to the days of the conversations she had with Trevion about cases she was working for Charlyn or when Charlyn would be at Quincy court, and it was all too coincidental. The only way McKenzie could've posted up as much as she did was if Trevion fed her the food. How else could she have known Charlyn's schedule so well? The thought of it all added to the bile that Royelle had towards Trevion.

When Royelle finally opened the file, she was disappointed to find limited information, although she wasn't really surprised. When she called the two numbers listed, both rang back as not in service, and McKenzie's phone went straight to voicemail. "Damn," Royelle whispered. She wished she had taken McKenzie's phone before Xandra took her, so she could try to get the numbers McKenzie had recently called, but it was too late for that.

Royelle quickly took pictures of McKenzie's street address, her employee photo, her social, and her date of birth with her phone and returned the file to Charlyn, explaining her findings, but Charlyn didn't seem surprised or pressed by any of it. When Royelle returned to her office, she jumped on her computer and, for the next several hours, searched anything she could find on Thomas Presley. She was surprised at the wealth of information she found. Of course, there was a lot she couldn't get access to without a court order, but she was content with what she did have and felt Xandra would be too.

Next, she checked her voicemails and listened to three of them before getting to Bella's. When she heard the contents of the message, she instantly became interested. She stored her number in her phone and committed to calling her later. Her last order of business was Xandra.

CHAPTER 20

When Royelle called Xandra and told her to be home by the time she got off work, she already knew Royelle was coming to her with a bullshit conversation involving McKenzie. As a protective sister, there were a lot of things that Xandra withheld from Royelle. Trust wasn't a factor; that was on lock; it was the pain that Royelle had been faced with that derived Xandra's movements. And at all costs, she was going to do whatever it took to avoid Royelle being impacted by it any further. As soon as she heard Royelle using her spare key to get in the house, Xandra went towards the kitchen to get them both a drink. "Here comes the bullshit," she murmured as she poured the tequila and pineapple juice into each glass.

"Sis!" Royelle yelled out.

"Kitchen!" Xandra hollered back.

When Royelle walked in, Xandra handed her the glass as a peace offering of sorts.

"Sis! You need to tell me what's going on. What did you do with McKenzie, sis?" Royelle cut straight to the chase.

"What are you talking about?"

"Sis! What did you do, and why didn't you tell me?"

"Man. What's going on? And why you questioning me like you're the ops. You wired or some shit." Xandra chuckled.

She knew damn well Royelle wasn't wired; she was just buying time to deflect the questioning off of herself. But, Royelle wasn't having it. She beamed her eyes hard at Xandra while waiting for an honest response. Xandra, quickly catching Royelle's drift, began to speak.

"Listen. I did what I had to do. Any snake that still slithers with venom flowing from their teeth—it's off with their head!" Xandra said, pressing her lips together, pretending to be slicing her throat off with her thumb running from one end of her neck to the other.

"So you killed her?!" Royelle hollered. "I didn't want the bitch dead! Beat her ass, sure, but dead, no!"

"Says the one who—"

"Shut it! We're not talking about me right now. Where's the body, sis?!" Royelle yelled.

"Sis. The bitch ain't dead. Not that I know of." Xandra nonchalantly responded.

Royelle peered her eyes at Xandra. "What are you saying? Where is she then?"

Royelle's questioning caused a tinge of concern for Xandra. This was the first time she had seen Royelle truly invested in what Xandra had done or not done. But then again, these were new days, and Royelle was gradually learning more and more about her sister. Knowing that Royelle was now fully aware of McKenzie's disappearance and seeing how troubled Royelle was behind not knowing the facts, Xandra knew the only thing to do now was to tell the truth.

She went into deep detail about knowing that Sion had people who enjoyed women like McKenzie, and since she knew neither she nor Royelle could have any more blood on their hands, she called him to make McKenzie someone else's problem that wasn't from the streets of Boston. She explained that there were already too many smoke signals around Royelle because of all the deaths, and one more would definitely start the fire; it was fumes that neither of them could afford to inhale.

The more Xandra spoke, the more Royelle wondered if she and Xandra were becoming the modern-day Thelma and Louise. She was beside herself. And as if things couldn't get any crazier, she watched as Xandra went into her room empty-handed, returning with a picture in her right hand.

"This is the other reason I couldn't risk letting McKenzie go or killing her." Xandra handed the picture to Royelle.

"Royelle jumped from her seat. "Sis! This is us!" Royelle panicked. "I thought you said that we were good?!"

"Sis, chill. We are good. Look at the picture again."

Royelle was hyperventilating. She could not believe what was happening. This was unfathomable. And if feeling like shit about everything that has happened wasn't enough, holding the picture of her carrying her father's body put the icing on the cake.

"Sis!" Royelle cried. "We're going to jail! They got us on camera!" She sobbed.

"Sis. I know you're worried, but trust me on this. We good! You're good!"

"Yea! That's what you said before and now look at us!" Royelle shouted.

Xandra looked at her with disappointment. "Are you for real right now? So you're questioning my integrity right now?"

Royelle's head lowered as she continued to cry.

"Sis, look at me!" Xandra sternly said.

Royelle picked her head up.

"Don't you ever say no shit like that! When have I, Xandra Valentina, aka Muneca Arroyo, ever let you down? Hmm? When?!" Xandra paused, waiting for the answer she wouldn't get. " When I tell you we good, you good, I mean that shit! Do you hear me?!"

"Yea, but—"

"No, sis! No fucking buts. I got us!"

"Sis, I hear you!" Royelle shouted back. "BUT! The evidence is looking back at us. How can you fix this?"

"Is it? Looking back at us?" Xandra questioned. "Look at the picture again."

Royelle looked down at the picture, trying to understand what Xandra saw because the only thing Royelle's eyes could feast on was that exact moment in time on the image.

"Do you see it?" Xandra curiously asked.

"See what, sis? It's you and me carrying Rayford. What else is there to see?"

"But is it, though? Come on sis, stop thinking about what you know is in the picture. Put your fucking paralegal hat on and look at the fucking picture. I mean really look at it." Xandra ordered.

Xandra could have easily told Royelle what she saw, but she wanted Royelle to see it on her own, hoping it would help lessen her fear. She knew that once Royelle got past the initial shock of it all, she'd be able to see the picture the way Xandra did. Xandra watched Royelle examine the picture, and when her eyebrows went up, Xandra knew that was the moment Royelle caught it.

"What do you see?" She quickly asked.

"I see us carrying something. But it's hard to say what we're carrying from this distance."

"Exactlyyy! So, to you and me, yes, it's us carrying a dead body because we know what it is and who. But to anyone else looking at this picture, it looks like something big, carried by two people. What two people? It's hard to say. And what item? No one can tell." Xandra said.

"Yea, but what if this gets back to the police. They will come back asking questions."

"So, let them! They ain't gonna find shit! But whoever it is ain't going to the police."

"How can you be so sure?"

"Sis, I've had this picture for a grip. And no one has come knocking yet. Trust me, if whoever this is wanted us in jail, we would've got bagged the day after he died. Somebody wants something from us or maybe just me since they left it on my truck, not yours."

Royelle began processing everything Xandra said, and a bit of anger towards Xandra began to emerge as the what if's crept up. What if the picture was clearer? What if the person who took the photo did go to the police? What if the police did come? What if the police had questions for her? How would she be able to answer their questions regarding the picture? Xandra withholding that information from her for so long had the potential of ruining her, and she didn't like that feeling one bit.

Her stress levels were at an all-time high. No one could've convinced her two years ago that this is how her life would turn out. And every time she looked at herself in the mirror, a different version of her appeared. She hated to admit it, but she was beginning to lose sight of who she truly was and remembered. She didn't know if she was coming or going. But one thing she did know was that she wasn't going to fold. She pushed her mounting feelings towards Xandra to the side and got back to it.

"So, what do we do now?" Royelle asked,

"You. You're going to keep going to work and therapy. Stay on script. Don't change your pattern, not even for a second. I'm gonna handle this, sis. Do you hear me?"

Royelle nodded. "I don't know how, but I trust you," Royelle said. Strangely, for the first time in her entire life, she was skeptical of her sister's possibilities.

"And that's plenty for me, sis. No salt."

"No salt," Royelle replied.

"You ok now?" Xandra asked.

"I'm not going to lie. I'm not ok. There's a lot going on all. But I'll be alright." Royelle panted. "Anyway, here's everything I have on McKenzie and Presley." Royelle handed everything she had over to Xandra and didn't ask any questions.

"Good shit, sis!" Xandra excited. "It might not look like much. But it's plenty. Trust me. I promise you sis. You good. I got you!"

"I know. But there's more."

"What more."

"That girl Bella, the one who was at the memorial service with McKenzie, left me a message and wants me to call her."

"What the fuck for?" Xandra frowned.

"I don't know."

"Well bitch, we gonna find out!"

Xandra advised Royelle to let Bella wait it out. Whatever she needed to talk to Royelle about would have to take a backseat to the Detective Preseley movement.

CHAPTER 21

Xandra sat at her dining room table with a notebook and pen writing down all the names of potential people who may have been responsible for the kodak moment she and Royelle were a part of. So far, she had Aruba, Bella, Detective Presley, and Detective Aveen. Trevion, along with Amadeo and McKenzie, were dead factors. They never even crossed Xandra's mind.

She closed her eyes and brought herself back to that night. She tried to zero in on any suspicious cars parked on the block, but none seemed to stand out. She looked back at the picture to try and figure out what direction the picture was taken from and quickly learned that whoever their eye-spy was, had parked on the corner of Woodward Park and Folsom Street. It made her chuckle as she remembered all the times she was in hiding taking pictures of Trevion and Amadeo in all their splendor of bullshit.

It puzzled her, though. She couldn't understand how their eye-spy managed to get such a shot in between the obscurity of darkness in conjunction with the fence and tree shrubs in the way; what should've been an impossible shot was clearly doable. It didn't matter now, however. What mattered now was trying to figure out why she and Royelle were being watched? Who was watching them? And what the hell did they want from them?

She thought about Aruba and Bella and immediately pegged them as being too dumb to pull something like this off. They just didn't seem like the type. But then she wondered if maybe that's why Bella wanted to talk to Royelle. Could she have been tailing them this whole time, just waiting for the right moment to catch her and Royelle slipping? This was another thought she quickly dismissed. She just couldn't see it. The way they acted at the memorial service let Xandra know they weren't the smartest of the bunch, and they definitely weren't built for this type of play.

That left her with Detective Aveen and Presley. She looked back at all the information she had gathered on them, thought about her interactions with both of them, and the consistency of ignorance lied with Detective Presley. Each time she faced him, he was either prying too hard, being a smart ass, cynical, sarcastic, or a know-it-all, which were red flags for Xandra. She never understood and still couldn't understand what his beef was with the members of the Blevins family, but her gut was telling her he was good for the stalker business. As she contemplated on what her next move would be, Royelle chimed in.

"What's up, sis?" Xandra asked.

"Sis. Go see Mrs. Lupe."

"Go see her for what?" Xandra questioned.

"Kameras!" Royelle said in German.

Royelle quickly hung up, saying nothing more. With everything, she now knew and all the storms she was a part of, talking over the phone about anything was the last thing she wanted to do. Xandra became discomfited when she was reminded about Mrs. Lupe's cameras. She had been so consumed in caring and covering for Royelle that she completely forgot about the clusters of videos that Mrs. Lupe housed. And even though she had no clue what Mrs. Lupe might or might not have, murdering her for the information was off the table. She was not about to recreate Trevion's Benton scene.

Now that Lupe's children were grown, married with families, and living on their own, things were pretty quiet in the multi-family home that Mrs. Lupe owned. She lived on the first floor with tenants occupying floors two and three. And although the neighborhood was pretty safe and always quiet, her children made sure their mother's safety was their first priority.

Therefore, they had the alarm system company come out and put cameras all around the house's perimeter, making sure not to miss a signal inch of the house's surroundings.

When Xandra finally pulled onto the street, all the cars in front of Adala's house were gone. "Bet!" She said excitedly, knowing that she wouldn't have to explain shit to Raylina or Raymelle as to her presence at Mrs. Lupe's. She got out of her truck and rang Mrs. Lupe's doorbell.

"Voyyy!" Mrs. Lupe hollered from her kitchen.

Xandra smiled when she heard the deep Boricua accent. It reminded her of her own.

"Munecita! Que haces aqui chula?" She smiled brightly, standing in the doorway with her floral muumuu and her hair in big Gray plastic rollers secured in place by huge Brown bobby pins.

"Hola Donya Lupe. I came to check on the house, and I wanted to ask you for a favor."

Xandra kissed Mrs. Lupe on the cheek as accustomed to their culture, showing respect and love. And when she entered the house, it was like walking into bliss. The house smelled like an array of spices—sofrito, sazon, adobo, garlic, cilantro, bay leaves, and pure Latina love. It wasn't often that Xandra got to whiff the authentic scents of Latino cuisine in the air, but when she did, it melted her heart every time, and hate quickly followed. It always made her think of her mother and everything she didn't do.

"So? Digame. Que favor?" Mrs. Lupe asked in her Sophia Vergara accent as she checked on her Arroz Blanco and Habichuelas.

"Donya Lupe, I know you have cameras. But do they work?"

"Claro nena!" Mrs. Lupe laughed, clapping her hands. "Por que? Que paso? Is some-fin wrong?" She asked in her broken English.

"Oh no! Nothing's wrong. It's just we think someone is trying to buy out the house and has been watching it. And so, we want to catch them so we can report it."

The whole way to Mrs. Lupe's, Xandra thought about what she could say that would sound plausible enough for why she needed to see the tapes. Telling her that someone was following them would've opened up the door to more curiosities. She thought about saying that a boy was stalking

Raylina, but that would've prompted Mrs. Lupe to ask Raylina questions about a boy that never existed. And telling Mrs. Lupe that she just wanted to see if she and Royelle were on camera was definitely out of the question. The best option left was the lie about the house. And since the small community of people on the street all knew about Rayford's plans once Adala passed, the story about the house fit perfectly, and Mrs. Lupe fell right into it.

"Tell me, mejia. What day did it happen?"

"I can't remember. Can we check for the last two weeks?"

"Hmm. Ok." She titled her chin towards her chest to see over her glasses.

Mrs. Lupe took the video back as far back as she could and ran through each day's footage until they reached the day that Xandra was looking for. Xandra intently watched as the cameras turned from right to left. When one finally landed on the corner of Folsom and Woodward Park, she asked Lupe to pause it. There she saw what looked like a heavy build, tall individual. She couldn't tell if it was a male or female, but by their stature, the way they stood, their height, and weight, Xandra presumed the person was male, but it was hard to tell, especially since their face was covered up by the black ski mask they wore.

"Donya Lupe. Can you zoom in a little, please?"

Xandra was trying to get a good look at the car on the corner, but the night air of darkness was too thick. She couldn't make out a license plate, but the car resembled that of a typical detective's vehicle. Since Mrs. Lupe's cameras weren't sophisticated enough to print stills, Xandra took out her phone and took as many pictures as possible; the pictures came out mediocre at best. But it was enough for her to work with.

Xandra watched for a few more minutes as the cameras looped back around towards the Blevins home, and it showed every move she and Royelle made that night. They were caught on tape from the time they drove up to the moment they carried Rayford into the house, and when Mrs. Lupe saw the expression on Xandra's face, she backed it up a bit and hit delete.

"Mejia. I didn't see anything. Did ju? Pasó, lo que pasó. Punto!" She said, kissing Xandra on the cheek.

Mrs. Lupe knew the real reason Xandra was there. She played dumb, but she was far from it. She and Adala had talked many times in the past about ways to take Rayford out but never had the courage. So to see that his daughter and step-daughter handled it gave her joy. It was payback as far as she was concerned for all that he had done to her best friend and sister Adala.

"Do you need some-fin else?" Mrs. Lupe calmly asked.

"No, Donya. Eso es todo. Gracias," Xandra replied, with a tear running down her cheek.

She was flabbergasted. She didn't know what to say. She couldn't believe that Mrs. Lupe had just pulled a gangster move on her. She never thought she would live to see the day that someone of Mrs. Lupe's age would do something Xandra would do without blinking. Her breath was taken away.

"Thank you so much, Donya Lupe," Xandra said, hugging her tightly.

She pulled away from Xandra to look her in he reyes. "Gracias para que?" She asked. "Haz lo que tengas que hacer y ten cuidado haciéndolo. Te quiero mucho." She kissed Xandra on her cheek and sent her on her way.

Xandra was still stunned as she got in her truck. For Mrs. Lupe to say that she didn't see, shit doesn't know shit, and for her and Royelle to handle their business while being careful doing it was the realest shit ever. Other than Sion, Xandra had never seen anyone move like that. But to come from an elder made it all the more authentic. She wiped the tears of respect from her eyes and called Royelle for a quick meet in twenty minutes.

"So. What happened?" Royelle eagerly asked.

"First things first, we're not on any of the cameras." Xandra didn't lie, but she didn't want to give her the truth. The less Royelle knew, the better. "Secondly, I think our stalker is one of the detectives on the case." Xandra passed her phone to Royelle.

Royelle gasped for air. "Are you serious?" She asked, looking at the pictures Xandra took. "Oh, wow!" She said. "But if it is one of them, why hasn't he said anything?"

"Like I told you. He wants something. But don't worry. I got this!" Xandra reassured. And now that we have this call, that bitch, set a meetup, and let me know once it's done.

CHAPTER 22

*B*ella couldn't believe that Royelle had actually called her back. As she anxiously prepared for their meetup, she wondered how she would even begin to tell Royelle all she had to say. How could she tell Royelle that she was one of the ones that Trevion had been fucking the entire time they were married, or did she even tell her at all? But Bella rationalized that Royelle deserved to know everything, especially now that danger lurked. Trevion being alive meant peril for everybody. Bella wasn't sure if Trevion would hurt Royelle or what he wanted from her, but she knew nothing good would come from him finding either of them.

It had been the first time leaving her place since her return from New York; she didn't know what to expect of the outside world. And since her apartment was in the back of the building, she had no way of peering out the window to check her surroundings. Being scared was an understatement. She quaked in her skinny jeans at the mere thought of Trevion being outside waiting on her. Despite having done nothing wrong, the idea of him being anywhere out there was terrorizing. At any given time, he could get to her or call her with demands that she better have complied with, or she was Aruba toast.

She heaved as she made it to the bottom level of her apartment building and looked out of the half-glass door. From what she could see, everything appeared normal. She quickly exited the building and ran to her car. She jumped in and immediately locked her doors. She breathed deeply as she started the engine being sure to look through all her mirrors for any sudden movements. "You got this," she said as she pulled out of her parking space.

She drove at a normal pace all the way to Sheesha Lounge on Cambridge street, looking out of her mirrors every ten seconds. She wanted to be sure she wasn't being followed, but the traffic was so dense it was hard to tell at this point. Finally, she pulled into Sheesha's parking lot and waited several minutes before getting out. She wanted to be sure nothing seemed suspicious or that other cars weren't pulling in behind her. When she felt safe, she got out and went inside, quickly spotting Royelle sitting in the far back corner smoking hookah with Xandra.

"Hey, ladies." She greeted with a smile as she walked up.

"Hey!" Royelle responded eagerly. Xandra said nothing. "You hookah?" Royelle asked.

"I do. But, I'm ok." Bella nervously responded.

"Suit yourself," Royelle said as Bella sat down.

"Would you ladies like a drink. On me, of course." Bella reassured as she called the waiter over to take her order of triple shots of Tequila.

Xandra and Royelle refused the offer.

"Must be heavy." Xandra sneered.

"What's that?" Bella asked.

"The reason we're here," Xandra replied.

Bella gave half a grin. "Something like that." She responded.

"Well, get to it, sweetcakes. Time is money." Xandra shot back.

Bella was already uncomfortable and having Xandra there only made it worst.

"Here you go." The waiter said, placing the drinks down. "Would you like to keep your tab open?"

Bella nodded her head yes and threw back the first triple shot. "Keep the rounds coming!" She shouted out to the waiter.

"Damn, girl! You good?" Xandra laughed. "You know that's a sign of stress, huh?"

"Ha! Stress. Now there's a word." Bella said, wiping her mouth with a napkin.

"What's going on, Bella? Why did you want to see me?" Royelle gently asked.

Bella looked over at her. "A lot is going on, Royelle, only I don't know where to begin."

"I don't care where you start; just start," Royelle replied.

"Do you believe in ghosts?" Bella asked, picking up her next shot.

Royelle looked over at Xandra with a perplexed look. "Umm, not in the literal sense," Royelle responded.

"Well, you should."

"And why is that?" Xandra asked.

"Because Trevion is alive." Bella quickly took her shot. "Waiter! Two more rounds!" She hollered.

The moment Bella stopped speaking was the moment Royelle's heart broke all over again. Instantly everything was frozen in time around her. It was like the Earth stood still. Everything was pitch black around her, and the only one at Sheesha was her. She saw nothing; she heard nothing. She was at a complete loss for words as she tried to process the enormity of weight that Bella had just laid on her lap.

Royelle's mind was sent reeling. She was catatonic and felt like she was living a nightmare. As she tried to process Bella's words, her thoughts ran through her like waves of rushing water, pausing periodically and rushing back in. There was no way possible Trevion could still be alive. The medical records proved it; the coroner said so. How could it be? She wondered. She remembered words that she read in a blog post, "If your heart acts like a gun in life, the person you face is a monster." Nothing could've been more real when she thought about who the monster was in this situation.

"Sis." Xandra shook her shoulder a bit. But Royelle didn't move. "Aye!" She snapped her fingers in Royelle's face, but Royelle still didn't respond. She barely blinked.

"Hey! Can we get a cup of water over here!" Bella yelled out to the waiter.

Quickly, he brought it over and handed it to Xandra.

"Uhh!" Royelle jumped when she felt the cold water that Xandra threw in her face.

"Yo! You good, sis?! What the fuck was that?" Xandra asked, frightened. It was the first time she saw Royelle in that particular state. Sure she had her frozen in place, but nothing like she had just witnessed. "Sis? You good?" She asked again. Royelle nodded yes. "Do you need a minute?" Xandra continued.

"No," Royelle said, darting her raging cold eyes at Bella. "Did I hear you correctly? Did you say that Trevion is alive?"

"He is," Bella responded.

"And how do you know that?" Royelle scowled.

Bella took a deep breath. "I saw him a few weeks ago in New York."

"In New York? Nah, you gotta be mistaken." Xandra said.

She questioned it, but she knew Bella was telling the truth. Everything Raymelle said about the body being burned in the car she knew was a lie then, and she was pissed about it now. Here she was trying to protect her sister from memory loss and all the calamity she was involved in, and they had been marks the entire time

"Look on some real nigga shit, you gonna have to give detail for detail about everything you know," Xandra demanded.

"That's fine. But before I do that, I need something from y'all." Bella responded.

"Bitch, we ain't up for no negotiations!" Xandra spat.

"Look." Bella calmly said. "I want the same thing y'all want."

"And how the fuck do you know what we want?!" Xandra questioned.

"You don't have to say it, but y'all want him dead like I do. Especially you, Xandra, because you're the next target."

"What the fuck did you say!?" Xandra questioned.

"I don't know what you did. But I heard him say you were the next target."

"Nah! You had to have heard that wrong." Xandra said.

The room was silent for a quick second. Royelle was still in shock, so no one knew if she heard what was said or if it went over her head, but the subject needed to be changed quickly.

"Moving on from that bullshit talk. What I'm saying is he couldn't possibly have done to you what he did to my sister. Why you mad, cause he fucked you and left you?!" Xandra remarked.

"Actually, I think it might be worst," Bella said, ignoring Xandra's cynicism.

At this point, Bella felt like, whatever was going to happen, just had to happen. She knew that if she didn't die at the hands of Xandra and Royelle, she was for sure going to die at Trevion's. So, rather than hold anything back, she laid it all out on the table. She started from the very beginning of meeting Trevion. She explained how long they've known each other, detailing the escort business he ran with men and women, what her involvement was with Detective Aveen and the murders, and how she got to Trevion in New York with the help of his brother D-Rock.

The more Bella talked, the less Royelle and Xandra felt they knew about the person that had been in their family for five years. Bamboozled was an understatement. They both felt had, hoodwinked, deluded, and entrapped all at the same time. They thought they knew all there was to know about Trevion, but they were wrong. And the more she talked, the more Xandra wanted to whoop her ass. But the information Bella had was too important. Causing her any harm right now would defeat the purpose.

Royelle, on the other hand, was ten seconds from wrapping her hands around Bella's throat. Her right leg was shaking at milli-second speed as she rubbed her hands between her thighs, trying to fight the violent urge building inside her. Bella could sense the impulses, but she knew what she had was like a money safe, and as long as she had value to add to the conversation, she knew she was good.

When Bella started talking about how Trevion's looks had changed, what he looked like now, how he killed Aruba, and what he did to her at the end, Royelle began to calm down a bit. She couldn't believe that this was the man she loved, the one she defended at all costs against her family, boss, and small group of friends. It was the same person she trusted with her money, life, family, and secrets. Her mother was right; Trevion was evil. He lied about everything in life and even now in his fake death. It was here that her mother's journal came alive. She wished she would've noticed then what her mother did.

After all that she had mourned, all that she did to heal, and all she did to try and recover what she lost, this news was a huge slap in the face. Royelle felt broken all over again. Only this time, this brokenness came with a new pair of red stilettos. Something ticked in Royelle. Something sinister, crimson red, and hot like lava was boiling inside. No one knew what she was thinking or how she was feeling, but the game had just flipped.

CHAPTER 23

*X*andra woke up the next morning in Royelle's guest room with much on her mind. Now she wasn't so sure if the person she saw in the picture was the detective, Trevion, or his brother. But her heart told her it had to be Trevion and his people. He followed the exact same move she did to him and Amadeo long ago. She figured the m.o. is the same, so it had to be them. Therefore, she ruled out the detective and figured it best to leave him be until she knew otherwise. When she finally came out of the room, she found Royelle already showered, dressed, and at the computer researching all that she could on Trevion and his brother D-Rock. But, based on Royelle's emotionless facial expressions, she knew something was amiss.

"Morning, sis." Xandra gently greeted.

"Morning," Royelle responded.

"Did you call Charlyn?"

"Yea. I told her I needed an immediate leave of absence."

Royelle was very dry and, matter of fact, with her responses. Xandra couldn't tell if Royelle was mad at her for what Bella had said or if she was just focused on her assignment and didn't want to be bothered. She prayed that what Bella said the day before went over Royelle's head, but it was hard to say. Whatever the case, though, now was definitely not the time for them to be on two separate wave links. So to give Royelle a minute to handle her business and get her mind right, Xandra grabbed her bag and headed for the shower. Royelle never uttered a word, much less looked at Xandra. *"What the fuck is her problem?"* Xandra thought as she turned the shower on. She really wanted to ask, but poking a bear in its disturbed state was never the right thing to do. Therefore, she got in the shower, handled her business, and by the time she was out and dressed, Royelle was gone.

"What the fuck?!" Xandra sneered. "No fucking see you later, no note, no nothing! This shit is starting to get old!"

She grabbed her phone and attempted to call Royelle, but it went to voicemail. Rather than leave her a message, she tried to track her location, but it wasn't visible. Xandra figured that Royelle must've had her phone off. So she sent her a text and made sure to exclude her emotions. Although she felt confident that Trevion didn't know where Royelle lived, she couldn't be too sure. However, she did know that he was walking the streets looking like a different person and had a brother named D-Rock, whom they only had a description of and not a very good one. With the way Bella described him, he looked like a typical hood nigga who could be confused for anyone. So Xandra had to prepare herself for anything. Therefore, before gathering all her things, she grabbed her gun, cocked it, and made sure she had one in the chamber ready.

Royelle was still burning on the inside from the day before. So while Xandra was sleeping, she was up, thinking, planning, and plotting. And although Bella casually left out the fact that she was the one creeping through the backyard, Royelle knew. She didn't have the concrete proof she needed, but her gut told her so. And women's intuition, as far as Royelle was concerned, was always right.

Royelle was confused. She hated Bella, but at the same time, she couldn't blame her for much. If Trevion could lie to her about everything he had in the five years they were together, then for damn sure, he lied to Bella about everything too. But she felt there was more that Bella didn't say. There had to be. While everything she said made sense, there were still things that weren't clear, like McKenzie and Aruba, for starters. Of all things that Bella talked about, she never explained how those two were involved and what they sought to gain out of Royelle's misery. Then there was their visit to the memorial service. Royelle wanted to know the reason behind that. Everything led to something, and Royelle wanted answers before snuffing Bella out. Regardless of anything, today, Bella had to die. In Royelle's mind, there was no way Bella could live and know all that she did, especially since killing Trevion and his brother was on the agenda. So leaving a witness to tell the story was out.

But when Royelle finally made it close to Bella's house, her neighborhood was blocked off a few streets up with yellow tape all around. "What the?" She said, parking her truck as close to Bella's street as she could. When she got out, she began briskly walking towards the growing crowd of on-lookers already at the scene. She made sure to stay as far back as possible and mix in with the crowd to avoid being seen or questioned by police for any reason.

As she got slightly closer, she noticed a lifeless body lying on the ground, covered by a white sheet. She couldn't be sure who was underneath it, but her heart was beating fast. Something told her it was Bella. And as the people started chiming in about the drive-by shooting that had occurred that morning at 6 am, her assumptions were validated. Bella had been murdered at dawn.

All the things Bella thought she was doing to be careful on her way to the meet-up failed. Trevion and D-Rock had been watching her since she returned to Boston. He was eager to find out if she was as authentic as he believed her to be or if she would fold, and she did. He couldn't believe his eyes when he saw who walked out of the lounge thirty minutes after she did. And at that moment, he had the right mind to kill her that night, but it was too hot on her block. So, he had to lay in wait. And when Bella left the house to get coffee the following morning, he lit her ass up with an AK-47, leaving her with some final words. "Death when you dishonor bitch!" They drove off, got breakfast, and waited for the scene to become active before returning.

When Royelle showed up, she had no way of knowing that Trevion was already in the crowd. But these were the moments that Xandra had warned her about. Royelle never had a plan when she moved on impulse and paid less attention to her surroundings, making it easy for her to become a target at any given point. The only thing that saved her this time was the police on the scene.

As she walked back to her truck, Trevion watched. He smiled, knowing that she didn't recognize his voice when he spoke to her about who the dead body was on the ground. She never even looked his way. In his mind, she was the same simpleton she had always been: all books, no streets. Getting close to Royelle was going to be much easier than he thought. But it wasn't her he was much concerned with at the moment; it was Xandra he sought-after.

When Royelle got into her truck, she was relieved that she didn't have to get her hands dirty, but it didn't negate the tinge of fear that had set in. She didn't know if Trevion was responsible for Bella or not, but it only made sense. No one else could've wanted her dead that bad. But, she figured, if it was that easy for Trevion to get the drop on Bella, then for sure, she and Xandra were next, especially Xandra since he didn't cut for her. So she had to think about her next move and strategy to take him and his brother out before they came for her and her sister.

Before leaving the house, she cut her phone off and didn't turn it back on until she was halfway home, all to avoid the police from pinging her location in case she came up as a suspect. She didn't think that she would, but she couldn't be too sure these days. Every turn she took, her name was in the mix, so this time she wanted to be careful not to get caught up.

When it powered up, she noticed Xandra's text message but didn't open it. She didn't want Xandra to know she saw it by leaving it on read. She needed time to think, time to be alone, and time to process everything from the beginning of her life with Trevion to where she was now.

She still had no idea how Trevion could have pulled something off like faking his death. To do that, she knew he would've had to have help from some high places and paid some serious money to get it done. A burned body in a car was for sure with the help of someone in the coroner's office or the funeral home. There is no other way for someone to pull off such a thing. It costs lots of money, lots of money. So, where was he getting it from? Who helped him then? And who other than his brother who was helping him now, Royelle wondered. Her mission was to find him before he found her but to do that, she had to find the people responsible for helping him arrange such a scheme.

She wanted so badly to call her brother and tell him everything that was happening, but she didn't want him involved. She knew he would kill on sight, but this was hers. She was no longer the Royelle everyone thought she was; she was different, and now killing for revenge came easy. If anyone was going to get Trevion's blood on their hands, it would be her, or she was going to die trying.

When she pulled up at her house, she saw Xandra's truck still in the driveaway. Although she wanted to avoid her, knowing she was still there was a good thing. Royelle had questions, and there was no better time to ask them. When she walked inside, Xandra was at the computer trying to check Royelle's search history, but Royelle had changed the password. She knew how Xandra operated and didn't want Xandra to locate or stop her from getting to Bella and Trevion.

"Welcome back. You cool now?" Xandra said, clicking out of the computer.

"I'm good."

"Where'd you go?" Xandra asked.

At first, Royelle was reluctant to say, but what was there to hide? She didn't do shit, and Bella's murder was going to end up on the five o'clock news anyway, so it was best for her to just spit it out.

"I went to go talk to Bella, but when I got there, she was dead." Royelle calmly said as she prepared a mimosa for herself.

"Are you fucking serious?! Why didn't you say you were going there?! And why did you go by yourself?! What's going on with you, sis? You been acting strange for real, yo."

Royelle looked over at Xandra. But it wasn't the look Xandra was used to seeing. Instead, this one had a questioning feel to it. It was like Royelle was trying to read Xandra's mind but kept coming up empty.

"Sis, have you ever lied to me about anything?" Royelle sternly asked.

"What? What kind of question is that?" Xandra asked with a screwed-up face.

"The kind that needs answering. Have you ever lied to me? Royelle asked again.

"Since when have I ever lied to you?" Xandra's face started turning red. She was taken aback by Royelle's questioning. "I may have kept things from you for your protection, but I have never lied to you."

"Fair enough. So, what haven't you told me?" Royelle flipped.

"Are you fucking kidding me right now?! You're questioning me like you the ops. Fuck is going on with you, yo?! Of all people, you're questioning me!?" Xandra hollered. "I've been nothing but a sister to you. You're muthafucking protector throughout life, and you got a nerve to question me?" Xandra yelled, slapping her right hand on her chest.

Royelle was unmoved. The more Xandra deflected from the question; the more Royelle knew that Xandra was hiding something. She was exhibiting the exact same behaviors guilty criminals did when they wanted the finger pointed at them to point in another direction.

"Sis, you have to stop protecting me. I know you. There's a lot you haven't told me, and maybe the secrets you're keeping can help us with this mess. We have to find him before he finds us, sis. So, whatever you know, I need to know. Bella wouldn't have said what she said if it wasn't true or if there wasn't anything to that. And even if she was lying, I still have to treat it as if she wasn't. So tell me the truth sis, what does Trevion have on you?"

Royelle was calm and compassionate. She wasn't trying to beef with her sister. She just wanted the truth from Xandra, and when she approached to hug her, Xandra started to cry. It was the first time she ever broke in such a way. There were so many times she wanted to tell Royelle the truth, but the idea of Royelle being too fragile to handle it kept Xandra from dropping bombs on her. All she wanted was to keep Royelle out of the way of hurt, and here it was backfiring on her.

Xandra sat for several minutes crying while Royelle watched. It felt weird to her. Normally, it was Xandra watching and consoling Royelle, but now it was in reverse, and that was confirmation enough for Royelle that Xandra had been withholding some serious stuff. After a short while, Xandra wiped her face with her hands and dried them on her pants. She cleared her throat, sat straight up, and looked Royelle in the face.

"Sis, I fucked up!" Xandra blurted out.

Royelle watched as Xandra went from a sitting position to a standing position as she began to describe the sequence of events and how she came to the idea of following Trevion that very first night. She recalled the day that Royelle came to her house with the yellow sticky note and how it made her feel when she saw how destroyed Royelle was because of it. She explained that the day she saw him and Amadeo together was the day that she started taking pictures and went twice as hard to follow his every move, all for the purpose of telling Royelle, so she could see Trevion for what he was and divorce him. But after witnessing the gnawing pains of all that Royelle had gone through and was still going through, she couldn't find it in her heart to tell her.

She painted out that she later learned about Xclusive after Royelle had kicked Trevion out, but by then, she felt there wasn't anything to tell because she knew there was no coming back once Royelle put him out. So, she didn't think it was necessary to add more to the plate when she was already dealing with Adala's decline and Rayford's bullshit.

Royelle gazed at Xandra as she gave explanation after explanation. She could not believe that this entire time Xnadra knew Trevion was a snake and a cheat and never once thought that telling her might be in her favor. She understood that Xandra was trying to protect her, but she also felt that Xandra undermined her too much. Royelle's perception of Xandra's protection made it look like Xandra saw her as weak, feeble, and incapable of handling things that had the potential of destroying her, and that left a bad taste in Royelle's mouth.

Royelle remained quiet, not once shedding a tear. She couldn't cry. There were no tears left. After everything she had gone through, all that she had done within the past several weeks, and all that she had lost, Royelle was like cold steel. On the exterior, she pretended to be the same timid, soft-spoken, always respectable Royelle. But, on the inside, she was quickly turning into stone, with no emotions, wrathful, and seething with anger. At this point, nothing could make her heart bleed any more than it had, or so she thought.

Before expressing the next part, Xandra went into the kitchen with Royelle following closely behind. She watched as Xandra cracked open the brand new bottle of 1800 Silver and drank it straight from the bottle. She drank as if it would be the last thing she'd drink in life.

"Must be heavy?" Royelle said."

"What you talking about?" Xandra questioned.

"Isn't that what you said to Bella right before she gave us some incomprehensible news."

"Touche," Xandra responded, taking another long gulp.

"Well, as you said to her. Hurry up, sweetcakes. Time is money."

"Well played again," Xandra responded.

Royelle was using Xandra's own words against her, and although Xandra was repulsed by it, she expected it. So she ignored Royelle's antics and continued. Although explaining what was coming next did not come so easy, it had to be said. And if she stood to lose Royelle because of it, it would be a hard pill to swallow, but at least the truth would be out. So she took one final gulp.

"Now, on this next thing, I need you to hear me. I see how you're looking at me, but I need you to hear me clearly."

"Royelle knew bullshit was coming.

"I kind of knew Trevion being burned up in the car was a lie. But I couldn't prove it at the time."

"And you knew this how?" Royelle sputtered.

"Because when he pulled his gun out on me, I pulled mine on him and shot him."

"Wha the fuck are you talking about, Xandra?!" Royelle hollered.

"Listen to me, sis. I had no choice! Somehow Trevion knew it was me who put those pictures on his truck. He followed me throughout the city and into Milton. When I got out of the car, we argued. He pulled his gun out on me, so I did the same. I didn't stick around to see if he was dead or alive, but when I heard he was burned in the car, I knew it was a lie."

Instantly Royelle felt like a million pieces of shard were seething through her skin.

"Sis, please say something." Xandra pleaded, knowing she fucked up.

"Xandra. Get out." Royelle said in a grim tone.

"What?!" Xandra was surprised at the response.

"I said get the fuck out!" Royelle hollered. "How the fuck could you? You knew what I was going through and said nothing! Nothing, sis! You said nothing! You saw me dying internally, and you said nothing. How could you sis? I don't give a shit what I was going through. You should have told me from the beginning, and we wouldn't be here now. Betrayal is a conscious choice, and you made yours. So, now I'm making mine. get the fuck out!" Royelle yelped.

For the first time ever, Xandra was fragmented. She wanted to explain some more, but Royelle had completely lost it. There was no more explaining that could be done. At this point, Xandra would just have to wait for Royelle to calm down and reach out to her. But since this was the first time that they had ever been at odds, she didn't know what to expect next.

As she headed towards the front door, she turned back to look at Royelle, hoping for a chance to reconcile the differences, but the look of death sat upon Royelle's face. None of which fazed Xandra, but it hurt to see it coming from her sister.

CHAPTER 24

Xandra drove home with despair riddled through her. Of all people, she was supposed to be the last one to cause Royelle any pain. Instead, she saw herself as Royelle's watchwoman, protectress, rescuer, and curator. She played no games about her. And to be at odds with her was the last thing Xandra was trying to be.

While Xandra understood the pain Royelle was in and why she thought she was betrayed, betrayal was the last thing Xandra would ever do. She knew that what she was doing was for Royelle's own good and wished that Royelle could see it that way too. But here they were, their first fight ever, and separated at the worst time. And with Trevion looking like who knew what these days, being separated was the worst possible thing they could be. This was when they needed to be by each other's side more than ever.

Xandra wished she knew where Trevion's apartment in Braintree was located, but it was a no-go. Only Aruba knew where that spot was, and she was dead. And since Xandra knew he'd be coming for them soon, she highly doubted that he returned to New York after killing Bella. She was more than convinced that he was still in the area somewhere, but she just had to do some more digging to find out where.

As she pulled into her driveway, she took a deep breath, relieved to be home, until she heard a popping sound. "What the fuck was that?" She said quickly, looking in all of her mirrors. She didn't see anything but immediately took precautions. Since she knew what she was up against, she made sure to have her gun loaded and ready before getting out. She called Royelle to let her know what was happening, but the call went to voicemail. Rather than hanging up, Xandra kept the phone in her left hand, letting the voicemail record everything just in case.

When she got out of her truck, she checked her surroundings, and everything was quiet. Since the sound she heard came from the tires, she looked down on the driver's side, and everything was intact. She walked over to the passenger side, and when she saw the front right tire, she bent down to get a closer look. "Shit!" She said when she noticed the massive nail in her tire.

"Don't move, bitch." She heard an unknown voice say as she stood up to go into the house.

When she felt the barrel of D-Rock's gun on the back of her head, she slapped it with her left hand, dropping her phone and shooting him with her right before Trevion hit her in the back of the head with a crowbar. When Xandra fell to the ground, Trevion limped over to his brother.

"Bro! Bro! You good?! Did you get hit?!" Trevion yelled.

"The bitch got me, bro-bro. She got me." D-Rock panted.

Trevion was in a heightened panic. He had his brother shot on the ground, Xandra was laid out, and he was in no physical condition to pick either of them up. He still had nerve damage in his left arm and a bad right leg limp from the gunshot wounds Xandra had blessed him with long ago. But he had to do something because he was sure the police would be coming soon.

"DaKari. I need you to get up, bro. We gotta get to the whip!" Trevion said worriedly.

DaKari struggled, but he had enough strength to get himself up and help with Xandra.

"Malachi, grab the bitch by her other arm. We gonna have to drag her ass." DaKari said, fighting through the pain. Once they got to the car, they threw Xandra in the trunk. DaKari got in the front passenger seat while

Trevion cleaned up any mess left behind. The only thing he could spot right away was Xandra's gun. Looking for casings was out of the question. There wasn't any time. He got what he could see and hauled ass as best he could back to the car, not realizing that Xandra's phone was under her truck, still recording on Royelle's voicemail. Finally, he made it back to the car in time to see that DaKari, although only being shot in the shoulder, was losing a lot of blood and struggling to breathe.

"Hold on, bro! I got you, man! I'mma get you to the hospital! Fuck man! Fuck!" Trevion hollered as he sped to the hospital. When he made it, he jumped out of the car and hollered for help. Immediately, the nurses in the lobby came running out with a stretcher.

"What happened?! What's his name?!" One of the nurses yelled out.

"I don't know! I don't know! I saw him laid out on the road!" Trevion lied, rushing back to the car. "Bitch, you better hope my brother don't die." Trevion directed towards Xandra.

He drove erratically to nowhere. He thought about going to his hideaway apartment, but he knew that was a bad idea. There were too many people living in the six-unit apartment building; he was bound to be seen with a woman who was visibly hurt. That was a chance he wasn't willing to take. "Fuck!" He banged his right hand on the steering wheel, realizing that their execution was poorly planned and he was running out of options. They were supposed to kidnap Xandra, torture her for fun, and kill her. Xandra letting off a few rounds and hurting DaKari in the process wasn't in the plans. Trevion had once again underestimated her.

He continued to drive down the highway with no direction in mind. He had to get rid of Xandra. But before killing her, he needed answers about Royelle's money and any policies she had on him where she stood to gain from his death. Trevion was ready for his payout, and he was dead set on Xandra being the guide for getting it. But first, he had to find a spot where no one would find her; only it was still daylight he was sure to be spotted anywhere he went.

When he drove through Lynn, he remembered some questionable landfill areas that were often unoccupied and an easy spot for a murder. As he pulled onto the gravel, he was content in knowing that the spot was as deserted as he remembered and expected it to be. He finally pulled over to the best spot he could find and got out of the car, holding Xandra's gun in his right hand. He vowed that he would shoot her right where she laid in the trunk if she tried anything.

When he approached the back of the car, he put his ear as close to the trunk as possible. He was trying to listen for any sudden movements or sounds, but since there was nothing, he was led to believe that she was still slumped from the blow to her head, and when he opened the truck, his suspicions were right. Xandra was still knocked out, bleeding from her head. When he put the gun in his waist to pull Xandra out, she hit him with the claw hammer that she found in the trunk.

"Ahhh!" he hollered, grabbing his arm to try and slow the pain.

As Xandra attempted to get out of the trunk, she swung again, but this time he caught it, yanking her to the ground in the process. The blow to her head had her weak and dizzy with no strength left. And even though the smell of her own blood had pissed her off, she had no energy to act. Her impulses were raging, but her body couldn't comply.

"Now bitch. Today you die!" Trevion said in a sadistic out-of-breath tone.

Xandra looked up at him strangely. She didn't want to believe it was Trevion, but being where she was right now, it only made sense that it was. "Who are you, and what the fuck do you want?" She struggled to ask.

"Who am I she asks? The bitch wanna know who I am!" He laughed. "If you don't know, then I don't know." He grinned.

Royelle spit out the blood in her mouth, mad as hell that she let someone get her. She got caught slipping, and she knew it was because of her recent argument with Royelle. She was never off her game, but things with her and Royelle were unsettled, which threw her off. She continued to stare at the strange person in front of her, and the only thing that looked familiar was his eyes. In her heart of hearts, she knew the person standing before her was Trevion, but she didn't want to believe that he looked that different. When she heard he had reconstructive surgery, she didn't think it was that deep; she was wrong.

"Trevion just kill me already. Why the fuck are we playing games? We both know I'm not making it out of here alive. So why waste my time and yours?"

"Ohhh?! So you do know who I am?" He laughed sinisterly. "How you like the new look?" He smirked.

"It's pathetic," Xandra said.

"Pathetic she says. But it's because of you that I've had to go through these extremes. It's cool, though, cause now that I got your ass, I'm gonna enjoy watching you die. You thought you killed me? Thought you had the drop on me? And look at me now."

"I'm looking, and it ain't much to look at," Xandra said through short breaths.

"Bitch still talking shit, even on her death bed." Trevion chuckled and clapped. "It doesn't even matter; what does matter is the money. Where's the money, Xandra? And before you say something stupid like you don't know, you better think about your answer."

Xandra chuckled. "Money? This is about money? Well, I hate to tell you this, but if you been broke all this time, you can expect to stay that way. There ain't no fucking money, and if there was, I wouldn't tell you anyway. You're a waste of space, not good enough for any bitch or nigga. But since you like fucking niggas, go juke one of them because whether I'm dead or alive, my sister is off-limits to fuck niggas like you." She spit at him.

And just before Xandra could say another word, Trevion hit her in the head three times with the same claw hammer she hit him with, and on the fourth swing, he struck her in the neck, turning it and leaving an open gash. He watched her for a few minutes to make sure she was dead, and when he noticed that she stopped breathing, he took off. His job with Xandra was finished.

CHAPTER 25

ear Brain Diary,

I know it's been a while since I've written, but please forgive me. I just had a lot going on and was trying to put the pieces together alone and with the coping skills that Dr. Angeli taught me. You know this thing of healing comes with a lot of pressure. Healing makes you look at every ounce of your life and forces you to re-evaluate how you may or may not have contributed to your own pain and trauma by revisiting some of those areas of your life that caused you grief first place.

Weird, isn't it? Like most of us want better, but choose the lesser. Well, for me, I choose a better me. A healed me. A solid me. A less afraid, timid, and pushover me. Royelle Amoire Belvins will no longer be the girl who people can walk over, talk crazy too or treat in any kind of way. Those days are over.

From now on, the only Royelle people will get is the one who will match what she is receiving. I think it's fair game. Don't you brain diary? People often think that what they do is ok, especially when your return is not the same as their applied pressure. I've never been confrontational and have always been the peacemaker. And I will continue to be those things, but with caution.

Well, that's it for now. I don't know when I'll write again, but just know I am doing better than good.

Royelle ~

Several days after the argument between Xandra and Royelle, Royelle had finally become clear-headed and calmed down. And although it took her a few days to rationalize and understand why Xandra did what she did, she knew full well that Xandra would never intentionally bring harm to her doorstep. And now, she had to reach out to Xandra and apologize for reacting the way she did and treating her like she was a common enemy.

She picked up her phone and tried Xandra several times, but each time she called, it went to voicemail. Normally, Royelle would've been upset, but this time, she understood a   different set of circumstances were presented, and the dynamics might have changed because of it. When she sat to reflect on what had taken place, she realized that she reacted without pause, and if she was in Xandra's shoes, she would've sent calls to the voicemail too. Rather than to call back, she sent her a text letting her that she was sorry, that she loved her, and wanted to talk as soon as possible.

While she waited to hear back from Xandra, she decided to get back on the computer and do more research on Trevion. She knew if she plugged in the right set of information, she was bound to find something that would stick. She remembered what Xandra told her about Sion and the different ways he taught her how to research people. So, she began searching every website on the list, and nothing came up. Finally, when she entered his information on archives.com, 2,726 death records for Trevion Kinglsey pulled up.

"You have got to be kidding me! This can't be right," she said, shocked that there were so many Trevion Kingsley's in the world.

Although it was a paid site, she knew that death records had to be reported and listed. Therefore, she made herself comfortable in the chair and began to apply filters to narrow down her search. She started with his first name, last name, and year of death; that only shaved off 37 people. Next, she added his date of birth to the search; it removed 1,112 people, leaving her with 1,575 people left. "Ok. We're getting somewhere now." She said as she added the filter to the state, bringing her count down to 15 people. "Now, this is what I'm talking about," she excitedly said.

One by one, she reviewed each file, reading their demographics and cause of death to see if they matched the information she had on Trevion, and so far, there was no relation. As her list began to get shorter, her excitement started to diminish. But when she got to record thirteen, a few things stood out, and the more she read it, the more the hairs on the back of her neck stood up. She wrote down the name of the mortuary responsible for picking him up and handling his remains and got herself ready for a day of uncertainties.

Since she knew she was no longer in a safe space, she was made to think like her sister. So she grabbed her Springfield 9mm and made sure it was loaded and ready to go at any given moment. But before leaving the house, she made sure to call Raylina and Raymelle. The last thing she wanted was to preach to them about checking in with her when she wasn't practicing it herself. But more than that, she knew things were in the thick of some shit, so she just needed to hear their voices, just in case.

She didn't want to assume something terrible would happen to her or them, but she couldn't be sure these days. So while the call may have appeared to be routine for Raymelle and Raylina, for Royelle, it was a *"just in case I don't make it home, know that I love you"* kind of call. Once the three of them talked and joked for a while, they ended the call with I love you's and Royelle headed out.

Stepping out of the house with no worries was now a thing of the past. These days, if it wasn't the detectives she was trying to avoid, it was death. Since Bella's confession, every time she left the house or made any sudden movements, her head continuously turned from left to right, just to make sure nothing was amiss, moving or acting strangely around her.

Luckily for her, the police, including P.I. Presley, was the least bit concerned with Royelle and the murders surrounding her. Police stations throughout the city were paired up in a joined task force trying to catch a serial killer that had landed its filth in the city, raping and killing young girls. What he was doing and how fast he was moving took rank over every other murder that was previously being worked on. Royelle was the least of any of their concerns.

When she got in her truck, she made sure to silence the radio so she could be aware of anything that might be strange or off. Then, as she drove to O'Donnell's funeral home, she made sure to keep an eye on her mirrors, watching for anything or anyone moving suspiciously. When she finally made it, she noticed that one car was already parked in the parking lot, and no other cars were driving past. It felt safe. She felt safe.

As she got out of the truck, she prayed that she wasn't making a mistake and was on the right track. She hoped that all the answers she needed were within the compounds and walls of O'Donnell's funeral home. When she got to the door, it was unlocked, so she let herself in. "Hellooo!" She yelled out. She waited a few minutes and yelled out again. "Hellooo!" She said a little bit louder.

"Coming right up!" The male voice hollered out. As he walked toward Royelle, he wiped his hands with his hand towel. "How may I help you?" He asked with a smile.

"Hi. Are you Mr. O'Donnell?" Royelle innocently asked.

"In the flesh." He grinned. "What can I do for you?"

"I have some questions about services." She responded.

"Sure thing. Let's go into my office. I apologize in advance for my mess. But it's just me here today. So, I've been all over the place." He said, clearing off his desk. "So, what can I help you with? You said you had questions regarding services." He sat in the chair.

"Yes, sir. I'd like to know what type of services you offer?"

"Well. We have traditional burial, cremation, and memorial services. What kind of service are you interested in?" He politely asked.

"I haven't decided yet." She responded.

"Ok. Well, let me see if we can make a collective decision together. But, first, tell me who it's for."

"My husband." She quickly answered.

"How old was he?"

"In his 30's."

"What did he like to do for fun?"

"He was into all kinds of things, especially hanging with the boys." She said, mocking Trevion's sexual desire for men.

Mr. O'Donnell chuckled and continued. "Any children?"

"None."

Chapter 25

"How about family?"

"You're looking at it." She shrugged her shoulders. "It's just me. "

"And I'm sorry, what did you say his name was?"

Royelle cleared her throat. "Trevion Kingsley."

Immediately, Mr. O'Donnell raised his head from his notepad and gazed at Royelle.

"Sir? Is everything all right? Did I say something wrong?" She asked.

She knew that she had hit the jackpot. Mr. O'Donnell was looking much paler, and he was beginning to sweat. The joyful expression he had greeted her with was gone. Pay dirt! That's what she thought. She hit pay dirt!

"Is this some sort of sick game?" His pale face was turning red as he stood up.

"No, sir. I reckon it is not, and I suggest you be seated." She said, aiming her gun at him.

He raised his hands and did as he was told.

"Now. This is how things are going to go. I'll ask the questions, and for every wrong answer, I will shoot you. For every right answer, you spare yourself pain. It's really that simple. Right answer equals survival; wrong answer equals torture. The decision is yours, really." She said thoughtlessly. To get a better angle of his position, she walked around the desk and stood inches apart from him.

Mr. O'Donnell couldn't believe that his bullshit antics and transactions would come back to bite him in the ass. Since Royelle never told him her name, he could only assume that she was the wife Trevion told him would never come seeking answers. But now, here he was staring down the barrel of her gun, defeated. She spoke properly, was calm, but was also very calculating, and Mr. O'Donnell could feel it. But given how Trevion described her as passive, unassertive, and faint-hearted, it was hard for Mr. O'Donnell to take her seriously. So, he decided to test the theory.

"Look. I don't know who your husband is or what you want to know." He spoke out.

Pop! Royelle shot him in the foot.

"Ahhh!" He hollered. You shot me in the fucking foot!" He continued.

197

"And I'll do it again if you don't give me what I want." Royelle calmly said.

"But I don't know what you want!" He cried out.

Pop! Royelle shot him in the other foot.

"Ahhh!" He let out an anguished, blood-curling scream. He tried to reach for his feet, but Royelle intercepted.

"Aht! Aht! Ahh! Don't you move." She pointed the gun at his head. "We can do this all day. I have nothing but time. But to spare you some, tell me what your connection to Trevion is. How did he manage to pull off his death? Who is involved in this scam? Now, before you open your mouth to tell me another lie, you better think long and hard about where this next bullet will land." She slowly went from aiming it from the center of his head to aiming it at the one between his legs.

Mr. O'Donnell thought about what Trevoion said in contrast to what Royelle was doing, and from Mr. O'Donnell's perspective, Trevion didn't know a thing about his wife. Actions spoke louder than words, and it was clear that Royelle wasn't playing any games. Therefore, Mr. O'Donnell started explaining that a few days after Trevion was in the hospital, he came up with a revenge scheme to get back at whoever shot him.

"Well, how did he know to come to you?" Royelle spat.

"Do you not watch the news?!" He drew back.

"Enlighten me."

Like everyone else in the hood, Trevion knew about the foul shit Mr. O'Donnell was doing to families who were mourning the loss of a loved one. The once well-respected Joseph O'Donnell was giving families the ashes of unknown people while storing the real bodies in a storage facility outside of the city, all so he could keep the money people were paying for services. And since he was still under investigation, Trevion took the opportunity to wave a few thousand dollars in Mr. O'Donnell's face to help him fake his death.

At the time of Trevion's death, the hood was accumulating so many murders a week of young black men that finding a replica for Trevion was a piece of cake. Once he was able to secure the right body, he went into action. For the sum of $30,000, Mr. O'Donnell secured his crooked coroner friend to identify Trevion through false dental records, and his doctor friend assisted with the signed fake death certificate. The process, as Mr. O'Donnell explained it was like any other business transaction, nothing personal.

"You are very clever." She said with a crooked smile. "No one would've ever guessed. But you know what's crazy about this whole situation; you enjoy stealing. Not just money, but the heart's soul, and love that people carry for their loved ones. I can see why Trevion came to you. You think just like him."

Royelle raised her gun and shot Mr. O'Donnell in the head.

CHAPTER 26

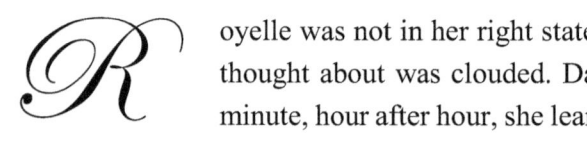oyelle was not in her right state of mind. Everything she thought about was clouded. Day after day, minute after minute, hour after hour, she learned more and more about the man she once loved. "What a cluster fuck!" She thought as she wiped everything off that she touched. As she casually walked back to her truck, she couldn't believe that Trevion was as demented in the head as he was.

She understood his brooding hate for Xandra, for what she had done. But to go through the lengths of faking his death and having reconstructive surgery was something that she could not understand or fathom. Royelle burned with more questions than answers. She wondered about the real issue concerning his identity crisis. Why did he have to go through everything he was going through just to get his revenge? Why couldn't he just tell her what happened? She understood it would've put her in a fucked up position, but nothing had her more fucked up than everything she was going through right now.

As she drove to the bar, she prayed that no one had seen her coming or going from Mr. O'Donnell's. She didn't see any surveillance cameras at the funeral home and doubted he had any, especially since he was already under suspicion and surveillance. She was certain that whenever Mr. O'Donnell's body was found, the community would've seen it as justice well served. She put herself in their shoes and wondered how she might have reacted if it was her mother that had been mishandled. She wasn't a vigilante killer of any kind, but she felt really good about taking him out after all he had done to those families. It was well overdue.

When she arrived at the bar, a few regulars were sitting in their usual spots. The television was going, and as usual, during the day, the bartender was a one-woman team, busy manning tables, taking drink orders, and making them. Royelle took a seat at the bar alone, sitting in front of the T.V. staring off into space.

"What can I start you out with? The bartender asked, placing a food and drink menu down.

"A sidecar, please. No! Make that two." Royelle said.

Royelle was in her head trying to make sense of not only everything Mr. O'Donnell had told her but how easy it was for her to kill him and not have any qualms about it. But what was more were all the things that Trevion had done to make his presence disappear. What was it all for? She wondered. Was their marriage that bad? Is what happened between him and Xandra far deeper than what Xandra described? Her thoughts scrambled. She couldn't understand the need for the deception.

"Here you go. Two sidecars."

The bartender placed the drinks down and walked away, leaving Royelle in her thoughts. With all the experience she had under her belt, she knew when a customer was up and when they were down. And from the moment Royelle walked through the door, the bartender knew something heavy was weighing on her, so she left small talk out of the bar etiquette equation.

Royelle picked up her first drink and sucked it down. And then, she sipped her second drink slowly while keeping her eyes on the television. "What's this? Royelle asked. "I didn't order any other drinks." She said to the bartender.

"That gentleman over there brought it for you." The bartender pointed in his direction.

Royelle turned to see who it was and she didn't recognize him.

"Send it back, please. I don't accept drinks from strangers." She said, turning back towards the T.V.

When he saw Royelle reject his drink, he got up and walked toward her. "So you're just gonna deny my drink?" He smiled, taking a seat next to her.

"As I said to the bartender. I do not accept drinks from strangers." She said, never taking her eyes off the television screen.

"Ok. Well, my name is Malachi. What's yours?" He asked with his hand extended.

Royelle looked over and rolled her eyes. " Royelle." She responded, falsely shaking his hand in return.

"That settles it." He said.

"What?" She asked.

"Bartender! A drink of whatever she's having and a Courvoisier for me." He yelled out.

"I said—

"You don't accept drinks from strangers." He interrupted. "But we're no longer strangers. We're on a first-name basis now."

Royelle cracked a smile.

"Ahhh! Is that a smile I see? You've been sitting at this bar looking like the whole world fell on top of you."

"Sounds like you've been watching me." She clapped back.

"Don't kid yourself, pretty lady. I just know a hurt woman when I see one. Just wanted to try and cheer you up, that's all."

Royelle looked over at him, scanning him from top to bottom, laughing on the inside. Dudes always came with some lame-ass game, trying to ease their way over to someone with repeated smooth talk. It was old and played out. But for the sake of entertainment, he stood out from amongst the other men in the bar because he made an effort to talk to her, so she went along with it. She would have loved to play his game some more, but today wasn't optional. Today she needed to talk to her sister, set some things right, and prepare for what might be war. She finished her drink and placed the glass down.

"Well, Mr?" She paused, waiting on his response.

"Just call me Malachi." He answered.

Royelle chuckled. "Ok. Mr. Malachi. I have to get going, but maybe we can catch up some other time." She said.

"Yea. That's cool. You pick the time and place, and I'm there."

Royelle opened her phone to the contacts and passed it over. He slightly smiled as he put his name and phone number into her phone.

"When can I expect to hear from you? He asked, passing the phone back.

"Soon enough." She smiled.

Royelle wasn't quite the drinker, so after three sidecars, she was feeling a bit tipsy driving towards Xandra's house. But it was the kind of buzz she needed to numb her pain and thoughts, even if for a moment. She often thought about calling Raymelle to tell him about all of her ordeals, but secrecy for her hit differently these days. More than that was protection. She wanted to protect him and Raylina from all the woes that came with being connected to Trevion.

Death was near; she could feel it. She just didn't know whose death. But the last thing she wanted was to get her brother and sister caught in the crossfire of something they had absolutely nothing to do with. As she drove toward Xandra's, she wished she would've listened to her intuitions at the beginning of her relationship with Trevion. Or, during the many times before the marriage, when Xandra tried to warn Royelle about Trevion. Or, when Raymelle told her, he had to give Trevion the brother-to-brother talk, and Trevion brushed it off like it wasn't shit. And although she felt messed up for not listening, it was too late for regrets.

When Royelle got to Xandra's, she was surprised to see her truck in the driveway, but the house was silent. That wasn't normal for Xandra. Anytime, no matter day or hour, if she was home, the windows were opened and the music blasting. But today was different. With a perplexed look, Royelle walked to the door, and out of respect for Xandra's privacy, she knocked first. When she didn't hear a response, she used her spare key to let herself in. "Sis!" She yelled out. It was dead silent as she slowly walked through. "Sis!" She yelled out again.

As she approached Xandra's bedroom, everything Bella said about how Aruba died came rushing back to memory, causing Royelle apprehension about opening the bedroom door. With everything that had been going on, she was afraid of what she might find on the other side. But, she finally opened the door and found nothing wrong. "What the hell?" She Royelle cawed. "I hope she didn't pull another disappearing act," Royelle said, leaving the house and locking the door.

As she walked towards her truck, she called Xandra's phone and paused when she heard the tunes of Eve's Love is Blind. "The fuck?" Royelle said. She quickly hung up and dialed right back, *"I don't even know you, and I'd kill you myself. You played with her like a doll and put her back on the shelf,"* played loudly. Royelle continued to let the lyrics play out and began walking towards the sound. She came unglued when she found the phone under Xandra's truck and saw the flat tire. "I know the fuck he didn't! I know he didn't!" She cried. The only thing that came to mind as she got back in her truck was Trevion.

She knew Xandra would never let anyone get the drop on her. The only thing that made any send was Trevion and his brother. She attempted to calm down, but her blood was boiling, and her tears wouldn't stop. She was in panic mode. She knew she needed to find them, but she didn't know where to begin. Everyone that knew about his existence was dead now. "Shit! Shit! Shit!" She hollered as she pulled over to the side of the road to regain her composure. "Think Royelle! Think!" She yelled. When she opened up her phone to scan her contact list, she finally noticed the little blue notification light blinking rapidly, indicating that she had voicemails.

Usually, she wouldn't check her voicemails for days, but this was an exception given the circumstances. She clicked the voicemail icon on her phone and let it play. Immediately the wrestling and popping noises in the background caught her attention. She listened closely as the voices spoke out, and the tussling continued. "Uh-uh!" She said, replaying the recording. This time, she listened more closely and could distinctly hear Xandra and the others talking. Of course, she couldn't make out everything being said, but the little that she could hear blew her mind.

"Stay calm." She said as she thought about her next move. She looked down at Xandra's phone, which was at ten percent. She knew if she went through Xandra's phone, something might stick out that would help guide her into what her next move should be. So she plugged it up and steadied herself. "Ok, Royelle Amoire Blevins. Get your shit together ." She said, wiping her tears. "You are who your mother raised you to be. What would you be looking for if this was a criminal case as a paralegal? What would Xandra do if it was you missing? Who would she call? Get your mind right and think!" She coached herself.

She took strong deep breaths and slowly released each one. Once she had her breathing under control, she opened up Xandra's phone, hoping that there would be something that could guide her to her next move. She started scrolling through the recent calls, but there wasn't anything worth looking into. Next, she went through her text messages, and there weren't any. "Yeah, right." She chuckled. She knew her sister well. Xandra not having text messages was like her not having a life. She knew Xandra must've deleted them to keep people out of her business.

Finally, she navigated through her contact list and came across Sion's name, and a lightbulb turned on. "Why didn't I think of him before!" She remembered Sion being the person who had helped Xandra keep track of Trevion. And as much as she hated him and felt that he was partly to blame for what she was going through and for her present suffering, she had to swallow her ego and pride pie for her sister's sake and make the call.

"Yooo! What up, X!" Sion answered excitedly.

The air was silent. Royelle hated the excitement in his voice.

"Hello?" He said when there was no response.

"He-Hello," Royelle stuttered.

"Yo! Who this man?!" Sion irritably questioned.

"It's Royelle. Xandra's sister."

Sion froze. Normally he would've questioned why she would be calling him. But, since she was calling him from Xandra's phone, he knew something was definitely wrong.

"I need your help," Royelle said, sensing the silence and shock. "My sister is missing."

Sion's eyes widened. "Missing?! What the fuck you mean missing?!" He spat.

"I mean like missing. Like gone. Like someone took her. Like —

"Yo! Yo! Yo! Say no more. How far are you from the Tavern?"

"Less than ten minutes."

"Come see me. I'll be waiting for you outside. I have on a Celtics jacket."

Royelle put the truck in drive, and in seven minutes, flat was pulling up in front of the Tavern. When she parked the truck, she and Sion were having a staredown as if they were getting ready for a wild wild west showdown. He didn't know if she was there on some murderous revenge-type stuff or if she was really there seeking his help. But he was prepared for either.

Royelle grabbed her gun and put it in her cross-body bag before getting out.

"It's about time," Sion said as Royelle got closer.

Royelle walked inside and followed him toward the back, keeping her right hand close to her crossbody. The inside, like the out, wasn't anything fancy; just a typical hood bar, complete with tables, chairs, a few pool tables, drinks that were dirt cheap, and air that was full of weed and cigarette smoke. And as hood as it was, she felt safe. When they reached the office, Sion walked toward his desk, and Royelle stood by the door, looking around the small office space.

"You can take your hand off your gun now. Ain't nobody here gonna hurt you." He said as he sat down.

Royelle didn't budge. Her body wanted to react, but her mind knew better.

"So you just gonna stand there? If it makes you feel better, I'll put my hands on the desk." He raised his hands to show he had nothing in them and placed them down on top of the desk. "Better?" He asked.

Royelle just looked.

"Look. You called me because you need my help. So tell me what's going on. Your sister and I have been friends for years. She's been nothing but a G.G. I would never jeopardize that relationship. Your sister is solid, and don't fuck with just regular people. So if she's solid, I know you gotta be too." He sincerely said.

"G.G?" She questioned.

"Yea. My gangsta girl."

Royelle crediting the sincerity in his voice slowly removed her hand from her bag and relaxed her posture. "There's a lot I want to say and ask, but none of that is important right now. What is important is that my sister is missing, and I need your help. She told me everything you did for her because of my fake dead husband, so I know you can help find her.

"You said, fake dead husband?" He questioned, wanting to make sure he heard Royelle correctly.

"Yes. Fake dead husband. Meaning, he's alive and is out here killing people, and I think he got a hold of my sister. In fact, I know he did."

To avoid going into full detail, she pulled out her phone, called her voicemail again, and slowly approached the desk. He methodically listened to the commotion in the background and stretched his ear to hear what the voices were saying.

"Ole boy is really alive?" Sion questioned again.

"Hmph," Royelle murmured. "You would know better than me." She snapped, unable to contain her disdain for him.

"I don't know what X told you or what you think you know, but I don't have shit to do with whatever the fuck it is y'all got going on. I did what I was paid to do. So we can keep going back and forth about this shit, or we can work together and find your sister. What's it gonna be?"

Royelle quickly changed her attitude and took a seat. She knew she'd never be able to do what needed to be done all by herself. So, she sucked up the hostility and let Sion do what he needed to do. He asked Royelle for her phone, plugged it to his computer, and downloaded the voicemail.

"How did you do that?" She questioned.

"I'm a computer genius." He smiled.

He asked Royelle to send him a picture of Trevion and asked her a few questions about his history and family life, and when he had enough, he demanded she goes home and stays there until he gave her the next set of instructions. Then, he ordered two of his soldiers to follow her home and stand watch until he said otherwise.

CHAPTER 27

ion could see the worry on Royelle's face as she left the bar with his partners. But he wasn't concerned. He knew he had a solid team that would make sure no harm met her as long as they were on assignment. More than that, this was Xandra's sister, and everyone that was tight with Sion knew about the love and respect he had for Xandra. So not only did he have to protect Royelle, but he had to find Xandra too, dead or alive. Not finding her was not an option.

Once the office was clear, he found the media file he downloaded and played it over and over and over again. He could hear all the shuffling in the background and some words being spoken, but the sound was a bit distorted. And since he was a computer genius, as he told Royelle, he did what he was trained in school to do, which was work his magic.

Although a thug all his life, he knew that the fast money he was making was chump change compared to what he could make in the tech world. So he combined his book and street smarts and went to school, graduating with a degree in computer engineering. Quickly after, he began installing surveillance cameras for businesses and trap houses. He was installing cable for people who didn't have a subscription, he was planting tracking devices on people's cars and phones, and hacking into computers for all kinds of clients, but his biggest source of income was the couples going through a divorce.

Xandra came to know him years before he enrolled in school when she entered the tavern on a whim to get a drink. At the time, as they talked about the ups and downs of life, places they wanted to travel to, and things they wanted to do, she had no idea that the reason the drinks were coming so fast and free was because she was talking to the owner of the bar, not an occupant. Learning his status came much later. Over time, they grew to know each other better, developing a tumultuous on-again, off-again relationship that she never shared with Royelle or the rest of her family. If it wasn't somebody permanent in her life, meeting her family would never happen.

Xandra could've been the mother of his children several times over, but she popped a plan B each time they had sex raw. She couldn't bear children for a man whose work consisted of impeding the privacy of others 24/7. That meant that she would be under watch at all times, and that wasn't how she operated. She couldn't function in a relationship with that type of soul-tie. So they agreed not to see each other in that way, remained tight friends, and met each other on the sexual side whenever the other desired it.

Although she knew he could still hack her shit at any time, if she wasn't his girl, he'd have less of a reason to creep, so the agreement worked out well. And no matter how much Sion wanted to do free business for Xandra, she would never allow it. Business was business, and she never wanted anyone to say, *"remember when I did this or that for you."* Being in debt to anyone was something she could never be.

With the technology Sion had, the once distorted recording he had was now clear as day. Listening to it made him a chuckle bit. As he repeatedly listened to the recording, it was easy to paint Trevion as a clown. The way Trevion spoke screamed bitch to Sion. It was easy for him to tell that niggas like Trevion were sweet on bitches, fake thugging it around gay men and pussy to niggas like him and his boys. He was more intrigued by the fact that even with Xandra being alone and up against two niggas, she was still his G.G. That was one of the many reasons he loved her so deeply. If she was going to go out, she was doing it like a "G," no matter what.

Once he got all the information he needed from the recording, he searched his databases for the names Malachi and DaKari Kingsley. When he found their adoption papers, he couldn't have been happier. Next, he searched the jail records on both of them just to see what type of niggas he was dealing with. DaKari he could see as a nigga from the streets. He had charges running back to the early 90s of armed robberies, weapons charges, assault and batteries, and an attempted murder charge that was later dropped due to insufficient witnesses; everyone knew what that meant.

Malachi Kingsley had no record. Not even a speeding ticket. So, he extended his search to look under Malachi and Trevion Pennington, and boom! Under Trevion Pennington, Sion found that Trevion had all kinds of financial charges against him, such as forgery, credit card fraud, embezzlement, identity theft, tax evasion, and money laundering, faking his death made sense now. He was facing big jail time, and unlike his brother DaKari, Trevion wasn't built for that. Sion's only problem now was finding the doctor who did the reconstructive surgery. He knew what Trevion looked like before, but that was no help now.

He looked back at the records to find the names of his biological and foster parents and started researching them. He learned that Tracy was departed and found the numbers listed for his foster father, Tony, and biological mother, Bessie. So he started the call out with Tony.

"Yah! Hello?" He spoke loudly into the phone.

"Is this Tony?" Sion asked.

"Yea! Who is this?!" He yelled into the phone.

The way he spoke only led Sion to believe that Tony was hard of hearing or on the verge of losing his hearing.

"I'm looking for your son Trevion. Is he around?"

"Trevion?! Why are you looking for Trevion?!"

"It's official court business, sir. I cannot discuss that over the phone." Sion answered.

"Well, son. I don't know where that boy is. I haven't seen him or his brother in years. I don't even live in that state anymore. But if he's anything like I remember, I'm sure he's got himself into a world of trouble." Tony said.

Sion never replied. He hung up the phone and called Bessie.

"Hellooooo." She answered cheerfully.

"Hi. Good afternoon ma'am. My name is John Taylor, I am with the investor's group, and I am looking to speak with Trevion Kingsley."

"With who?!" She yelled out.

"Uh, yes, ma'am. Trevion Kingsley."

Bessie laughed. "Son, how did you get this number?" She questioned.

"Our database shows you listed as his mother."

Since she didn't have any other children after Trevion, she knew exactly who Sion was referring to; she just didn't know his name had been changed. She took a deep breath and giggled before answering.

"Son. His biological name is Malachi Lucifer. I named him that because I just knew he had the blood of satan running through him. When he was born, I tolddd those nurses and social workers that he would be trouble. He is no son of mine, sir. I gave that demon child to the social workers right away!" She emphasized. "I don't know what investor's group you are with, but I can assure you that having him a part of it will cause it to crumble. Now I have to go. Please do not call here again. The thought of his name or him finding me gives me chills." Bessie hung up the phone.

Sion wasn't shocked by any of it. But the way his parents spoke about him gave him great insight. Trevion may not have been a killer on paper and portrayed as sweet, but parents often knew best. What Sion was hearing without it being said was that Trevion was not only crafty, but he was cunning, devious, and ingenious. He was worst than his brother DaKari. DaKari was out in the open, an on-purpose type of nigga. Trevion was judicious, sneaky, and underhanded. Based on what he now knew, chances of finding Xandra were probably slim to none. But he had to find him before it was too late for Royelle.

He called her up, told her to get a pen and a piece of paper, and gave her all the details he had on both brothers. None of it surprised her. Again, he demanded she lay low and wait on his next set of instructions while he and some of his other partners did what they needed to do to find and rid Trevion of his misery once and for all.

CHAPTER 28

*I*t had been a few days since Royelle got the call from Sion. And each day, he called in to check on her and make sure everything was good. Of course, his same partners were still on guard, so he didn't expect anything less. But he wanted to assure her that he was still on the hunt and hadn't forgotten about her. But over those days, while he was doing his part, she was doing hers. She had plenty of downtime to think, plan, and prepare an execution, so she asked him to stop by so she could share the specifics.

When he arrived, he was proud to see his soldiers in position like he expected them to be. He dapped them up, gave them some bread, and Royelle let him in the house. The two sat in the kitchen as she explained that after he had given her all the details about Trevion and his brother, she felt she knew a way to scale him in. She ironed it out step by step, and Sion was pleased.

"Man, you and your sister, bro." He laughed.

Royelle was not only thinking like Xandra; she was thinking like the law too. The idea was brilliant.

"I could use someone like you on my team for real. Your sister too, but she won't hear of it."

"Me either." She laughed. "This is a one-time shot. But who knows what the future might bring, right?"

He smiled, shrugged his shoulders, and rolled the conversation over to how they weren't going to stop searching for Xandra until they found her. He knew that was one of Royelle's biggest concerns, but survival came first, so she had to do what was first. She told Sion that she needed to get out of the house to go see her siblings before she did anything else. She had been talking to them over the phone daily, but she needed to see their faces. He agreed and told her that he would be waiting for her outside when she was ready.

Forty-five minutes later, Royelle was driving to Raymelle and Raylina's with Sion sitting low in the back seat of her truck and another one of his soldiers following behind in Sion's blacked-out Tahoe, all to ensure her safety. When they arrived at the house, all the cars were outside. Sion called his partner and told him to park away from the house, but to remain in a position where he could see everything in case anything popped off. He looked around and assured Royelle that everything looked good. He told her to take her time, and they would be outside waiting on her when she was ready.

Finally, when Royelle was inside the house, she felt a strong peace come over her. It felt like her mother had been there the whole time waiting on her. The house was clean, the blinds were open, the aroma was fresh, and Raymelle and Rayline were chilling in the living room watching T.V. with no worries. These were the moments she had been missing. She could've been right here with them day in and day out. But instead, she was running around town, killing people and quickly losing herself in the process.

"Heyyy loves!" She surprised them.

"Sisss! What's good?!" Raymelle shouted out. "I thought you forgot we lived here or some shit." He continued.

"Boy! Don't start! I've been busy with work, therapy, and everything else." She lied. "How y'all been? Y'all miss me?" She smiled.

"Duhhh! Of course, we do." Raylina said.

Royelle hugged both of her siblings tightly and didn't want to let go. But hanging on too tight would've been a big indicator that something was wrong.

"Where's Xandra?" Raylina asked.

"Chileee, you know that girl be on the run. She had some business to attend to out of town, but she'll be back soon." She lied again as she took a seat on the couch next to Raymelle.

For the next hour and a half, the three of them talked, joked around, and made preparations for dinner. It was the first time they had done it in a long time, and it felt great. Royelle needed this. After all the bad she had done and all the wrong she had endured, nothing else felt so perfect except for the present moment. The things to come came with no guarantee, so she had to soak the feeling up now and make it stick. After they were done bullshitting and clowning around, Royelle gave them hugs and kisses and told them she would check in later.

When Sion saw Raymelle come to the door, he was surprised to know that he was one of the dudes he ran ball with at the courts. *'Damn, it's a small world.'* He thought. He had mad love and respect for Raymelle. Every time he saw him on the court, they shot the shit, and through conversations, Sion could tell that Raymelle was A1. And now, the stakes for protecting Royelle and finding Xandra were even higher. As Royelle approached her truck, Sion slouched down a little more so that he couldn't be seen and waited for Royelle to hop in.

"Yo! I didn't know Melle was your brother!" He said as she drove away from the house.

"You know him?!"

"Yea, I know him. He's my running partner on the courts."

"Wowww! It's a really small world."

"It's a small ass city." Sion laughed. " A'ight. Let's get back to the house, so you can do what you gotta do, and I'll do what I gotta do. You good now?"

"Yes. I'm good now. I just needed to see them."

She continued the ride quietly back to her house and was relieved when she made it to see Sion's boys still there and unharmed.

"Listen. Don't make any sudden movements and make sure that everything you do, I know about it. Put this in your bag and make sure it goes everywhere you go." Sion handed her a tracking device that was disguised as a pen. "It will give me your exact locations, not approximates. So make sure you keep it on you." He said again.

"I got it." She replied.

Before getting out of the truck, she called Malachi and asked if they could see each other tonight. She said she would be at the Red Rose hotel for a conference staying in the penthouse suite, and didn't want to spend the night alone. He agreed to the time and place that Royelle set forth, and they both disconnected the call with excitement foreboding.

Sion waited for Royelle to go into the house and pack her bag for the night before taking off. Then, he ordered his boys to make sure she made it to the Red Rose safely and into the suite before leaving her. They did as they were told and scanned the suite before she went inside. Once it was clear, they told her where they would be when she was ready, and they left the room.

CHAPTER 29

oyelle wasted no time showering, doing her makeup, and getting dressed so she could attend the women's empowerment conference that was expecting several hundred women. Before leaving the room, she made sure to put everything in its proper place for the night and stuck the pen Sion gave her into her clutch. Finally, she texted Sion and his boys and used the code to let them know she was on the move.

When she made it downstairs, women of all races were in beautiful gowns and two-piece suits swarming the lobby. It was a beautiful sight to see. When they made it inside the function room where the conference was being held, she felt like she had walked into royalty. There were tall gold acrylic pillars in the center of each table covered with red roses and hanging baby breath. The table settings were complete with crystal dinnerware and glassware that gleamed as if it had never met the greeting place of dust. The entire setup was phenomenal. She was certain that the women paid a pretty penny to be a part of it. Lucky for her, she had cold ass Sion, who hacked into the hotel's system, giving her the penthouse suite, uploading a fake ID and credit card information into their database, and getting her a ticket to the event.

Once the conference was nearing its end, she texted Malachi, and he let her know that he was at the bar in the lobby waiting on her. When she walked out of the conference and began walking his way, his eyes gleamed at how beautiful she looked.

"Well, hello, hello." He greeted with a smile.

"Hello to you too," She greeted back.

"How was the conference?" He asked as she took her seat.

"It was amazing!" She smiled brightly. "Do you see the number of women flowing out of that place? My goodness!"

"Yea, I do. Women could do many great things if they stayed in this energy." He remarked.

Royelle smiled and ordered her drink. "Thank you for coming. I really needed a friend tonight."

"Everything ok?" He asked.

"Everything is fine." She said as the bartender placed her drink down. "I just have a lot going on personally, and I wanted to not think about it for one day."

"I can dig that." He said. "Well, I'm here now. What would you like to do?"

Royelle smiled seductively. "I have the penthouse suite. The ideas are endless." She stood up and slowly began to walk away. When she noticed he wasn't walking beside her, she turned around. "Are you coming? I know you didn't come to sit at the bar all night."

They hopped the elevator to the penthouse suite, and when they made it, Malachi was astonished. The suite was 1,000 square feet with three floors, which most people booked for entertaining purposes. The living room was on the first floor, the bedroom with the California king-size bed, spacious bathroom, a rain shower, and claw foot tub was on the second floor, and on the third, is where the entertainment happened. It came complete with an entertainment area, with large bay windows, a full bar set up, a kitchen, and a large covered, fully-furnished outdoor rooftop with amazing views of the city. It was paradise for sure.

"Damnnn! This is nice!" He excitedly said.

"Isn't it?! I could live here forever. And it's so beautiful outside." Royelle replied, walking towards the bar on the terrace. Malachi followed behind. "Something to drink? Let me guess, Courvoisier?" She asked.

Malachi grinned. "You remembered."

"Of course I do. I mean, how could I not. You were persistent at the bar." She giggled.

"I was, huh?"

"Indeed." She passed him his drink, and they cheered.

For the next few hours, Royelle was astounded by how well put together Trevion now looked. From their conversations, she couldn't tell if he knew she was on to him or not. But three things gave him way at the Dublin House. From the moment she saw him, she knew it was him. His appearance was different, but his eyes never changed. When he sat next to her and raised his arm to get the bartender's attention, she noticed his warrior tattoo, and when he ordered his Courvoisier, she was almost 100% sure that the person sitting next to her was Trevion. But when Sion called and told her all the details about him, it sealed the deal for her.

This was the moment she had been waiting for. The moment she could be in the same room with him and get the answers she had been seeking. But now, she was out for blood. She was scorned, sold for sex, lied to, manipulated, deceived, destroyed, and because of it, turned killer. Now the only question she needed an answer to was her sister's location.

She continued to play her role as the unknowing drunk and drank Vodka to her hearts content pretending to be tipsy and ready for sex. Unbeknownst to him, he continued to drink his Courvoisier while she drank water disguised as Vodka. She refused to be caught slipping. So, when she left for the conference, Sion had his boys enter the room and empty most of the Vodka from the bottle, diluting it with water to kill its effects on Royelle.

"I feel soooo good!" She screamed, twirling in a circle. "It's been such a long time since I felt something like this, you know." She smiled at him.

"I can make the night better." He suggested as he stood up.

"Oh, I'm sure you can." She said.

She walked up to him, and as she began kissing him, she slipped a needle from under her garter belt and stuck it in his neck.

While Malachi continued in his slumber, Royelle cleaned up all the mess they had made, quickly putting everything back in its proper place. Sion offered his assistance, but Royelle refused. Therefore, Sion sent his boys in and had them place plastic all around the area where Royelle and Trevion were located. He told her that whatever she did, to try and keep it clean. She agreed. She pulled all of her stuff out of her bag, and thirty minutes after, he was awake.

"Royelle!" He yelled, waking up tied to a chair naked. "Wha-what the fuck are you doing?! Why the fuck am I naked?! Where the fuck are my clothes?!" He rambled.

"Shhh! Don't get into hysterics. It's not becoming of you, Malachi."

"Stop fucking playing and untie me, Royelle!" He angrily spewed.

"Now! Now! Dear Malachi, in due time."

Royelle slowly circled around him sizing him up as he tried to shimmy his way out of his hold, but Sion's boys had him on lock. There was no way he was getting out of the death grip. One thing she knew for sure about him was that he hated to lose control. So to witness him in this state of mind was a joy for Royelle to see. Finally, the one who had caused pain in and out of the city was about to experience the same pain, if not worse.

"Yo Royelle! I'm not fucking playing. Untie me!" He continued to wiggle around in the chair.

"Shhh! Quiet down, Johnny boy." Royelle placed her index finger over her lips. "This will be over soon enough, but right now, I need you to settle down."

"Fucking untie me!" He hollered. "I'm not playing this fucking game with you!"

"Game, he says! You've been playing games for the last five years; nowww, you want to quit? It doesn't work like that, baby. We're just getting started." Royelle laughed sinisterly.

"Just tell me what the fuck you want! So I can get the fuck on!"

Royelle continued to walk around him, staring. He looked desperate, pitiful, and pathetic. She couldn't believe that the man sitting in the chair was once the man she married. To see all the thing he did to conceal his true identity and the shit he had been doing was astonishing to her. She couldn't believe that there were people in the world who actually lived doubled lives and pulled it off like cashing a check. The fact that she trusted him cared for him, and went out of her way for him, doing all the things that good wives do, only to get back a life full of dogshit, was jarring to her.

Royelle had one hundred things brewing in her head as she stayed quiet, angrily staring at him and his naked body. She remembered all the times they shared sexually, and it angered her even more. Used and abused is what she was feeling at the moment. Despite that, a part of her still loved him, and she couldn't understand why. This wasn't how the night was supposed to go. Feelings weren't supposed to get in the way of tonight's purpose. Yet, here it was, a slight conviction presenting itself.

"So what? You gonna keep me tied up in this chair all night?" He smirked.

"How could you?"

"How could I what?" He asked.

"How could you?" She asked again.

"Man, I don't know what the fuck you're talking about."

She walked over behind the bar and pulled out everything she could find between them. Then, she walked back over to him and began flicking pictures of the two of them together towards his face. Finally, she flung their marriage certificate and his birth certificate at him, and they landed at his feet.

"How could you? I was nothing but good to you? How could you do this to me? What was it all for?" She let her tears fall.

It was hard for her not to cry, not to feel pain and hurt. He was the first person she gave her everything to, her heart and soul to, and he crushed her idea of love for good. No one coming stood a chance to get from her what she once gave to him. But like men, they never see the damage they have manifested onto a woman until the woman snaps. But then it's too late. When he finally looked down, he was surprised to see the pictures they took as a couple, the marriage and birth certificate all looking back at him. He didn't say it out loud, but he knew the jig was up.

"Was I not enough? You had to have Amadeo, Aruba, McKenzie, Bella, I mean everything and everyone, but me! Wasn't I enough?"

He didn't respond. He continued to stare at the items on the floor, knowing that he had lost.

"Answer meeee! She hollered, lunging a blad through his left thigh.

220

He let out a howling scream as she turned the blade. He looked at her as she looked at him with emptiness in her eyes. It surprised him that it was Royelle inflicting this pain on him. He would've never guessed in a million years that the one person he thought would never hurt a fly, would be the one to take him out.

"Royelle! What the fuck are you doing?!" He yelled through panting breaths.

She let out a sinister laugh. "Malachi. It is Malachi, right, or should I call you Trevion? I don't really know what to call you these days. I'll just call you Trevion since that's what I know you as. But, you asked me what I'm doing?! Well, that's easy. I'm doing everything to you that you ever did to me."

Trevion was sweating, and his breaths were going a mile minute. He was trying to ignore the pain from the stab wound in his leg, but it was impossible. He was bleeding and weak, but he didn't want her to see any weakness in or on him.

"Roy—

"Shut up!" You don't call the shots here; I do!" She hollered.

"I need something for the bleeding." He said.

"Pussy! It's a flesh wound. You'll survive."

She knew it wasn't, but she didn't care.

"Listen. At this point, what you've done to me is over. I can get past that; in fact, I already have. What I can't let slide is my sister. Where is she, Trevion?"

"The fuck you asking me for?! I don't fucking know!" He yelled.

"Listen, You have no idea how much I have changed since I woke up from the coma, went through therapy, and learned about myself again. The Royelle you once knew is no more. She's gone, out of here. What you are looking at right now is what you created. So, when I tell you that I will stab and shoot you until I get the answers I want, I mean that. If you have never taken me seriously before, now would be the time to start. So, it's up to you how this pans out. We can make this fast and easy or slow and torturous. All I want to know is where my sister is. What's it gonna be? " She pulled her 9mm out from under the sofa cushion, cocked it back, and attached the silencer Sion had given her.

Trevion laughed aloud when he saw how Royelle was trying to pose a threat to him. And since he figured she had someone helping her with his capture, he knew he wasn't making out alive. Telling her where Xandra was made no difference to him. He knew that the grim reaper was on stand-by awaiting his arrival. He continued to laugh and looked up at her.

"You stupid bitch! Do you think any of that shit scares me! You minus well kill me right now because I ain't never telling you where your sister is. Fuck that bitch! I hope she's dying a slow fucking death! That bitch is the reason I fucking look like this! Fuck her! Fuck you! And anybody else that got beef!"

"You know there's a famous quote written by Jason Jones that I absolutely love. It says *Justice is blind until she gets the person that blinded her. Then it's payback time.* I couldn't agree more."

Royelle walked over to her bag, grabbed her last syringe, and stuck it in his neck.

"See, I wanted to shoot you, but I didn't want to leave a huge mess for the cleanup crew. Shooting or stabbing you is bloody, messy, and quick. This here is much easier, cleaner, and I get to watch you suffer through it. So now you suffer, bitch!"

"What did you stick me with, bitch?!" He asked, feeling his body go numb.

"Stressful, isn't it? Sitting there wanting to talk or scream and can't. That's how I felt when I learned you were dead, had another wife, were selling me for sex, and doing god only knows what else. No worries, though. It will all be over soon." Royelle said.

As Trevion's heart began slowing down, she texted the boys and let them know she was ready. When they walked in, she started gathering all her belongings, making sure not to leave anything behind.

"You good?" One of them asked.

"Yes." She replied in a soft voice.

"What about X?" He asked.

"Nothing." She replied.

"A'ight." He nodded his head up, signaling her to leave.

Chapter 29

As she prepared to leave the suite, she turned back to see Trevion take his final breath. It was officially over. She was happy for his end and sad for Xandra's. She couldn't believe that this was how it would end for her. But, now or later, she knew they would find her sister. And as long as she could give her a resting place, she was good with that.

She hit the button to her remote starter as she casually strutted back toward her truck. As she got closer, she began to sub-woofers bass beats ring out to the tunes of Leslie Grace's song, "I Call The Shots." When she opened the door, an ill-omened expression came across her face as she began to sing out the lyrics.

"I'm laying down the law, cuz I'm the, I'm the boss. So move, just move along
Step aside, step aside, I'm changing up the game, putting you in your place. Yeah, it's a brand new day, recognize, recognize. Oh, oh, never knew the power in me. Now you see, I got it So, don't ever underestimate me. Tread carefully; I got this! Look who's on top now I call the shots now!"

She continued to play the song over and over again, replaying what she had just done. This was the end. She had killed Trevion. And like everyone else who died at her hands, she justified the killing by reminding herself of all the hurt that was imposed on her first.

"Don't look at me like that. What would you have done?" Royelle said, looking into the rearview mirror. "How long was it supposed to continue before it ended, huh?" She looked into the mirror again, and her reflection was the only thing looking back at her. It served as a reminder that no matter where she was raised, what circumstances she survived, the killer in her was always there; she was just dormant.

A few minutes into her drive back home, her phone rang from an unknown number. She looked down at it and was reluctant to answer it. But knowing that it could be Sion or one of his friends, she went ahead and answered it.

"Hello?" She answered.

"Hello. I'm looking to speak with Royelle Blevins." The unknown voice said.

Royelle frowned. "This is she. Who is this?"

"My name is Lisa. I'm calling on behalf of your sister Xandra—

"What?! Where is she?" Royelle hysterically yelled into the phone.

"She's here at St. Martin's hospital in the ICU."

"What?! What happened?! Is she alive?!" Royelle hollered.

"Yes. Ma'am. She's here and she's alive."

Acknowledgments

Almighty Father! Here we are again... Book 3, The Finale! Without your grace and mercy, the air you have breathed into my lungs, and your desire to see me make it day after day, I would not be here. Thank you! Thank you! Thank you! You've allowed me to make it this far, and I pray I live to see another eighty years. Until the day that I sit at the right hand of your throne, I pray that you will strengthen my creativity and writing abilities, give me strength in my hands to write and type and keep my memory afresh and renewed every day and alive with ideas.

TK, here we are, baby! Three down, so many more to go. Thank you for continuously pushing me into greatness, for believing in my work, and for making me see things that I place doubt on. I can't believe the direction we are heading in, and I thank you for keeping me in line with it. SHE is up next!

My children and Grandson, all that I do, I do for you. When I depart this place, you will have a legacy to follow. It may not come in the form of millions, but it comes in the form of following your dreams, never giving up, and always showing those who think you can't that you can. Never let those who don't believe in your worth stand in front, beside or behind you. They will be the first ones to knock every aspiration out of you. So stay connected to those who forever want to see you win!

Moe The Writer! Thank you for showcasing me on your podcast Straight Coffee, No Tea! It has been a pleasure to work with and beside you. I cannot wait to do more and to see where your book, I Made Him Leave, takes you. You have great energy, spirit, and drive. The sky is the limit, baby. And remember, we are writers, my love. We don't cry; we bleed on paper. Thank you for being who you are. I can't wait to work on future projects with you.

To Tiff and Remi, thank you for the endless love and support. For the encouragement along the way, the many dinners and talks about life, succeeding, and more importantly, God! For all the fellowship and for bringing his word to the table when times are rough or when a reminder is needed. It is always great to have wonderful friends, but wonderful friends who know the word of God and help you apply it are rare. Thank you for it all! I love y'all!

Devin Monterio and Michelle Hill (The Bracelet Lady), Thank you! Out of sheer love and genuine friendship, our bonds have been strong. No questions asked, just straight love, check-ins, and random days. That's all it takes! Thank you, both for what y'all do when y'all don't even realize that you're doing something. It's the little things.

To all of my family and friends...Y'all are so spread wide marking names, and states would be a short story, and I just can't even fathom that idea right now LOL! But, I wanted to thank each and every one of you near and far. You may not know this, but you are a driving factor in what I do and why. Some people cheer for you and don't mean it; others only clap because they see other people doing it, but don't genuinely care. But for those of you, who only see the best in me and love me for me, THANK YOU! Life is grand when you have real people in your life.

To my haters, doubters, and those who don't believe that I can, thank you for existing. You make striving for better that much more fascinating. I say I wouldn't make it without the love and support from my family and friends, and that is true. But I need you, my haters, just as much. Nothing drives a person harder than the people who think they can't. We take pleasure in knowing that we can and showing it.

www.ingramcontent.com/pod-product-compliance
Lightning Source LLC
Chambersburg PA
CBHW061454030726
47503CB00005B/1701

* 9 7 9 8 9 8 6 1 5 6 0 2 6 *